Underworld Queen

Sharon Hamilton

Sharon Hamilton's Book List

SEAL Brotherhood Series
Accidental SEAL (Book 1)
Fallen SEAL Legacy (Book 2)
SEAL Under Covers (Book 3)
SEAL The Deal (Book 4)
Cruisin' For A SEAL (Book 5)
SEAL My Destiny (Book 6)
SEAL Of My Heart (Book 7)
Fredo's Dream (Book 8)
SEAL My Love (Book 9)
SEAL Encounter (Book 1 Prequel)
SEAL Endeavor (Book 2 Prequel)
SEAL Brotherhood Box Set 1 (Accidental SEAL & Prequel)
SEAL Brotherhood Box Set 2 (Fallen SEAL & Prequel)
Ultimate SEAL Collection Vol. 1 (Books 1-4 + 2 Prequels)
Ultimate SEAL Collection Vol. 2 (Books 5-7)

Bad Boys of SEAL Team 3 Series
SEAL's Promise (Book 1)
SEAL My Home (Book 2)
SEAL's Code (Book 3)
Big Bad Boys Book (Books 1-3 of Bad Boys)

Band of Bachelors Series
Lucas (Book 1)
Alex (Book 2)
Jake (Book 3)
Jake 2 (Book 4)
Big Band of Bachelors Bundle

True Blue SEALs Series
Zak (Includes prequel novella)

Nashville SEAL Series
Nashville SEAL: Jameson (Books 1 & 2 combined)

Silver SEALs
SEAL Love's Legacy

Sleeper SEALs
Bachelor SEAL

Stand Alone SEALs
SEAL's Goal: The Beautiful Game
Love Me Tender, Love You Hard

Bone Frog Brotherhood Series
New Year's SEAL Dream (Book 1)
SEALed At The Altar (Book 2)
SEALed Forever (Book 3)
SEAL's Rescue (Book 4)
SEALed Protection (Book 5) Coming Fall 2019

Paradise Series
Paradise: In Search of Love

Standalone Novellas
SEAL You In My Dreams (Magnolias and Moonshine)
SEAL Of Time (Trident Legacy)

Fall From Grace Series (Paranormal)
Gideon: Heavenly Fall

Golden Vampires of Tuscany Series (Paranormal)
Honeymoon Bite (Book 1)
Mortal Bite (Book 2)
Christmas Bite (Book 3)
Midnight Bite (Book 4) Coming Fall 2019

The Guardians (Paranormal)
Heavenly Lover (Book 1)
Underworld Lover (Book 2)
Underworld Queen (Book 3)
Immortal Valentines A Paranormal Super Bundle

Audiobooks
Sharon Hamilton's books are available as audiobooks narrated by J.D. Hart.

About the Book

Audray has just assumed the title as first-ever Queen of the Underworld. As she attempts to consolidate her rule, characters from the past threaten to destroy her and the love she shares with Jonas Starling, a 300-year old dark angel. When she discovers she has been the recipient of a miracle, suddenly their whole immortal lives are changed forever. Will they survive the coming war or get snagged in the power struggle over not only the underworld, but the human world as well?

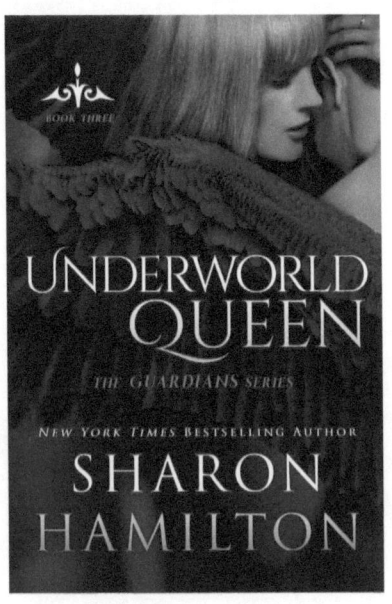

Go here for the video trailer for Underworld Queen.

youtube.com/watch?v=0tPuymIysRs

Chapter 1

AUDRAY LOVED BEING the first-ever woman Director of the Underworld, but she preferred the title "Queen" even better. Jonas had begun calling her that and it became part of her persona almost immediately.

Maybe it is the way Jonas whispers it to me just before he takes me.

That word was something she would never tire of hearing, just like the sounds her paramour made as he pleasured her to distraction and beyond. And the best thing of all was that he did it out of love, not obligation. His need to please her was equal to her need to be ravished over and over again.

And worshiped as only a queen should be.

Jonas was still wearing his black leather vest, but was naked everywhere else that counted, sleeping like a baby. She tucked her back into the warmth of his chest, feeling tiny against him, and reveled at how safe and protected she felt. She'd never had such a big man, big everywhere, but especially big in the way his soul screamed for her. It took a lot to distract her from all the pleasures in the Underworld, but being in bed with Jonas outshone them all.

When they'd gotten back to her home in the human world, he'd barely caught the bike when she jumped off. He saved it, of course, cursing softly, before it could tip and fall into her blood red Maserati. Even hearing him curse gave her chills.

All afternoon she had been touching him as they flew past rows of vineyards and redwood trees on their way home, her breasts pressed against the back of his thick torso. Her cheek rested in the place she smelled his maleness the strongest: at the back of his neck, just under his hairline. She watched the light brown tendrils of his shoulder length hair dusted with gray, catch fire in the late afternoon sun, coaxing her to reach down and squeeze his package, making him swerve the bike. But he was laughing, and she felt they didn't have a care in the whole world.

She had thought she would enjoy the powerful Directorship more. Jonas had been an unexpected distraction. Ever since their explosive first meeting, Audray felt her whole world had changed.

As happened so frequently, when they got to her home they were so intense with need, she ran up the stairs peeling off clothes and leaving them behind for him to gather, which he did, adding to his own bundle of discards. He'd barely got his chaps off in time. Hopping across the bedroom floor he pulled off one boot, then the other, quickly shed his jeans and then dove into her bed and took her without being careful.

Now resting, their bodies cupped together, her chest pressed against his back, they lay on the grand bed of her queenly suite. He turned her over and snuggled up behind her but didn't awaken, one huge arm was tucked around her waist, pinning her in place.

As if I would want to be anywhere else but here. She heard him stir to her telepathic thoughts.

She could feel the silver buttons on his vest as they pressed into the flesh of her back. He stirred as she pushed her rear into his groin, and yes, there was something there for her already.

With one powerful arm he propped her to her knees. His finger laid a path along her slick peach from front to back, and then he gave her two large fingers. The muscles in her sex devoured them both.

Taste me.

"Yes, my queen." Kneeling to her, he spread apart her cheeks and lapped her wetness with the sandpaper of his tongue. She felt her release instantly and he drank her juices as if she was the elixir of his life. "More, give me more, my queen."

His demand sparked another ripple of pleasure as she jerked, burying her face into the pink satin pillow. While she moaned in ecstasy, he suckled every drop she could give.

His two hands were on her breasts, as he fondled and squeezed her senseless. She felt his enormous cock as it slowly pressed against the crease between her cheeks, playfully pressing over her anus to find the slit of her peach and plundering her to his hilt, splitting her with need.

He held her body at her ribcage and slowly moved her up and down on his shaft until she shuddered. Her knees and thighs hugged the outsides of his, giving him full access. It was impossible to get enough of him. Wanton with desire, she was beyond trying to couch her thoughts but let her fantasies run rampant telling him the stories she'd never dared to tell anyone before. The stories of her passion.

"Ah, yes. And I shall never tire of filling you."

"I HAVE A few things I need to do today at the Directorship in the Underworld, Jonas," she said as she tied the thirsty cotton robe around her.

He removed his towel and massaged her wet hair, running his fingers through the long blonde tresses. He kissed the side of her neck and whispered in her ear, "And I have a few things I need to do to you today as well." He polished it off with a kiss.

Audray turned to face him and smiled. "I think I need to take you with me to the office," she said as she lost herself in his dark eyes.

"I promise to inspire you," he beamed, reaching under the robe and squeezing a breast.

Audray frowned. "Ah yes, I especially like it when you inspire me." She placed her hands on either side of his face. "I love it when you surprise me."

She felt his groin lurch as he drew apart the two folds of her robe, looking down at her naked body and licking his lips. She opened her eyes wide.

Again?

THE TRANSPORT STATION was located in an abandoned warehouse district, not far from the house Audray had inherited from Peter when she assumed power. The non-descript rusty metal building could only be accessed with a pass key no human possessed. A series of black limousines shuttled dark angels and their belongings between the human and Underworld like a well-run mass transit system, except there were rarely drivers and there was no timetable, but existed on an "on demand" schedule.

The ride today to the Underworld was quick and efficient. Like getting back to work after a long vacation, Audray felt her body tense and stiffen. She checked her messages on the red palm device. One message troubled her. There had been an incident at the re-entry room, that place where dark angels first stepped out into the Under-world as immortal beings. Several novices were hurt and one was killed. She had been torn limb from limb.

The perpetrator had been caught and was in chains. Her staff wanted to know what to do with him.

"Burn him." She spoke into the palm device as they exited the door of the transport. Jonas took her hand and led her up the steps of the Directorship offices. She thought it odd he said nothing.

Her staffer squawked back another objection, but Audray cut him off. "I don't care about his story. Only the Director—" She'd slipped up and corrected herself quickly. "Only *I* can dish out corporal punishment."

"Ma'am, with all due respect," the scratchy voice on the other end of the phone persisted, "He says he was sent here to meet Jonas. And he says there are others who follow."

Audray looked into the dark eyes of her lover, her rock, and now her whole world. Jonas did not plead for the life of this recruit to be spared.

"You know anything about this?" She asked her paramour, covering up the device.

"Of course not. But it cannot be good news," Jonas muttered in return. "Some things from the past should remain in the past."

"I agree."

Regardless of the reasons for this dark angel's entry, he'd violated one of the few rules of the Underworld in causing the true deaths of innocent dark angels. She needed to demonstrate her unwavering regard for law and order. She had to rule like a queen. She knew Jonas had a past, just like she had one. There wasn't any reason to make it complicated.

"I said, burn him."

Chapter 2

PROFESSOR CARL CARRINGTON looked over the bowed heads of his World History class at Meriwether and Grant College. He adjusted his bow tie, stretching his neck up out of his shirt and fingered around the top of his heavily starched off-white collar. One of his colleagues said the students' nickname for him was Indiana Jones. Glancing over the clutch of seated bodies, he didn't see any painted messages on any of the girls' eyelids. He'd always attracted the attention of the younger women, and just as easily dismissed them as typical teacher crushes. But he did think he had Indy beat in looks, with all due respect to Harrison Ford. After all, the actor was getting a little long in the tooth, and Carl was in his prime, at a mere thirty-two years of age. He didn't mind at all he could pass for Mr. Ford's son.

"Time's up," he said as he double-clicked the stopwatch. There was a groan and some shuffling of feet as his freshman class began, one by one, to sit up or untangle themselves from their favorite test-taking posture. One male student in the back row scratched the inside of his ear with a paperclip.

"Okay, now pass your papers to the front of the row, and Jeremy here will pick them up."

A young auburn-haired girl with enormous breasts, wearing a low-cut sundress and too much eye makeup handed her paper in directly to Carl, ignoring Jeremy, who was fuming.

"There you go, Professor. I left my number on top in case you can't read my writing."

Carl's face flushed and his groin bulged, in spite of the internal scolding he gave himself. It had been months since his weekend with the yoga instructor who took him to a couples Kundalini retreat and blew his mind. Who knew? It was the most intense sexual liaison of his life. He'd come prepared for some stretching and relaxation. What he got was a weekend so hot he couldn't remember any of the exercises or techniques, and he had to drop out of his Pilates class because the sight of his instructor's ass was so distracting he thought he might hurt himself. Today he was in desperate need of a lay, but balling one of his students was out of the question.

"Thank you, Darlene. I'm sure I'll be just fine."

"I'm sure you are, sir." She winked and turned around slowly. He watched her ass swizzle out the door in spite of himself. He laced his fingers through his curly hair.

Get a grip, Carl! He looked at Jeremy who obediently stood before him with the stack of collected papers.

Jeremy also wore a bow tie. In fact, he had even begun to wear sweater vests just like his Professor wore every day. Carl had five of them, one for each day of the week. This being Thursday, he wore the green one.

"Here you go, sir."

"Thanks, Jeremy." He took the test papers and smiled at the short youth who had become his shadow of late. All but a handful of students had shuffled out of the class. "Um, I'm not going to be in my office this afternoon. I have some research I have to attend to," Carl said to Jeremy over the sheaf of papers.

The youth looked crestfallen. Carl would have felt worse, but he'd begun to figure out the boy had formed an attraction for him, of the sexual kind. The obvious signs were growing daily and made him extremely uncomfortable.

At first, he was flattered Jeremy had such a love of 17th century England, which was Carl's own interest. He willingly agreed to tutor him, become a mentor. But later, as the meetings between the two got longer and more regular, a different type of relationship was beginning to develop, at least on the boy's part. He could see Jeremy found something else in him besides facts of history—something that was not returned, and never would be.

Time to nip this in the bud.

"Well, sir, I shall see you on Saturday then, at the library." Jeremy's pink cheeks were dimpled with a smile between them. He never showed his teeth.

"I'm thinking you are spending too much time on your studies and not enough time with your family and friends."

The boy frowned.

"Jeremy, forgive me, but all these meetings…it's making me a little uncomfortable." The boy looked at his feet so Carl was forced to speak to the top of his light brown curly hair. Jeremy's large ears protruded out at the sides, reminding Carl of a Hobbit. "Maybe I'm making too much out of this, but I'm feeling a little ill at ease, like maybe it isn't appropriate to be alone with you so much."

There, now you've said it. Hope to God his parents don't have a direct line to the department chair.

At first, the boy's hazel eyes shot up in pain. But soon Carl saw his gaze returned with the steely blue-green stare of a dangerous young soul fueled by something very dark. He shuddered as he watched a slow smile to creep onto Jeremy's youthful face. The smile was Cheshire cat wide, but his eyes were cold and cruel.

Carl realized he never really knew this kid, and perhaps underestimated his motives. He was suddenly glad he had decided to distance himself from him.

Jeremy is a ticking time bomb.

CARL DASHED UP the shallow steps to the library's three-story domed lobby, immediately turning right. He was eager to start the research the strange dark lady had hired him to do.

Stopping at the glass-walled entrance, he straightened his hair and snapped his bow tie, smiling. His perfectly white teeth smiled back at him in the reflection, prompting a grateful inner nod to his mother for having insisted he wear braces as a child. He swiped his teacher's card and was admitted with a couple of loud clicks. He had an uncharacteristic spring in his step, and sauntering to the reference desk like a young pup, leaned over. To the right, two abandoned tables bordered a two-story picture window. He was disappointed the reference desk was empty. Carl didn't want to use the bell, but was left no choice. The metallic tinkling sound made his heart flutter.

Molly, the red-haired goddess of the reference section, magically appeared. Every time Carl saw her he thought about doing unspeakable things to her in the stacks room, with the smell of their passion and the old leather books filling his nostrils. She reminded him of Tess in the Highwayman poem:

Tess, the landlord's daughter.
The landlord's red-haired daughter
A long red ribbon
Tied to her chest.

"Professor Carrington, are you alright?" Her green eyes sent the taste of lime to his tongue, as his mouth watered.

How long have I been staring at her?

The girl was blushing, and he was suddenly glad for the counter between them.

"So sorry. I was thinking about one of my students, and I forgot where I was for a second."

"Well, whoever she is, I think she's one lucky girl." Molly smiled easily. That was one of the reasons he liked coming here, when he could have gone to the large University library downtown.

Then her words drifted into his consciousness. He was fairly sure he was blushing.

"Not what you think, Molly."

"Really?" She leaned forward and showed him the natural line of her ample cleavage. She pressed the light pink pillows of her breasts into the top of the counter and rubbed them back and forth with a slight turn of her body at the waist.

Carl swallowed. He adjusted the smooth brown belt on his tweed pants. Then he remembered his mission. The mysterious lady had paid him a month's salary for his research.

In advance.

She'd descended on him while he was attending office hours the week before. When she entered the room she locked his door behind her. As she introduced herself and extended her small hand, sweat had collected on his upper lip and he found it difficult to even tell her his name. She asked him to help her with some historical information about one person in particular.

"Molly, I need some information about a Jonas Starling, an 17th century British landowner who had interests in the Caribbean.

"Well, if that's all, Professor." She gave him a smile that almost bowled him over.

"Um, yes. Thank you." The room's temperature had climbed a good five degrees.

Molly punched a few keys on her computer and instructed him to wait while she went to the back. He thought about how she wrinkled her nose and how it accentuated the creamy pinkness of her skin and the light dusting of freckles across her bridge. She was kissable. Probably everywhere she was kissable.

She brought out a large volume, slapping it down on the counter-top with a whack, sending a small cloud of dust up and out at the sides. Carl was surprised to read the title:

Pirates of the Americas.

Chapter 3

THE CHARRED REMAINS of the executed dark angel smelled like the soil at a slaughterhouse Jonas had seen as a child. It was disgusting then, and it was even more disgusting now, as his black boots trudged through the crispy black flakes, kicking up a fine dark-grey dust that got lodged in his nostrils. He forced a sneeze to clear himself out, but was rewarded with a whirlwind of fine particles—the remains of the dark angel who had come to meet him. Jonas had not told Audray everything about his past and this now festered like a splinter under the nail of his moral code. He might have to reveal things he'd hoped he could bury forever, along with the story of his youthful love and her family who had died, partially because of who he'd become.

He had to see for himself what was left of the fellow. He found a melted silver medallion, like a large dollop of shiny wax, still attached to the grape wreath silver chain some of his ancestors wore when Jonas was a boy. He couldn't make out any indentation or markings as he cleaned the smooth surface from the black grit of death. It reflected back his distorted face.

Although already dead, Jonas had begun to cherish his afterlife as an immortal dark angel. His relationship with the new Director made him feel strangely alive for the first time since becoming immortal some three hundred years ago. After his disastrous years at Court, where he'd been conscripted into doing despicable things, he'd slipped aboard a vessel bound for the Caribbean, and set up a new life on several of the islands there, until he'd been discovered and then took the only option available to him as a last resort: join the Underworld as a dark angel.

It had been a long three hundred years, and he'd considered ending himself in a true death. Until recently, he'd wondered if he could tolerate living forever. But finding Audray had changed everything and opened up a brand new bright future for Jonas. She was every bit his equal, in intelligence and strength of character. Her desires in the bedroom also matched his perfectly. If he could have a thousand nights with different women or one night with her, he would take her anytime. He'd thought of himself as completely dark and brooding. But these past few weeks he was beginning to feel the warm afterglow of—could it be—love?

Nah. Impossible. It's lust. I'm thinking with my other brain. He would have to think more on this.

He'd denied himself anything but an occasional quick and simple no-talking tryst, just to take care of his basic needs. But now he carefully explored her body, asked her questions, told her things about being the man he really was, being careful to edit out the parts he wasn't ready to reveal. He thought about their conversation and her questions that very first day they were together.

"I made kings for a living."

Audray had looked puzzled. "Explain," she said as she walked around his body that afternoon and touched him…places…that came alive and ached for her. She was looking at him, picturing in her mind what they would look like together, what they would feel like together. His grandfather had the same gift of sight, but only with women he loved. Audray stimulated in him *something* like that. He'd never before been inside a woman's head, and he was intrigued with her strength, as well as her sensuality. He'd never thought much about how women saw things. But he wound up wanting to know how she thought. And what she wanted him to do.

"I pleasured royal ladies whose husbands could not father an heir."

"I see."

"I was very good at it."

"I'm counting on it," she'd answered. They'd been inseparable ever since.

His smile abruptly left his face as his thoughts returned to the macabre scene at the cell as he fingered the melted medallion in his palm. "Anyone get a look at this before it melted?"

Two guards shook their heads, but the third said he had seen one before, on a new recruit who came to the Underworld a month ago.

"Strange fellow. Pink skin, almost womanly, if you know what I mean."

The other two guards burst into laughter and Jonas had to wait to find out the guard checked under the man's clothes, and yes indeed, he was a man, albeit a small one.

"So what about the medallion?"

"It had a design in the middle with lines radiating outward. Three little balls, lined up like a triangle, with an eye in each one. There was a serpent that bordered the outside, eating its tail."

"Never-ending cycle of evil," Jonas whispered, recalling the old fairy tale his grandmother had scared him to death with at night when he was young, as well as a few nights as a teen. "Everything for the kingdom," he whispered, recalling the ancient prophecy of a ruling dynasty that would never be vanquished. It had been a long time since he'd thought of it. He'd supposed everyone from that cult were long dead.

"Never heard of it or seen it before."

"No, you wouldn't have. Wasn't your story. It's mine."

The guards started to clean up the floor, getting out their mops and long-sleeved bright blue rubber gloves.

"Anybody come after, looking for this guy?"

"Nope. And the viewing room was empty, except for the regulars."

Regulars were female dark angels, the reviewers, who liked to be on the receiving end of a man's first night as a dark angel, when they discovered for the first time their prowess, able to make love indefinitely. They could finally be the men they bragged about being. These ladies would haunt the viewing area, watch the human's last dying vision on the big screen and then vie for the privilege of treating the reconstituted dark angel like long-lost lovers. They'd pounce on him just after he walked through the padded blue door to the viewing reception area. Sort of a "welcome to hell and the rest of your dark life, sucker." It was usually an emotional time for a man—or a woman.

"Any idea why he ripped her apart?" Earlier, Jonas had peeked over Audray's shoulder at the images. In his three hundred years, they were the most disturbing things he had seen here.

Everyone shook his head as one guard offered, "You can get the disc from the viewing office."

And that was something he hadn't considered. Certainly could get a better feel for the bastard by watching him alive than watching what was left of him being mopped up.

The viewing office resembled a large multiplex theater. Each time a new recruit was admitted to the Underworld, they had to be confirmed as a suicide, which was the only way a human could gain entry in the afterlife. For this purpose, while the recruit was in a waiting or "stasis" pattern, viewers were gathered in one of the small viewing rooms similar to an earthly theater and were given the task of confirming that the recruit's last minutes did properly reflect a suicide. It couldn't be a murder, murder for hire or accidental death. The recruit had to willingly throw his life away.

Occasionally someone didn't pass. Jonas had no idea what happened to the prospective Underworld citizen, but they were never heard from again.

Jonas had to wait an hour in the viewing office while the record he was looking for was located in the archives. The extremely short grandmotherly woman with a bun looked like a woman who had killed a string of husbands for their Social Security. Her face was sweet enough, although heavily lined and smelling of tobacco and Red-X, the preferred drink in the Underworld when one truly wanted to forget who and where one was. But Jonas knew he'd never drink anything those hands of hers gave him, even if it looked like it came right out of the Underworld well itself. What made her particularly dangerous to Jonas was the fact that she looked bored. People without focus and purpose scared him.

Finally at the window, Jonas waited impatiently for his video to arrive while the woman took an incoming call. "Honey, like I tried to tell you, we don't always get advance billing," she said into her headset. "Sometimes we know, most the time we don't. Not everyone is lucky enough to have fans down here before they turn."

She rolled her head from side to side, showing her annoyance with the caller. Jonas saw the whites of her eyes—the whites only. It freaked him out.

He heard a deafening sucking sound and thunk, rattling the glass partition in front of her desk.

"That's fine, dear. I'm sure you'll locate your husband eventually. Good day." She removed the headset and squealed. "Oh, looky here." She held up a clear yellowed pneumatic cylinder containing a compact disc and rattled it around like a castanet. She carefully wiped the disc clean before handing it to him.

"There you go now. Have fun."

Jonas was sickened by the suggestion she thought he was viewing the man's coming out party and crime of murder as fun. He sniffed the disc.

"The Red-X gets everywhere," she stated. It was a fact.

But Jonas smelled traces of blood. "Someone get hurt retrieving this?"

"Oh gosh, I hope not!" Then she gave him a broad grin. "Wouldn't want any of my girls' civil rights trampled on, would we?"

Jonas slipped the disc into the zipper pocket of his vest and patted it once. "Thanks."

"No problem." Granny lit a cigarette and lasciviously looked him over. He thankfully couldn't read her mind, but he guessed she was wishing she'd been turned at an earlier age.

He was halfway out the door when he remembered the other dark angel with the silver medallion.

"You keep records on every turning?"

"No. Some are expunged."

"Who orders that?"

"Depends." She took a long drag on her cigarette, spitting out the bits of tobacco that had stuck to her tongue.

"Who has the authority to expunge? Come on, I need some answers."

"Why don't you ask that pretty little blonde you've been humping day and night? She knows." The woman blew a cloud of white smoke in his face; the foul-horse-dung-smelling fumes made Jonas cough. "Or don't you two talk about things like that?" Her grin showcased red-stained teeth.

"Fine. I'll discuss our little conversation with her. I'm sure she'll be interested in helping me out, seeing as how you're so busy."

Granny abruptly stood up. "Hey, wait a minute. I'm trying as best I can. I don't want to step on any toes here." She put her cigarette out and waved the smoke away with her right hand. "Look, I've got something for you." She rummaged through a desk drawer and pulled out a clipboard with yellowed sheets of manhandled paper. She lifted up the top page, peeling it back and pointed to a line on the page underneath, tapping her finger on a particular entry.

"What's this?" Jonas crossed the room with two long strides.

"It's the address of the other one."

"What other one?"

"The one who didn't kill the girl. Arrangements were made for him to stay above the Pink Pussycat bar."

Jonas looked down at the address and the beautifully scripted letters. "Who wrote this?"

"I did. Used to teach penmanship in high school."

Jonas knew she had changed her mind and was now being truthful with him, almost helpful.

"Who set this up, the apartment and all?"

"Peter," she answered.

The former Director of the Underworld who Audray helped eliminate. Peter had spent nearly a full year jockeying for position, even cheating, to get himself elected as Director of the Underworld, a position he only held for a short time. What always had bothered Jonas was why Peter wanted the job so badly. Did this have to do with the prophecy of the "second coming?"

His blinding obsession with power eventually caused his demise. It put him in direct conflict with a much older dark angel, Jonas' friend, Joshua Brandon. Audray had been Joshua's newest recruit, and together they toppled the greedy Director, who had been vaporized in the process. Was this a loose end that Joshua had overlooked? Part of the former Director's grand scheme to consolidate his control over the Underworld?

But as Jonas mulled over these things, he came to the conclusion that this was something personally directed towards him, stemming from his past. Since Peter was now truly dead, perhaps this surviving new recruit, with the right coaxing, would reveal the secrets Peter took to his Underworld grave.

He didn't like unearthing the past. But, in an attempt to protect Audray, he had to find out what schemes were afoot that might put her in danger. He'd dealt with danger his whole life, both his human one and his longer immortal one. But with Audray, his new reason for living, he found new passion to keep her safe, no matter what the cost. He was glad Audray agreed to give him a few days to satisfy his concerns.

The Underworld seemed suddenly too small. Jonas felt a knot in his stomach. He touched the inked entry with his fingers, and then quickly removed them, wiping his hands against his jeans. He looked at the older dark angel and knew he wouldn't like what she said next.

"They were family, I think."

Chapter 4

I T HAD BEEN a long week in the Underworld. Former Directors, with the exception of Audray's predecessor, had never learned to read. Joshua, her sponsor, had told her that was a good thing. An educated dark angel was more dangerous to the "live and let live" lifestyle of the Underworld and was someone to be feared, according to him. "Remember, my dear, Heaven is imperfect by *design*. The Underworld is imperfect by *accident*." He warned her that anyone who mastered the organizational skills and could read would enslave all dark angels to a life of obedience, something he detested.

So Audray had spent the entire time working her way through reversing several bureaucratic layers Peter had imposed on the Underworld, relaxing some of the ridiculous rules he'd set in place to restrain and control his dark angel subjects.

She studied the new requirements Peter had imposed on the number of new souls recruits were to achieve or risk elimination. He'd made lists of dark angels who had not fulfilled that quota and she noted a number of long-time allies of Joshua's had been eliminated. Then she found Joshua's file about her own past, with the official transcript of her own turning, which intrigued her.

Jonas was sitting with one leg over the arm of a new red leather high backed chair she'd brought into the office, waiting to escort her home for the evening.

"Listen to what Joshua says of me, *'She is easily the most well-*

equipped dark angel I have ever turned. Although I don't believe in predestination, Audray's existence makes a case for it.'"

Jonas' bedroom eyes and crooked smile told her he agreed. "You are indeed a natural. Never met anyone so perfect for this job, my love."

"And I would have said Joshua was the natural. A born leader," she answered back.

"Who never wanted to be a leader. He just didn't like people messing with *him*." She was reading the report further, when he asked, "Does that ever bother you that he thought your higher calling was being a dark angel?"

"Never. As a human, I felt limited." But it still hurt when she thought about her past. The unfinished business of her revenge should have left her, she thought, but instead, the growing urge to strike back was consuming more and more of her thoughts. She read on, but kept her emotions quiet and shielded from Jonas.

'I have given her the right to seek revenge against her human abuser, something I've done only a couple of other times, and with disastrous results. I believe Audray can handle it, like she has handled every other task I have given her.'

"You are worried about something?" he asked her, finally. The man was patient, but protective.

"Not really. But I do have some unfinished things up top." She hoped he wouldn't be able to feel her true intentions. She didn't like to mislead or lie to Jonas, but she wanted this part of her life to remain private, at least for now.

"Then I'll make arrangements. When do we leave?"

"Jonas, I'll be fine on my own. I know you have work you want to complete down here. When I'm done, and you finish your investigation, we'll meet for a few days in the human world, how about that?"

"I do have some leads I'm working on. But I don't like you being alone for too long."

"Just a few days. Four or five at the most, okay?"

NEXT DAY, AUDRAY was finally back in the human world, fulfilling the promise she'd made to herself. She had thought about making this trip hundreds of times since she was sixteen. Though Jonas had offered to go with her, this was something she had to do, and do alone. She wasn't ready to tell him that she had a living human mother. It had continued to nag at her after she assumed the role of the Director. And while part of her just wished for another few days off with Jonas to kick back and enjoy the way their bodies mingled and played, she was feeling something stirring in the air—something dark and dangerous. So, while he was consumed with his research about the two new dark angel recruits, now seemed like the perfect time to confront her past. There would be time for the pleasure—an eternity in fact—later.

When she was offered immortality in exchange for her life as a human, she was promised she could go back and seek revenge against the man who raped her just a week after her sixteenth birthday: her mother's live-in boyfriend, Burt.

It was time.

She'd spent hours thinking about how to kill him, how to exact as much pain as possible. After the brutal rape, which occurred the evening before her dance competition, she took the five hundred dollars she won despite her emotional and physical pain, and hitch-hiked to LA in a big rig driven by a Christian trucker. She hadn't seen her mother since.

The truck driver dropped her off at the YWCA and even paid for a night, leaving her damaged body without touching her, as if she was the young virgin he thought she was. He'd given her his cell number in case she ran into trouble anywhere, but she never talked to him or saw him again. He was the sort of man Audray wished her mother could have chosen to share her trailer and bed with.

Shaking her head to scatter the disturbing memories, Audray focused on the task at hand. Stepping off the Underworld transit, Audray exited the warehouse and walked to her house near the station to grab a few things and pick up her red Maserati.

The freeway was a pleasure to drive. Though Peter had purchased the red machine, Audray's taste in cars was identical, and she rather liked the pitchfork design on the grill.

The seedy outskirts of her birthplace announced the town as surely as any billboard. Recalling how close the trailer park was to the freeway, she had no trouble locating Riverbend Estates, though the sign was still unrepaired from the rifle shots fired at it some twenty years ago.

Bet that would be a story.

She entered the potholed drive, avoiding two white chickens as they scurried past. There certainly wasn't a river in sight, and these trailer homes were not estates—they were dumps on wheels. A small band of bedraggled children were playing with sticks at the side of the road. Girls in dirty rags and bare feet carried naked dolls by the hair.

Nobody was smiling, but they looked at the car.

Slowly, Audray pulled up to a concrete parking pad near the trailer with a torn front door screen. The door was open.

Is she home?

At that moment, a thin older woman with graying blonde hair pulled back in a ponytail stepped onto the front stoop and dumped an ashtray full of cigarette butts onto the ground. Tapping the plastic bowl on the metal railing twice, she turned and just as she reached for the door handle, saw Audray's car. She stopped, frozen in place.

Audray turned off the motor, opened the driver's side door and stepped out into the dusty air. She removed her sunglasses and stared into the lined and tormented face of her mother.

"It's me," Audray said, just loud enough to carry above the noises of the freeway nearby.

Her mother set down the ashtray as if it were a piece of crystal and shuffled with a limp across the metal porch to the top of the steps. Her cheeks were sunken and her face had a definite green pallor to it. When she smiled, Audray could see half her teeth were missing.

She could have been beautiful at one time. Audray glimpsed a flicker of recognition, but suspected it was through an alcohol-induced haze. Her mother's eyes appeared to have trouble catching up to her head movements.

"Auddie? That you?" The woman hesitated as if confused what to do, but all of a sudden, her legs seemed to propel her on their own, as the older woman hobbled down the stairs. She stopped at the bottom, hanging on to the railing for balance, breathing with difficulty.

Audray crossed the yard and stood in front of the woman who gave birth to her. As much as she had tried over the years to tear her own heart out, she could not find it in herself to hate the disheveled sack of bones before her. The unhealthy woman was obviously close to the end of her human life. For her mother's sake, as well as for her own, Audray hoped this would silence the pain forever. Audray was surprised to find that she didn't want her mother to suffer.

"You came back. I always thought you'd come back." The woman weaved. Her right hand clutched the handrail, but her left arm shot out, fingers splayed.

"Yes, Mama." Audrey grabbed the woman and hugged her carefully, as if too much pressure would shatter her brittle bones. The woman began to shake, and Audray thought she was crying, but soon realized they were tremors. She looked at the grey-green closed eyelids and wondered if her mother was dead.

Audray picked her up easily and carried her into the trailer. She figured her mother weighed less than ninety pounds. She walked down the clothes-strewn promenade of liquor bottles to the rear of the trailer, where she knew her mother slept.

She nested her in a pile of dirty clothes and sheets, propping a pillow under her head and kneeled at her side, rubbing her hand until the woman came to. Her first breath of raspy air came with difficulty, as if her mother hadn't expected to still be alive. But soon she opened her eyes, recognized her daughter, and exhaled the foulest breath Audray had ever smelled.

She was mumbling something to her. When Audray leaned her ear in, she heard, "My cigarettes. Where are my cigarettes?"

"Not now, Mama. You don't need them."

The woman righted herself and with amazing strength, sat up and hoarsely barked, "I want my goddamned cigarettes now!"

Audray dropped her hand and searched the countertop in the kitchen, finding them atop a pile of plates with spoiled food and empty pill bottles. She walked out through the screen door to retrieve the ashtray and heard her mother yell out to her.

"Hey! Don't go stealin' my cigarettes. You can afford some of your own."

Now this made Audray smile. She hadn't smoked since she was sixteen. Removing one from the package, she held it up to her nose and confirmed how she loathed the practice. With the smirk still fresh on her face, she held the white stick out front at arm's length and lit the end with a red ray of fire from her index finger.

Pleased with herself, she put it to her lips and took a long hard drag, filling her lungs with the awful smoke.

"When in Rome," she whispered as she exhaled and coughed. She surveyed the park as she leaned on the railing and took another drag. Rarely did it happen, but the scene was worse than she had remembered.

The fit of coughing and spitting up something otherworldly reminded her that her mother was calling her again.

"Coming."

Audray bent down to hand over the lit cigarette, but it got ripped from her fingers. Seeming to get strength from a couple of deep puffs, her mother addressed her with a scowl, "Thanks."

Yes, Mother. You were right. There are things that are worse than death.

"How'd you like to live like this forever, Mom?" Audray raised her eyebrows and gave her a sultry smile.

Her mother looked back at her with squinting eyes, holding the cigarette in the lower right quadrant of her purple lips, and responded, "You nuts?"

Audray took a seat on the corner of the bed, careful to avoid getting punctured by an empty needle. Her mother noticed.

"Vitamins."

"I didn't figure you for the health nut type." *Why can't you just will yourself to die? Or do you hate yourself so much you want to linger on and make everyone else miserable too?* She looked at her mother's shriveled breastbone and blotchy yellowed skin and wondered how she could have suckled from this woman as a baby. *What kind of poison did you feed my soul?*

As if her mother could read her thoughts. "Well, missy. Look at you, all growed up and 'sophisticated' like. Here you are, driving around in that beast and lettin' your ol' mother waste away in this shithole."

"I've paid my dues." Audray gave her a steely stare, tinged in red, hoping to scare the woman.

Her mother didn't notice. She was trying to whisk away ashes that had fallen from the cigarette onto the blue and yellow daisy quilt. "You weren't the only one. I had to put up with that man's beatings nearly every day, even when I was pregnant with you."

"You should have left."

"I did, moved here, moved a hundred miles away and thought maybe he'd leave me alone. But he found me.

"You took the scumbag back? What were you thinking?"

"Audray, your father had been killed in the war and I was all alone. I was pregnant and I was a mess. He took care of me at first. He seemed so nice. But then he changed."

"He nearly ruined my life," Audray whispered as she stared out the small porthole window to the dump of the trailer park.

"Well be grateful. He did ruin your sister's life."

"My sister?" Flashes of a recurring dream about being in danger, and someone, some blonde angel protecting her. Her mother had always told her she was crazy.

She'd blocked out so much about the rape, despite her best efforts, she began experiencing the nightmare of that day again. She saw Burt's body looming over her, taunting her.

"Go ahead, I'll do to you what I did to her," he'd growled. Audray had always thought he was talking about her mother. Did he mean her sister?

Her mother turned her head to the side and wept, her chest caving deep as her painful gasps punctuated the stale air inside the trailer.

Audray used her fingers, digging into the woman's cheekbones under her jaw and righted her face so they could look into each other's eyes. "Tell me about my sister."

Her mother looked like a little girl. Her lower lip quivered as her eyebrows tented. Silently, she nodded. She stared at Audray as if in fear, as if she expected to be struck. "Burt—Burt strangled her and ran off."

Audray was filled with rage. She wanted to snap the woman's neck. "So he came back, and you let that man back into our house? Why didn't you have him arrested?"

"They arrested someone else for it at first. I couldn't believe he'd done it. So when they arrested someone else, I just figured Burt had taken off on a bender."

"I want to know about my sister."

Her mother reached across the bed, opening a drawer in the built in cabinet, pulling out a fistful of yellowed photographs. She clutched them to her chest in her gnarled and reddened fingers.

"She protected you. Protected you with her life. They found you wandering the park site, looking for me. She was babysitting you while we were at work."

"How old was she?"

"Twenty-two. She lived up north, but was here for a few days, helping us out. We were in a real bind. She never liked Burt, just so you know."

She looked down at the curled photographs, tucked and cradled in her breast and drew a smile. Audray could see the beauty of her face at one time, at a glimpse of a woman who was happy before she'd succumbed to her addictions. "She was a sweet girl, and the apple of your father's eye. She'd taken your father's death hard, but had started a new life. I asked too much of her." Large tears streaked down her mother's cheeks.

Audray wanted to see what her mother was hesitant to share with her. She wanted her hands on the photographs.

"They could never prove anything, you see," her mother began again. "Burt came back all healthy. Stopped drinking. Was helping me clean up too, but then we just—we just couldn't stay that way."

Audray's anger was tempered by the understanding her mother was just basically a weak person incapable of handling the double tragedy, let alone life itself. Her mother's wounds were self-inflicted. Knowing what she did about the dark angel population, Audray realized she could become prey to some cunning dark angel looking for another convert. She vowed not to allow this to happen, though the taste of it was a bitter pill.

"Let me see the picture. You have a picture of her?" Audray asked.

Her mother handed her a faded photograph of her much younger and happier self, standing next to a handsome man in uniform, with a blonde young woman between them whose face she recognized.

Claire.

Her friend Daniel's Claire, the Guardian angel that Joshua Brandon, Audray's mentor, had fought with—*that* Claire stared back at her through space and time. Stunned, Audray realized Claire had become a Guardian angel by dying to save her.

The Director of the Underworld's own sister was a Guardian—a sworn enemy.

Chapter 5

CARL SET THE large book down on the dark wooden table at his favorite Irish pub. He sighed, pulling back a lock of hair that had fallen over his forehead, anxious to begin his research for the mysterious dark lady who paid him handsomely. Straightening his bowtie, he noticed a shadow fall across the table.

The perfume cloyed his senses, and for a moment he thought of luscious Molly and her breasts offered him so shamelessly this afternoon.

The barmaid's name was Caitlyn, he noted as he looked up at her nametag. Probably not her real name, since the girl was Asian.

"You're new here, Caitlyn," Carl said as he flashed her a quick smile she seemed to warm to.

"Actually, I'm Caitlyn's roommate, filling in for her tonight." She smiled and shook her head.

"Did I miss something?"

"No, you didn't miss a thing. You're the first one who noticed." She repositioned the brown serving tray under her arm and extended her right hand. "I'm Uma."

He took hold of her delicate fingers and a part of him wanted to kiss them, decorated with purple nail polish. But he shook her hand instead. "That's a beautiful name for a lovely lady."

"Yes, and you'll get me fired if you don't order soon."

"I'll have a Newcastle draft," he said, adjusting his collar again and repositioning his lap.

"Coming right up."

Carl thought perhaps he imagined she was intentionally exaggerating her tail feathers—until she looked over her shoulder and nodded to him demurely.

He quickly got back to examining the book.

"If I let you take it overnight, you must bring it back first thing in the morning," Molly had said.

Of course he could do that.

"And you'll owe me, Professor Carrington." At first Carl wondered if she meant he had to pay a fee, but then when he caught on to her implication, he straightened his bowtie and felt his cheeks flame.

He reached into his tweed jacket pocket and pulled out the index card with Molly's phone number on it.

"Call me if you want to turn it in tonight. I'll take very good care of it until morning, I promise."

He felt his cheeks blush again. He had just been able to accept that he had dirty thoughts about the young redheaded library science student. But now that his attraction was being returned, he wasn't sure how he felt about it.

Conquering new territory here.

The soft purr of a female voice jolted him back.

"One frosty Newcastle. Anything else I can get you, Professor?" She finished it off with a wink.

Carl winced and glanced around the room to see if he had attracted anyone else's attention. He was sure his voice would sound like a ten-year-old, so he just shook his head and gulped his beer, holding it with both hands.

The ice-cold liquid settled his nerves. His throat had been parched. The stuffy smoke-filled pub was noisy and hot. He removed his bowtie, put it in his pocket and attempted to undo his collar. It was like unbuttoning two pieces of cardboard, but at last the tiny button yielded and his neck was free.

He took another sip of the draft and, drying his fingers on the thighs of his pants, flipped open the heavy navy blue front cover embossed in gold and black lettering. The first few pages were clear onionskin in a cream shade, crinkling as he turned each page carefully. He looked at the date of the publication.

1860.

Pirates of the Americas, by Sir Anthony Markham.

Carl began to read the short prologue.

I have attempted to explain the life of piracy certain brave young men took to when their families stopped supporting them and their fortunes waned. Lured by the call to adventure, they engaged in practices we might today consider criminal, yet they were in fact sanctioned and often openly supported by the Royal houses of England, France and Spain.

These men, and a few women, were pawns in a much larger chess game played out by the kings and queens, knights and bishops of their time.

And yet their bravery and gallantry, their respect for the code of the high seas made them royalty, without the golden robes and crowns. For wealth can be defined in many ways.

Unlike their earthly masters, some even cheated death itself. I would like to think they rule over kingdoms we have yet to discover, that their graves house a bundle of bones but their souls reign supreme and live forever.

—Sir A.M.

June, 1856

Carl thumbed through the list of chapters, not knowing which one he needed. His finger stopped at the Sixteenth Chapter entitled: The Life and Tragedy of Jonas Starling.

Jonas Starling was born in 1667, the youngest of four brothers, and grew up in the country surrounding the town of York, where his father, the 3rd Earl of Stratoven, had considerable lands and tended a well-managed family farm. He also had developed plantations in the Caribbean, and, as a young boy, Jonas had accompanied his father there to learn about overseeing his family's interests in the islands some day.

A tall handsome lad as a youth, he came to the attention of the ladies quite early. As the youngest son, he would not inherit, but if he married well, could advance his station in life considerably. So, at the age of eighteen, he was betrothed to the lovely Anne Mackenzie, only daughter and heir to Ian Mackenzie, a very wealthy Scottish Laird. This match would also secure Mackenzie's ties to England, as his father had been rumored to be a supporter of the restoration of the Scottish monarchy, though Ian Mackenzie swore otherwise.

Carl looked around him. The tavern had filled to near capacity. A number of couples were eyeing his booth with the empty bench seat across from him. He had a twinge of guilt, but was anxious to get back to his reading.

Before the marriage could take place, however, in 1685 Jonas was summoned to the Court of Charles II, who was in desperate need of a male heir, having fathered a dozen children, illegitimately. The Queen looked fondly upon the young lad so, as a test of his family's loyalty and to help cement the Mackenzie alliance, he was asked to spend the summer with her and to become her lover. He was to bring about a male heir, under the cloak of secrecy. A high Catholic, the superstitious Portuguese-bred Queen secretly believed enemies of her husband's had cursed her womb.

Heartbroken, at first Jonas refused, but when even his betrothed urged him to do his part for his family and her clan, he relented. He came to live at the court, ostensibly to advise the King on farming techniques.

"Excuse me. Can we join you?" A fresh-faced coed leaned toward him, her arm entwined with a young man's. He was laughing, conversing with a couple at an adjoining table, oblivious to what his companion was trying to negotiate.

"Yes," Carl said despite the fact that he felt like his private life had been intruded upon. When she looked down at what he was reading, he covered it with his right hand. The young woman pulled her companion down next to her, across the table from Carl and his book.

"I'm Robert. Thanks." The kid held his hand out as he snuggled close to the girl.

Carl shook his hand and then pulled the book into his chest a bit, checking the surrounding area to make sure no one else could read over his shoulder. The couple began to make out furiously. Even though Carl was trying to find his place, he couldn't help but notice the young man's hand slipping under her shirt. When he looked at her face, she was smiling at him, over the top of her friend's head as he kissed her neck and upper chest.

It reminded Carl of how long it had been since he'd made love to a woman. He quickly found his place and soon forgot about the room and the randy young couple.

In short order, the Queen's pregnancy became known. Anxious to return to his home in York and the arms of his young betrothed, he was disappointed to learn the Queen had no intention of releasing him. In fact, she believed he was good luck to her, and rewarded loyalty by allowing childless ladies in her court to lay with him in exchange for favors. He threatened to escape many times, but was warned that he held the fortunes, if not the lives, of his father and his soon to be father-in-law, in the palm of his hand.

The scandal of his real purpose at the Court broke just as the King died, leaving the country in disarray. As a male heir had not yet been born, an uprising ensued. Jonas refused to join the cause. Before he could get home, armies slaughtered all of the Mackenzies, including Anne. Jonas' father and his two brothers were hanged in the public square as traitors. Jonas fled to the Caribbean.

Though he was rightful heir to the family's interests in the Virgin Islands, he was thwarted by numerous slave uprisings. A huge infusion of capital was needed to help stabilize the disrupted operations. Hindered by a lack of funds, the plantations were taken over by several managers and agents who had been previously loyal to the elder Starling.

Carl heard her moan. She was straddling him, and it appeared they were doing it right there. In spite of himself, Carl blushed. He no longer felt it was his table.

"Excuse me," he whispered as he stood and left them to their lovemaking. He didn't even get a look from them as he parted his way through the crowd and into the night air. It frustrated him he had to be so close to so many people.

Three doors down was a much quieter place, a coffee house with tons of vacant tables. He chose one in the corner and ordered a cappuccino.

Jonas turned to the seas and joined what he thought was a salvage operation, in order to raise funds to defend his claim. Through mutiny and demise of the captain on one voyage, he was pressed into service as a pirate, or face death.

Jonas excelled at being a corsair or pirate. He soon rose through the ranks and became known as the Blackbird, using a black starling symbol on his ship's colors. He brought great wealth to his crew and investors who hired him. But he tried to spare human life whenever possible, and had a reputation for protecting women, especially beautiful women. This made little difference to the authorities, and he became a wanted man, unable to have a permanent home without fear of being arrested. One day, his luck ran out.

The barista brought him a large-handled brown ceramic cup and saucer. He inhaled the frothy foam at the top and savored the warm elixir he loved on Sunday mornings while reading his newspaper. Had the world gone crazy? Kids having sex in front of him at his favorite tavern? Promising students with perhaps a dark agenda? Lovely Molly who haunted him and made his groin lurch whenever he thought of her? A mysterious lady wanting information about a 17th century man who turned to a life of piracy after losing his entire fortune and his family?

I'm merely a professor. Am I a magnet for these things? He didn't have an answer.

He read on:

Having lost all he held dear, and now a wanted criminal, he perished in a prison somewhere on Antigua in his early twenties.

Stories are still told in dark places in some of the shantytowns dotted throughout the Caribbean, that Jonas lived, and was found leading a quiet life in several places around the islands. Rumor has it that each time he was found, he would disappear again.

Carl wondered why he had never run across this compelling story before.

Why is she interested in him? He considered the sultry dark-haired young woman who asked for his help, who had agreed to advance him a month's wages to give her a dossier on this intriguing character from history. He was to meet up with her on Saturday at this very coffee shop.

He thumbed through the book, looking for other references to Jonas Starling, but could find none. He finished off his coffee, declining a second cup and tipped the girl generously. He cradled the book under his left arm and made a path to the front door.

Grateful for the cool night air, he decided to walk the few blocks to an all-night copy store, instead of taking his car. There, he duplicated the short chapter.

"You have permission to copy this? Ever hear about copyright laws?" The clerk had greasy hair and pink skin, dotted with red blemishes. His dark eyes studied him.

Carl opened the cover of the book and flipped to the publication date. "You ever heard of Shastra Publishing? Do you think anyone is still alive who cares?" The clerk looked down at his finger tapping on the 1860 notation.

"Never can tell."

Carl looked at his watch. "Look, man, I'll just go somewhere else. I come in here all the time and make copies of manuscripts. I'm a history professor."

"I know who you are."

Does he have a smile on his face? Who the hell is this kid? Carl felt a chill tingle down his spine.

"Ah, probably nothing to worry about, right?" The kid broke into an evil smirk. "I mean, who could possibly care after a hundred and fifty years?" He rang up the fee and Carl paid with his campus credit card.

He felt the clerk's eyes on his back as he left the store. Carl raised his hand to adjust his bowtie and then discovered he had already removed it. He undid one more button on his shirt and rolled his shoulders.

Maybe I should have stayed for the second beer. Walking back to his car relaxed him.

The cottage Carl lived in was part of the campus housing for single staff. But he would have chosen it on his own. He loved the cobble-stoned entryway and random brick patterns on the outside walls covered with vines of ivy. The windows were small-paned in a criss-cross pattern, like some of the thatched cottages in the Cotswold district he loved to visit in England. He could almost live the history he studied, as if, once stepping into the little dwelling, he was transported back in time.

The mailbox at his front door was nearly empty. He unlocked the heavy oak door and entered his domain, setting the book down on a steamer trunk that was his coffee table. The house was in need of a fire. He stoked it quickly and sat down on the brown leather couch, watching the flames take hold.

When he removed his tweed jacket he remembered his bowtie, which he carefully extricated, along with the folded index card with Molly's number on it.

Molly, what would you look like here, on this couch by the fire? Would you let me unbutton your...

"Oh, God help me," he muttered. *Perhaps it's been too long since I've had a woman.* He wondered if he would even know what to do.

He stood up, kicked off his shoes and walked in his Argyle socks to the kitchen and poured himself a Scotch.

Now this is what I really wanted. He poured himself another and took it over to the couch, setting the short glass next to the heavy book. The light of the fire danced on the dull dark green paint of the trunk, on the wooden stays and brass studs holding it together, and on the curled index card. He saw the numbers flickering as he leaned over and picked up the paper.

Without thinking, he retrieved his cell phone from the inside pocket of his jacket and dialed her number. He leaned back into the soft leather and sighed, listening to the rings. He licked his lips and tasted the warm liquor residue there.

On the third ring, she picked up.

"Well, hello."

Had she expected me really to call?

"I've read the book, and I…" *What was it he really wanted to say?* "I have something to do in the morning, and thought perhaps your suggestion of returning it to you tonight might work out better." His exhale drew static on the line, but Molly was patient with her response.

"Okay."

"Well, I don't want to get you into trouble, you know, with the book and all."

"No. We definitely don't want me to get into trouble."

Carl's face flushed again. He'd always envisioned doing things to her in the stacks, but now he saw other possibilities.

"Well, I could…"

"Why don't I come over?"

He had been holding his breath and released a sigh she no doubt heard. "That would be good. I think I will be up for a bit."

There was a pause. Molly whispered into the phone, "Oh, I hope you'll be up for more than a bit. I won't make you wait long." The phone went dead.

Should I call her back and cancel? Does she know where I live? He looked at his cell phone keypad and almost hit redial to cancel. Was this sound judgment on his part?

But as he stood to hang up his jacket and put another log on the fire, the growing bulge in his pants was beginning to call all the shots.

MOLLIE'S BUG RATTLED up the driveway and abruptly stopped mid-sputter. Carl had brushed his teeth, reapplied aftershave, and changed his shirt. He opened the heavy front door and tried to stand casually in the doorframe. He could feel the warmth of the fireplace at his back. Molly's red hair shone in the blue light of the streetlamp at the bottom of the driveway. As she walked to him, he could see her soft white cheeks, her moist red lips, and the hint of cleavage, covered demurely by her nylon jacket.

In one fluid motion she touched his chest with the mounds of her breasts, and even through their clothes he felt the heat of her body. He lowered his head and she met his lips with hers, parting them, giving him a tiny moan which melted deliciously in his mouth.

He pulled away to look into her eyes, which sparkled green. He held her cheeks with the palms of his hands and rubbed his thumbs over her lips, devouring the feel of her flawless pink skin, the look of her red hair and the beautiful emerald green hue of her eyes. "Beautiful. You are so beautiful, Molly."

She smiled, and guided one of his hands to her breast. His thumb traced the bulge created above her pink satin bra, and, as he unbuttoned her shirt, saw there was a clasp in the front, which he quickly undid.

His groin lurched at the sight of the two pink orbs waiting for him to touch with his tongue.

A car drove by, and Carl was reminded of where they were. He pulled her inside his bachelor cottage by encircling one arm around her waist and closing the door with the other. Her scent enveloped him.

I've captured you.

It had been a long time, for he suddenly didn't know what to do next. She removed her jacket and let it drop to the floor at her feet. She finished unbuttoning her shirt and let it drop. Then she removed the gaping bra by letting the straps slip down her arms as she squeezed her breasts together, distorting them, pushing up the rose-colored nipples.

She unzipped her jeans and slipped them down her hips, her eyes still nailing him. She wore no panties, and the light red fuzz of her sex called him to explore.

Her body was perfect in every way, the body that would adorn a porcelain plate as Venus herself. She could have posed for a large nude portrait that would hang in a gentlemen's club to be lusted after for generations. *She could have been the mistress to kings.* He imagined being alone with her in a tent in the desert or kissing her body amongst vines and lush dark leaves in a rainforest jungle like in the adventure books he read as a youth.

She turned, showing him her backside, the rounded perfectly formed cheeks of her heart-shaped ass, as she pulled out several pins and her hair fell down her back.

Carl felt his knees buckle for just a second. He knew he was thoroughly entranced. His fantasy woman had come to life, just as if she had risen from the pages of history to claim his soul.

I'll take my time. I will savor every square inch of your perfect body.

He would make her moan under him and beg for more. He wanted her body to consume him in the fire of her red hair.

All night long.

Chapter 6

JONAS FLIPPED OPEN his sat phone.

"Hi there. It's so good to hear your voice." Audray answered.

"Same here. You okay?"

He heard the hesitation in her voice.

"Audray, tell me. What's happened?"

Again she hesitated, but she took a deep breath and then began, "I found my mother, Jonas."

"Good. And? Is she what you thought she was?"

"Worse. But there's more. Jonas, I have a sister. Not only that, but she died trying to protect me when I was still in diapers."

"How does your mother know all this?" he asked.

"I saw her picture. And I saw a picture of my father too. She is Claire, the Guardian, remember? She's Daniel's Claire. The one Joshua was trying to turn, remember?"

"Claire is your sister, was your sister?" He couldn't believe this to be true. He'd helped Joshua in his attempts to snag the little Guardian.

"Well, since she's alive she's my sister still."

"Are you going to try to meet with her?"

"Not yet. I'd like you with me when I do."

"Sounds fair enough. What's next then?"

"My mother told me where their bodies are buried and I'm going to go visit tomorrow, before—before I run one more errand and then I'll meet you."

"We still on for San Francisco on Saturday?"

"Can't wait. I need to get out of the Central Valley as soon as I can. This place is sucking me down into a pit of despair. I hate it here."

He paused.

"Jonas, is anything wrong?"

"No. Not unless you didn't get the bridal suite at the St. Francis."

Audray laughed. "Oh, ye of little faith. If it's truly your favorite, I'll buy it for you as a wedding present."

"Wedding?" Jonas wasn't sure he was hearing things properly. "I said bridal suite, as in the nice room with the view of the city and the big jetted tub?"

"Yes, love. And I want something more. I want to make you my legal tender."

We haven't discussed this. With any other woman it would have made Jonas panic, but he didn't mind the liberties Audray took when it came to claiming him. He smiled.

"Oh, I can be tender."

"Yes, I know. The problem is with the legal part. Jonas, can you be legal?"

"No. I've always been told I am over the legal limit."

It was Audray's turn to laugh. "I've noticed."

He remembered what he had to do in the next twenty-four hours. "Audray, I want you to be careful."

"What's happened?"

"There's another one just like the one you had executed. He's been down here a month or more."

"So, find him. You have my permission to kill him."

"Well, there's something else."

"Yes? You are beginning to worry me, Jonas. Or is this just a way for you to stall parading your luscious ass down a red carpet to say 'I do'?"

43

"Funny."

"Or maybe you don't want the tailor measuring you all over for a tux…"

"I've cut men's arms off for less."

"There you go. But I'm not going to give up until you are mine. Truly mine in every sense of the word."

In the old days, this would have been his cue to disappear again. But now, there was the smell of danger all about. *Tides are changing. War is brewing. People are going to die.*

"Audray, I don't want to lose you."

"The only way I want to lose myself is in your arms and in your bed. You probably couldn't be rid of me if you tried with all your immortal might."

Wish that were true. He didn't like thinking Audray could become someone's target because of her relationship with him.

"I mean it, Audray. There are things going on that are not good. Not good at all."

"What things?"

"Peter sponsored both of them."

"Well, he was supposed to troll for souls, in addition to running the Underworld. I don't find that odd at all."

"They were both related to him, blood related."

"I never thought family was important to that bastard. He seemed so consumed with himself. I didn't think he had any family. Odd he never told me."

Jonas never liked to think about how close Audray had gotten to Peter, and what she had to perform to be given the ability to vaporize, which was usually something only the most powerful dark angel possessed. Even past Directors failed to have the skill.

"So you can see how this changes things," Jonas continued.

"I misjudged him. That could be dangerous in my current occupation," she said. Her voice was strained, a little hoarse. Her internal chatter seemed purposely jammed so he couldn't tell what she was feeling. But he knew she was getting nervous.

"That's why you have me here, my Queen. Remember? I am the keeper of your soul."

He heard the satisfying exhale and then came a flood of images he liked much better.

"Thank you, sweetheart."

"I guess I'm just missing you, Jonas. It's getting harder and harder to be away from you."

"Me, as well."

Jonas knew about family and what desperate people would do to retain power. He had lost himself in the Underworld, thinking he could escape it all. If Peter hadn't been eliminated, who knew what he would have done? Would he have been able to establish a family dynasty that could never be overthrown? How far along in this process had he gotten?

"I just want you to be careful, until I can be by your side again. I think there's someone out there worse than Peter, Audray. And I think he's coming here. Just watch your back."

If he had known about all of this, would he have involved her? *Probably no fucking way I would have been able to control myself.* Were assassins being sent to eliminate him so they could have a clear shot at Audray? He was beginning to feel they both were being sought after.

After all, Audray had already helped to bring down the former Director. That would have made her a target without the added burden of being the one woman in the whole universe Jonas wanted to keep from harm's way.

Chapter 7

AUDRAY HAD TO stay at a motel a hundred miles away to find something decent enough that didn't make her skin itch. So it was after ten when she pulled into the parking lot of the dilapidated metal building that was her old dance studio. There was one car parked near the front door.

On hot days, and there had been many of those, her instructor, former skating sensation Michael Murphy, would roll up the metal corrugated door and turn the music up to play over the slogging water cooler that managed to sound like it was working. As she approached the glass door with the tinkle bell over the top, she heard music coming from inside. Some light jazz.

She looked through the glass, all of a sudden shy about invading this man's space—probably the only man who truly cared about her way back then when she was 16. She used to go to bed at night and fondle her own breasts, pretending Mr. Murphy was doing it. Every correction he made to her form was an intimate act to Audray, and it left her skin burning in strange places, not just where his fingers had been.

Audray had been tall for her age. She smiled as she remembered Mr. Murphy was always getting on her about leading her male partners around.

If he only knew who I am today.

Michael Murphy walked across the padded blue floor in his bare feet, shirtless, wearing a towel over his shoulders. His grey warm-up pants were filled with stains and holes. He rolled his neck and arms, stretched his calf and thigh muscles to complete his warm up exercises.

The muscles in his chest were still well defined, and Audray knew he would look fit and handsome until he got sick and could no longer dance. She found all the things she had wanted to say to him over the past ten years well up inside her. She pushed open the door and the little bell warned him.

She could see he recognized her immediately, but waited, his hands pulling down on both edges of the white towel as it draped over his neck. His breathing was just beginning to go back to normal, but Audray could see a small catch in his chest a couple of times as he watched her approach him.

She tried to walk towards him as if she were a ten-year-old. It was impossible to do. Her female equipment and years of training got in the way.

"Hi, Mr. Murphy. Do you remember me?"

"Audray. There isn't a day that goes by when I don't wonder what became of you."

She spread her arms to the side and did a full turn in front of him. She had on a red nylon slicker, black stretch pants and white mohair turtleneck. She hadn't put on her thigh-high red boots because Jonas wasn't around to help her remove them, but her red spiked heel ankle boots felt just as constricting.

"Still wearing red and black, I see." He grinned. "I'd say you did okay after all. I was hoping…"

"I'm fine. You heard what happened?"

Murphy nodded his head and looked at his toes. "Yeah, and your mother took it pretty hard too. We thought perhaps he came back and killed you, but then the police found a truck driver who…"

"He was my Guardian angel that day."

"I'm glad he was." He stepped closer to her, the space between them reduced to only two feet. "I wish you had waited for me after the contest. I looked for you. I wish you had trusted me enough to let me help you. I would have, you know."

"I know."

"It's been the biggest regret of my life. I should have been there for you."

"You aren't my father." Audray didn't like excuses.

"But I should have protected you."

Audray broke the space and walked toward the center of the floor, then remembered her red heels and slipped them off. She looked at the rusted walls and beams of the metal building, the broken window repaired with duct tape, the metal chairs surrounding the floor she used to sit on impatiently awaiting her turn.

This was my world at one time. This was where I came to escape.

"Of all the things my mother didn't do, at least she got me dance lessons," she said at last.

"Actually, she stopped paying after the second month. We taught you all those years because it was the right thing to do. Couldn't see you spending your time hanging around the trailer park or begging for coke money at the truck stop. You can thank my wife for that."

Always been able to find people to save me, heal me. Is this a natural gift?

"So, are you dancing?"

This amused her. "In a manner of speaking." She turned slowly and cocked her head. *Should I tell him?*

"Every time we go to the movies I look for you. I was so sure I would see your picture up on a big screen some day." As he approached her, he frowned. "Your eyes—are those contacts?"

Audray forgot about the change in her eye color due to the turning. Her emerald green eyes were now deep black.

"It's just something I prefer now. I'm not who I was back then. I've changed, in many ways."

"Haven't we all?"

No, some people don't change. Like my mother. Like Burt.

"Thank you, Mr. Murphy, for all the kindness you shown me over the years. I think my dancing gave me the courage to leave this place."

"Well, you survived. And now look at you."

It took me years to recover. Ten years of my life. It would have been more if it hadn't been for my acquaintance with the dark angel who turned me, Joshua.

Michael Murphy walked over to her and placed his hands tenderly on her shoulders, causing Audray to start. It was the first time they had touched since that afternoon before the competition, when she stole from him a dangerous kiss. But as Audray looked into his grey eyes, she saw the pain there, not the sensuality she expected from his touch.

All of a sudden the pathetic, dirty town became too much for her. Overcome, Audray fell into Murphy's arms, sobbing. He held her shaking body carefully, rubbing her hair and saying soothing things to the top of her head buried deep in his chest.

"Audray, we all worried, but hoped for the best. You were—are such a strong woman. I knew somehow you'd survive. I just knew it."

If he only knew what things I'm battling now. Her whole life she'd wanted to get even with Burt, prayed for this day. And now there were things brewing which were much worse, things perhaps outside of her control.

But that wouldn't stop her from fulfilling the promise she'd made to herself as her body healed, as she emotionally survived, every time she looked in the mirror, every time she was admired, every time she did something worthy of praise.

She hoped Jonas would understand. She had to pay Burt back for all the pain he'd caused her family.

She'd do it for Claire too. She was her sister before she was her enemy. She wasn't going to ask for permission. She'd ask for forgiveness later. Much later.

Chapter 8

CARL AWOKE TO the feel of warm flesh on his chest and down his thigh. Molly's perfume had permeated the bedroom, coating his dark heavy oak furniture with her femininity. Her smell would be all over the brown quilt his grandmother had made him. His bathroom would no longer be the place where he readied himself for the day, but the place where she had him ram into her rear over the sink counter, as he watched her lips form the O of her moan, matching the color of her blushing cheeks. Seeing her face in his mirror, he knew he would recall that moment every time he stared into it to shave.

For the rest of my life.

He had never brought a woman to this home, let alone a grad student. He closed his eyes again, unwilling to wake her. Feeling her skin on his skin, he dreamed of what a future encounter could be.

He felt twenty years old again. He imagined he had rescued her from the clutches of an evil prince, so grateful were her affections. All evening he starred as the hero of her movie, the conquering victor taking the spoils. She would bring him to the point of exhaustion, and just as he was falling off to sleep, she would do something, like suck on his dick or bite his nipple, and the romp was on. He was Don Juan, Casanova and the Highwayman all in one, with a cock that would not be denied and utterly refused to quit. He never knew it was in him.

This had been the greatest night of his life.

His fingertips laced down her creamy backside as she melted into him again. Her bent knee nuzzled his groin. He had to be at work early, so glanced over at the clock beside the bed.

Six-thirty.

His first class was at eight, but it was only a five-minute walk from his house. She felt willing, and he had just enough time. He let his fingers move down the crease in her rear cheeks, and tickled her furry opening until he felt her slick fold. He held his breath and inserted a finger there. She moaned and lifted her head, spearing his chest with the point of her perfectly dimpled chin.

"Professor, I love your lesson plans." Her eyes were half-lidded. She licked her lips and slowly brought her hands to his temples. Her fingers sifted the few early gray hairs there as her mound began to press into his upper leg. And then she squeezed his thigh between hers, rubbing her moist peach against him.

"Molly, Molly. If I'd only known."

"I was trying to land huge atom-bomb-type hints on you for weeks! What took you so long?" She smiled.

Am I that dense? "Well, I was having some wonderful fantasies about…being…with you in the stacks."

"Oh, good! We should do that too sometime."

Carl was thrilled she was thinking about another date.

Is this a date?

Molly straddled his hips and undulated back and forth, arching her back so her perfect rosy breasts protruded out, then presented them to his face as she lowered herself on his shaft. She rode him with soft movements, the light blue veins under her milky white skin becoming places he wanted to kiss. Her red hair hung down over her right shoulder and bounced on her breast as he pumped her. His hands smoothed the surface up her belly, between her breasts and then up to her neck. She sucked on his fingers, rolled her head to the side as he felt her muscles take hold of his cock and milk it. Just under her earlobe he saw a large reddish hickey.

Did I do that?

And yes, he remembered he did. He touched the bruise with his thumb and felt himself lurch, as he dug his cock deeper into her. He tipped her on her side and rode her at side angle. Her pink knee and leg rested over his shoulder. He held her little plump ass like a pillow, gripping it at the sides with both hands and plunging in over and over again to his hilt. When she raised herself up on one elbow and pushed herself against him he exploded, spilling his seed into her. Her muscles held him tight, and then released him as they both exhaled and collapsed.

HE STARTED WORRYING about being late for class when she insisted she shower with him. Again. But all she managed to do was get him rock hard and make him promise to get together with her tonight.

How could I refuse? Besides, he had to even out the mark on her neck by making another one on the other side. And there were a few positions he wanted to try…

JEREMY WAS IN class early, as usual. Carl had on his red sweater vest, but today, Jeremy wore none. He wore a long-sleeved designer tee decorated with skull and crossbones mixed with red hearts.

"No bow tie today?" Carl asked, as he turned and began putting notes on the chalkboard.

"I decided I didn't like the way they looked."

"Well, it is for older folks. Stuffy teachers, like myself." *If he only knew how perfectly young I feel this morning!*

"Well, I figured they'd be even too stuffy for you, so I burned them all last night."

Carl thought this was an odd statement. He continued writing on the board as several students walked in and took their places. Jeremy stood his ground.

"Saw you last night, you know."

"Oh really? Well, class is about to start." Carl leaned around his troubled student and said good morning to several others as they filed in. But he wondered if the little creep had been looking through his bedroom window.

Why in the world would I think that? There was something strange in the air.

"Saw you at O'Toole's. You were drinking a beer and reading a book. You left before I could come over."

Was Jeremy following me around?

"Jeremy, please take a seat…"

"My friend works at Copymagic, said you made some copies."

"Yes. I'm doing some research."

"Need any help with that?"

"No thank you, Jeremy. Now take your seat, please." Carl looked out at his class. "Okay everyone, today we start on chapter seven of the red book."

Jeremy nailed him with an icy stare that chilled him all the way to the bone.

Chapter 9

J ONAS NEVER FREQUENTED the dancing dens in the Underworld, mostly because he couldn't stand the stench of Red-X and he didn't like being pawed over by the men and women who haunted such places. But his mission was to find the other dark angel with the silver medallion, Rupert Blade. He didn't recall if Peter's last stage name—the name he was born with as a human—was Blade. Peter had been Director for such a short time no one knew much about him. Jonas grew an immediate dislike toward him, despite the fact that Jonas was part of the security force and was charged with protecting the Director. His quick assessment of the man sprang from some place deep within his soul. Trusting his instincts had kept him alive all these years.

Would he see a family resemblance between the Peter he knew and the elusive new recruit who dismembered the girl? What chilled him most was that the cretin who murdered the girl was looking at the camera the whole time. Though her friends were all over him, trying to make him stop, he completed his deed with the cool grace and strength of a trained killer, grinning into the camera, defying the consequences.

He's goading me.

Jonas would look for someone with very pink skin, someone who resembled a pimple-faced youth, but was really much older. And someone who looked sick.

That's going to be a tall order down here.

The Pussycat had large elevated pink cages set up at various places around the room amongst the small black tables and chairs. The dancers inside were in various states of undress. Part of the sport was for the patrons to rip off the clothes as they danced, which would occasionally cause a bloody scratch, or a stiletto heel through the hand, rejuvenating in less than an hour if the injury wasn't too grave. To even the odds, the girls were chained by one ankle to the cage floor. It was exciting, but dangerous to sit too close to the cages, as some of these dark angels were expert in harvesting themselves a patron's eye with their spiked heels. Eyes didn't grow back like wounds to other body parts. It was rare to see a man with a patch sit too close to a dancer.

The room was packed.

Jonas walked to the bar and greeted his old friend, Simon.

"Well, well, when the Director's away the boys will play." He reached his multi-tattooed forearm over the bar and gripped Jonas' hand.

"Yeah, well I'm meeting up with her tomorrow. I'm sort of here on official business."

The bartender made a sweeping motion toward the crowd and said, "Take your pick, son. I'm sure there's got to be at least a few officials here." He threw his head back and laughed, showing off his red teeth. Then he leaned over toward Jonas and whispered, "And officially, anything that dances in one of them cages is the best piece of ass anywhere in Undertown."

Jonas knew the older angel had firsthand experience. But his own appetites had changed since meeting Audray.

"Simon, I'm looking for a new recruit, someone who came down here within the last month. He'd have a place upstairs, arranged by

Peter. You know such a lad?"

Simon looked at Jonas and scowled. "Now what would you want with the likes of him?"

"I'm not allowed to say."

"Don't go messing with that lot, Jonas. They's up to no good."

"They?"

"Well, before his demise, the former Director had been turning souls left and right. It got to be like some kind of frat house upstairs. After your Audray took charge, I figured it was safe so kicked 'em all out two days ago."

"Where'd he go?"

"I have *no* idea."

"How did he learn to turn so quickly?"

"To be honest with you, I always liked the way Josh did it. He really trained them, gave them guidance on the ins and outs of claiming souls. These lot are real butchers, almost grabbing people off the street. They've been lied to, told all sorts of things. Then they would hang around here moping, crying in their X, pick up a girl and get lost for a few days. When they was ready, they'd come back and then they'd start bringing more new ones in." He wiped down the counter with a pink-stained rag. "Never saw so many new recruits in my life, almost like they was building a freakin' army."

"What about Peter's involvement?"

"Well, they was totally pissed the day he got whacked."

"But Peter must have taught them how to turn, before he was killed?"

"Yeah, they spent a lot of time in his office. And he came here, too."

Jonas looked out at the mob of people. One of the girls had gotten her leg caught in the grip of a huge dark angel. He had her body pulled against the cage, her flesh being pressed by the metal rods. Jonas could see the angel had a mind to rip her leg off for sport, an injury she wouldn't likely survive.

Not today.

Crossing the room in one long leap, Jonas quickly grabbed the man's shaved head and twisted it with a loud crack. The hulking body slumped to the floor.

He looked at the girl, who was climbing down from the cage, limping. Blood was soaking the towel she held to her groin area. She hurried off without stopping to issue a thank you. Jonas hoped she would heal.

Though the music blared on, the crowd stood still and glared at the man who'd just eliminated one of their favorites. Jonas was also the man their new Director had chosen to share her bed. As he looked from each hungry face to another, there wasn't a friend among them.

Until he saw a Cheshire smile coming towards him, wearing all black, sporting a silver medallion around his neck. His skin was light pink, but his hair was dark, like Peter's. He looked to be almost Peter's twin, but Jonas saw he was bigger built than the former Director. A large scar traversed his cheek and ran down to his jaw line. A deep groove encircled his neck as if the fellow had been hanged.

This bastard is hard to kill. And he's seen serious battle.

The dark man looked around him, playing to the crowd, as he walked casually toward Jonas. Conversations resumed and the dance floor began to writhe again. The man stopped a short distance in front of Jonas and stuck out his arm.

"Jonas Fucking Starling."

"That's me. Am I supposed to know you?"

The man smiled. "As charming as I thought you would be."

"There a point to all this bullshit, or do you just like to see which way your piss flies in the wind?"

"Now there, you see?" He spoke to his smaller companions. "He's got two good quips in on me, and I haven't been able to land a single one." His buddies stared back at Jonas, eyes wide.

Jonas adjusted his stance so he could reach for the long blade he stored in his boot.

"You're a hard man to find." The stranger matched Jonas' open stance with one of his own. "We've been looking nearly three centuries for you. You are a living legend. Took us awhile, but we finally found out how to get here."

"I didn't catch your name."

"Rupert Blade, but then I think you already know that."

He'd have gone for his weapon, without thought for his own safety, since he had the approval of his Queen, but as much as he coveted this man's death, he needed information more.

Rupert must have seen the tenseness in Jonas' upper body.

"This isn't a place or time to fight, my friend, if I can call you that."

"I'm not your friend."

"Acknowledged." Rupert motioned Jonas to join him in one of the quiet anterooms, away from the crush of the dance floor and the awful cages. "You want something to drink? Some wheatgrass perhaps?" Jonas might have been surprised, but the look of Rupert's smirk told him he was playing with him again.

"John, go get us some Sexual Apricot." Rupert's dark eyes sparkled in the dimly lit room with the six-foot stone fireplace. He sat down on a dark leather couch, and motioned for Jonas to do the same across from him. Rupert watched him, then leaned over a black marble table, elbows on his knees. "I imagine you dally a bit when she's gone?"

"How do you know she's gone?"

"Because I happen to know she's in Bakersfield as we speak."

This is not good. Jonas wished he'd just killed the man who knew fully where his soft spot was: Audray.

"Okay, so you've got my attention. Why don't you just spill it and we'll both be on our way." Jonas forced himself to relax, but his training kept him alert, heart beating fast, ready for anything. He left his knees wide and open, his back straight up.

John arrived with a tray laden with a dozen shot glasses of pink-ish-amber liquid. Two glasses were placed in front of Jonas, and two in front of Rupert. John and his companion each helped themselves to one, and took a seat near the fireplace, within earshot. The balance of the tray was left between Jonas and Rupert.

Rupert tossed back his first shot. Jonas didn't move a muscle.

"I happen to know you love Sexual Apricot, or have your tastes changed in that direction as well?"

"Like I said, why don't you tell me what you came here to say? I know you enjoy the witty dialog, but it's a little annoying, no offense."

"None taken." Rupert leaned back on the couch, extending his arms to the sides and crossed his legs. "I'll be honest with you, Jonas. I came here to find you but I'd rather kill you, and if you turn on me, I will."

Jonas jumped to his feet. Rupert didn't flinch, looked back at him with a casual smile, signaling his two readied companions to seat themselves again. Jonas noted he was fully primed and ready for a death fight, something Jonas wanted to avoid.

"Look, asshole, I'm tired of your games." Jonas started to leave.

"I want to make a deal, in exchange for your life and the safety of your woman."

"I don't make deals."

"Oh, but I have it on good authority you do."

"Your information is wrong."

"You forget your past, sir. Remember when you were eighteen and the dandy of the ladies at court? Remember when the Queen and her cousin couldn't get enough of you, even after she was well with child? Your child?"

Jonas saw the peach and golden brocades of the Queen's boudoir, her "Pleasure Palace" she had called it—a place even Charles himself was not allowed. She'd not gotten around to making it a nursery when the king died and she had to flee the castle. He'd spent half a year of his life screwing any woman who came to him there, on the Queen's orders, under penalty of death. He'd stopped caring about his own life shortly after he arrived at Court. He did it to preserve the lives of his beloved Anne and both their families.

"Ever wonder what became of the child?"

Jonas assumed the child was stillborn, as the Queen's other thirteen offspring had been. His hands balled into fists at his sides, as he remained standing.

"I can introduce you to descendents of his. Yes. He *was* a male child. And he became a very rich and powerful man." Rupert frowned. "Just not a king."

Despite himself, Jonas was curious, mesmerized by Rupert's words. But he also felt his past reach up and grab him by the balls.

Rupert got up and extended his hand again. "Welcome back to the family, cuz."

Chapter 10

NOW IT WAS time for Burt. She wondered where his remains would wind up some day. Hopefully not in a well kept cemetery. She wished it would be at the bottom of a drainage canal or woods. He wouldn't have a headstone. There would be no angel looking over him.

The freeway was snarled with afternoon traffic. The hot, dusty and flat surroundings looked like hell itself, except for the lush green rows of crops that splayed out like spines of a fan as she drove by. She watched the automatic sprinklers spread their shimmery goodness over the green rows, spraying as if sugar-coating everything. She smiled and checked her rearview mirror. *The only sweetness in this godforsaken place is long dead and buried.*

Traffic crept along until the turnoff to the VA Hospital, which must not have been a popular destination. The brown and cream two-story brick building looked like an old military base, complete with a jet fighter cemented into the dry crabgrass turnaround in front of the building. A few children were climbing up on its wings and trying to pry loose the bars keeping them from the cockpit.

Audray was conscious that her car was attracting attention everywhere she went. In LA she would be one of many. And at her home in Northern California, where she kept the car, a red Maserati wasn't commonplace. But it wasn't odd, like down here. Some of the wealthy farmers might be able to afford one, but would never even consider it.

She'd always been taught that if you showed your bling in the Central Valley, you were putting your life in danger.

The car chirped as she locked it and made her way up the concrete steps bordering a meandering ramp that zigzagged to the hospital entrance.

The cool lobby was a welcome relief from the hot late afternoon, but it smelled of urine, disinfectant and dust. Audray's heightened senses brought it in so fast she needed a surgery mask. The waiting room was filled with several patients and family members, some of both in wheelchairs.

She felt instantly tired, not sure if she had the energy to do what she came to do. But she took a deep breath and walked up to speak to the black woman seated behind a window enclosure, dressed in a blue smock. The whites of her eyes were as yellow as her teeth.

"Can I help you?" she gave Audray a rather murderous glare.

"I'm here to visit a family member. His name is Burt Foreman."

The receptionist looked over a clipboard and shook her head. "I'm sorry, Mr. Foreman is not able to have visitors." Her smile was wide, as if she enjoyed dishing out the news.

"Yes, well I understand he is in rather poor shape, but it is urgent I see him."

"I'm sorry. Hospital rules."

Audray inhaled and blew over the woman while she pled her case again. The woman's eyes half closed as she leaned back and almost tipped over in her padded rolling office chair.

Audray continued staring down at the woman, breathing hard, adding another dose of her influence, due to the woman's extra girth. At first she thought the receptionist would pass out. But then she shook her head.

"Boy, is it hot in here?" She fanned her face with a stained file folder and looked back at Audray, who kept her jaw tense and allowed her eyes to rim in red, ready to flame her in an instant if it became necessary. She had no intention of going away until she got the permission to finish her deed. The woman exuded fear and confusion, her lower lip beginning to tremble. A tiny bit of spittle resided in the corner of her mouth.

"Oh, what the hell. He's gonna die any day now. I doubt you'll be able to speak with him." She stood up. The woman was easily six-foot-two and the size of a professional football player. "Five minutes." She held up a hand that could palm a basketball, fingers spread wide. "You got five minutes, you hear?"

More than enough time.

The woman answered the phone and held up her five-minute sign like a small pizza platter. Audray was careful not to appear unnaturally quick, and entered the room Burt shared with three other male patients. Everyone was sleeping except for a younger man who was a double amputee, heavily medicated. He nodded as Audray passed him to get to Burt, whose bed was next to the window. Both televisions were blaring.

She looked down at the gray face of the man she saw in her dreams as she cried herself to sleep in those early days. He wore death like a blanket all around him, and it wasn't becoming. He had a tube down his nose secured with a white piece of tape. A yellowish green liquid was being sucked from inside him, ending up in a clear jar with an inch of the frothy buildup at the bottom. He was hooked up to an IV on the back of one hand, but his other flaccid arm had large purple and red bruises on the inside at the crook. One purple trail snaked up from the bruise almost an inch.

That probably hurts. The thought gave her courage.

Audray picked up the yellow plastic water pitcher and poured a stream over his face and onto his chest. Burt opened his rheumy eyes and mumbled, trying to wipe the water, getting his arm caught in the plastic tubing. His eyes got small as he squinted to see who was next to him.

"Don't have your glasses? Guess you don't read much."

"Who…?"

Audray leaned into him so that her face was no more than five inches from his. At first there was no reaction, but then his eyes became wide.

"Bumblebee. My little bumblebee."

Audray looked up and out the window. It should have hurt, this reminder of what he used to call her in perhaps happier times before the rape. She noticed her heart was completely stone cold.

"That all you can say to me after you what you did?"

"I'm sorr… I couldn't help…"

"I'm not here for an apology. You're beyond redemption."

She blew on his face, grimacing down at him. *It doesn't hurt a bit. Not anymore.*

"You want to live forever just like this?" she asked him.

His eyes contained nothing but questions. Audray continued. "Yes, that could be one solution. I could let you live forever in a bed, hooked up to a tube, your ass wiped not as often as it should be so it gets nice and red."

"Wha?"

"Or I could cut off your pecker with a pair of scissors I bet I could find. Maybe then the government might try to sew it back on, maybe backwards. I could arrange that if you like. Or make you leak like a punctured garden hose, hmmm?"

She found a small pair of nippers for cutting surgical tape. "Now these look good. Nice and dull."

Burt was trying to scream, but was having difficulty mustering the energy, from the whoosh of air she deposited to his face. A buzzer started going off. Someone in the room was beginning to have tachycardia. It didn't matter to her who it was.

"I had more than enough reason to kill you. But yesterday, I found out you also killed my sister." Audray reached under the sheets and pulled his hairy unit, yanking it sharply to the side, twisting it. Burt's face got bright red, the veins in his neck and at his temples bulged, but no sound came out of his mouth as his eyes crossed.

See what it feels like to be helpless? Can't save yourself? Should I kill you?

She released her grip and watched him fall back into the bed. She thought about leaving him alive to experience the bruising and pain in his cock with every muscle he tried to move, every breath he tried to take until his last day, which was coming up very soon. It wasn't eternity, but it was the best she could do, and not nearly what he deserved. He wasn't worth killing. Much better to let him suffer out the rest of his miserable days.

She gave him a dose of her dark energy, causing his heart to start racing, which set off more alarms. *Oh, how I wish I could rob ten years from you like you robbed me of mine.* With satisfaction, she witnessed his grimace as his pecker began to harden, making a mound in the sheets at his lap. His eyeballs were bulging, but she'd silenced his tongue so his feeble efforts to speak only frustrated him more.

"You won't live out the day, but every minute of it will be in pain. You reap what you sow, Burt."

She heard staff coming down the hall so she shifted through the wall of the adjoining room, setting off another series of buzzers as the three older male patients were all awake watching the TV mounted on the wall above the spot she'd just walked through.

Audray quickly took the other way around and back out to the lobby, passing the now-vacant reception area. She knew that he wouldn't survive the heart attack that was racking his body. In those last few minutes, he'd be in the most excruciating pain of his miserable life, and he'd be lying there knowing she did it, got even, and wouldn't be able to tell a soul. She hoped their attempts to resuscitate him were long and equally painful, and that he would die slowly.

There was a guest bathroom down the hall, where she washed her hands to rid herself of any remains of the sack of flesh known as Burt.

THE RED MASERATI growled through the gates of Central Valley Cemetery, rumbling up the drive to the top of the hill. Her mother had said to look for the big Guardian angel statue holding a little lamb—the section where her sister was buried, next to her father.

She parked the car under a hulking willow tree, its ancient branches hovering over and touching the red beast, hiding it in shadows. The afternoon's heat was coming to a close. Puffs of dandelion seeds blew in the breeze, dotting the air, dancing with moths and flying insects, against the ever-present background noise of the freeway.

It took her several seconds to exit the car. She saw no one, but she felt watched. Stepping out into the light of day, she noted the birds had stopped chirping. She expected something, not sure what it was. The hairs at the back of her neck and on her forearms bristled. She'd gotten her revenge, and it felt good to have that chapter of her life closed forever. But she also had the eerie feeling someone had been following, watching her every move. She felt like a target.

Her lunch, what little of it she ate, hung undigested in her stomach. Her red boots ascended the crown of the hill and stopped just before the looming statue with wings, which protected the little lamb. The white marble had turned gray and was streaked as though crying.

Birds had dallied there and an abandoned nest sat in the crook of the large angel's arm next to the body of the lamb.

Audray had never experienced grief before. This emotion had always been just out of reach. But the devoted expression on the face of the angel moved something inside, and she was surprised to find tears rolling down her cheeks. *Something has been lost. Something is gone forever.*

She bit her lower lip as she leaned forward to read the inscriptions on the ground. To the left she read:

Lt. W. Michael Steele

December 25, 1945 to June 4, 1980

Rest in Peace. Your earthly work is done.

Husband, Father, Soldier
Guardian of the Weak
Protector of the Weary

Audray's eyes moved over to the right, and she gazed upon the gravestone of her sister:

Claire A. Steele

February 14, 1970 to June 1, 1992

Gone to be with her father,
Who will protect her throughout eternity.

Rest in Peace, Little Guardian

The warm wind caressed her cheek, chilling the tears streaking down her face as she realized something perhaps her psyche had known all along: that she loved her sister, who had given her life to protect her. In turn, her sister's love for Daniel gave her a second chance as a human, and the love of the man Audray had tried to take away from her.

"I am so sorry, Claire," she whispered as she bent down to brush the dried leaves and debris off her sister's name. She traced the letters on the cold stone. Her heart felt cold as she relived the pain she'd caused them both. Had she known, would she have acted the same way? Done Josh's bidding to try to plunge Daniel into darkness?

Kneeling on all fours, she looked up at the face of the Guardian above her, basking in the gaze of her sister's protector. She couldn't remember ever being loved like this by anyone in her life—anyone but Jonas.

Perhaps Jonas has awakened this part of myself I never knew was there. She wondered what her childhood would have been like if someone had cared for her like this Guardian, if someone had looked down upon her like this stone angel watched over her sister. She searched her memories and she saw Claire's face again, smiling down at her.

If Claire had lived, would I have become something other than a dark angel?

Were there seeds of goodness that went unwatered?

She lowered her lips to the cold stone and kissed it. "Thank you. Thank you for saving my life," she whispered.

Audray stood up and dusted her palms against her thighs. She wiped her cheeks with the backs of her hands and straightened her clothes, brushing her hair back off her forehead. A funeral procession was making its slow way up the hill, but at the last minute, the black hearse diverted to the other side, a long trail of cars following behind.

Someone else's family in pain.

She took one last look as her car passed by the gravesite. No one would ever know that a dark angel had stopped, kissed the stone of her long-lost family and was humbled at the thought of an ever after filled with warmth and love.

She knew, if she had to make the decision today, she might choose a different life for her and Jonas. *But that's silly. Dark angels don't have hope. They just have forever. We have forever to be together.*

And for the first time in her life, she was full of remorse for her actions.

IT WAS GETTING dark when she drove down the freeway and came to the Riverbend exit. A large traffic jam impeded her progress, so she was stuck on the two-lane road, searching the horizon. A pyre of smoke ahead of the string of waiting cars told her an accident had happened. She checked her watch. She wanted to get this meeting with her mother over with as quickly as possible. Then she could get out of this dusty town.

Should I tell her I took care of Burt, that I found Claire?

Audray thought about Burt and what her mother had told her.

"Because of your little wings. You used to dance around all the time with those little wings. Sometimes, you'd get so furious at Claire when she made you take them off for bed."

She'd forgotten this until today. She heard the buzzing and some giggling and for the flash of a second saw a young beautiful face with short blonde hair smiling at her.

Claire. I do remember you. I loved you once. I love you still.

A car horn interrupted her reverie. The trail of cars began to move and there was a gap. Her Maserati roared to life, and she soon exited. A handsome uniformed policeman gave her a polite bow and smile as she passed.

The smoke was not coming from the freeway, but off in the distance a short way. Like a beacon, her car followed. It was on the way to the trailer park. The closer she got, Audray realized it was coming from the park itself. Red fire trucks had blocked the entrance, and men in yellow slickers were running like ants all over the area. A white Coroner's van with flashing lights pulled in front of her and was admitted to the park.

Audray stopped in the middle of the road, causing a loud cacophony of honking behind her from impatient drivers. But she barely noticed. She was staring at the sight of her mother's trailer, fully engulfed in bright orange flames, sending thick black smoke up to the darkening sky above.

Chapter 11

CARL FINISHED UP his third class at two o'clock, and had the urge to pop in at the library unannounced in order to see Molly. He thought about calling her first, but was afraid she had changed her mind or decided he was too old for her.

Ten years. That's not too old. And the way he felt right now, he was up for anything she could dish out, perhaps more. The day was brighter as he sprinted over, his laptop case flapping against his rear in the warm afternoon sun. He removed his bowtie, slipping it into his pocket and then unbuttoned the two top buttons of his shirt.

He zipped his card through the security monitor, and with a sucking sound the automatic doors opened.

He thought he could smell her already. It was a thrilling but ridiculous thought. He searched around the reference desk, between shelves of books in the area. He closed his eyes and yes, he could smell her. *Is this some new power she has awakened in me?* He couldn't wait to feel the moist softness of her lips slathered with cherry lip balm, or to delicately pucker her white flawless skin just under her left ear; cause her a bruise with his passion.

His dream was rewarded by the feel of her breasts against his back, as a soft perfumed hand snaked its way between the buttons of his cream colored shirt and worked lower. He whirled around so his eyes wouldn't miss a single second of her look of lust for him.

God! How I need that look. His arm encircled her waist and he pulled her into his chest, lowering his lips to hers as he burst into flames inside. She was his. His in every imaginable way and he willingly became lost in the folds of her clothes, the tendrils of her fiery hair and the smell and feel of her flesh pressed against his.

The long feeding kiss was beginning to attract attention as he heard someone clear her throat. He stared into the disapproving jowls of the head librarian, standing not more than ten feet from the two of them.

"Professor. This is not the place."

Carl looked from her stern face to Molly's. "No, it's not," Molly agreed, smiling.

"I'm sorry," he barely got out before Molly grabbed his hand and led him in the opposite direction. The librarian's body stood rigid. Carl knew he would hear from the Dean about this.

But I don't care anymore.

Molly slipped them through a side door into the stacks room she opened with a pass card. He reached for the lights, but she grabbed his hand and placed it on her breast. The smell of old books and curled yellowed sheaves of paper sent a thrill up his spine. He felt called to adventure, daring, young and bold. The perfect place for a tryst, second only to his own bed.

"Will she follow us here?"

Molly held up a card. "I have hers. I'm doing some maintenance here today."

"So we won't be disturbed?"

"Prof…"

"Please, call me Carl."

"Carl." She blushed at the use of his name. Carl's groin jolted so hard he almost fell over. She leaned into him, kissed him slowly, warmly breathing all over his face before pulling away, taking several long seconds. "I didn't say we wouldn't be disturbed, but we have a few minutes. Do you think…?"

Carl boosted her onto a wooden worktable and climbed on top of her. He unbuckled and unzipped his pants quickly and let himself be found by her searching fingers. He urgently needed to get inside her before someone else stopped him. He moved her head, lying back in the nest of long red tangled hair. He wanted to see her eyes, sparkling green pools smiling back at him, underscored by her pouty pink lips. His hands searched for panties as she giggled.

No panties!

He adjusted her skirts and plunged in.

This is better than before.

Her back arched as he pumped inside her to the hilt. She exposed the long stretch of her creamy white neck. He saw the light blue vein under her ear pump and pulse, covered with the reddish purple bruise he had put there last night.

You are so delicious.

She brought her hands to his rear and pulled him deeper, moaning, eyes closed. He delicately moved her chin to the left and licked the unblemished skin on the other side, sucking a kiss from her flesh until he felt the welt developing. She went wild; her internal muscles squeezed him over and over until he could not control himself.

He was lost in the flow of his seed and her need of every drop when they heard the main door open several shelves away.

Molly was up and on her feet so fast, he had no time to get his pants hiked back over his hips. As they stepped into the library from the side door, they escaped discovery by whoever had entered the stacks.

Carl quickly tucked his shirt back in, turning away from students as Molly led him around the corner to the safety of unconcerned library patrons.

He hugged her, but tried not to show passion. "I am so sorry, Molly. I fear perhaps I have cost you your job."

She nodded her head and smoothed her pink fingers over his chest, toying with his pocket, his buttons, waving her long auburn lashes up and down as if cooling him. It only served to further fan the flames of his desire.

I just can't get enough of her.

"I think I have a different job, now."

Job? What job?

She must have seen his confusion. She pressed her mound against his thigh and whispered, "My job is to pleasure you for as long as you'll have me."

SOMEWHERE CARL FOUND the strength to look the head librarian in the eyes shortly before he left. "It's a new relationship. We are both consenting adults, and she isn't one of my students," he managed to say.

"It's a library, Professor!" She spat out with disdain.

"Yes, and you have my word it won't happen again. But I have to say, I've been at this college for almost eight years now, and I've seen worse. Much worse."

She glared back at him, speechless.

"And so have you," he added before he left the building.

CARL HAD A big glass of wine ready for Molly when her green Volkswagen rattled up the driveway and sputtered twice after the ignition was turned off. He had prepared a special dinner, complete with some chocolate dessert, anticipating she had lost her job.

She accepted the wine happily and walked past him into the house, carrying a bag over her shoulder. Carl looked down at his canvas slip-ons and smiled. "So, how bad was it?" he asked as he followed her to the living room and took a sip of wine.

"Bad," she said without turning around. She dropped her bag and her right shoulder, with a sigh.

Carl was quickly behind her, "Well, then can I make it better?"

"Yes. I would like that." She leaned into him as he folded his body around hers, removed her clip, letting her red curls cascade down to her waist. He pulled her hair aside gently, kissing the bruise he had made on her neck this afternoon.

"I am so sorry that I caused you...pain..."

"No pain. It was wonderful and worth it."

"Worth it?" he said as he allowed a forefinger to trace down her low cut sweater and breech the top of her bra and then inside. His hand squeezed the wonder of her left breast. It felt like it was her heart he held.

"It was worth every agonizing minute of the two-and-a-half hours I had to stay there, waiting to be with you again." She turned around and smiled.

"And your job?"

"Well, I've lost my stacks privileges, for now. But my advisor called me on the way home, and he said he'd had a pleasant conversation about it with the head librarian, and they shared a good laugh."

Carl kissed her, almost spilling their wine.

"Not sure what you told her, but my advisor said to let you know you were right."

Chapter 12

JONAS DIDN'T TOUCH the angel in front of him who claimed to be a distant relative. He stiffened his spine, stuck his chin out straight and lowered his gaze over the next several seconds until their eyes met. He wanted Rupert to get the full import of Jonas' size, notwithstanding the fact that he stood a good foot taller than him.

Rupert retracted his arm and grinned, his eyes sparkling in their blackness, his breathing clipped short. Jonas felt inspected like a rare piece of meat served to a diner who hadn't eaten in a week. Blade's fingers twitched at his sides, finally making their way into fists. The two companions rose to standing position again and put down their drinks.

Jonas was studying the room, the angles he would have to achieve to slay all three of them. He wasn't going to look behind him to give away his thoughts, but it concerned him he didn't know who might have walked into the room. But he would be no use to Audray dead, and he sensed Rupert didn't care one way or the other.

He who cares least wins.

Jonas worked on his emotions and took a couple of deep breaths. The agitation in his stomach dissipated. Rupert wouldn't give him the satisfaction of being a hothead or a sacrificial lamb for any cause. He was a little smarter than Peter, although clearly they were both cut from the same cloth. Or from the same womb.

Jonas bent a knee and slanted his stance, putting his hands on his hips like he'd just righted himself after falling off a horse. He used the opportunity to casually look behind him while he spoke. Two strangers blocked the doorway. "For a second there, I thought you said we were related." Jonas knew it sounded dumber than he thought it would. But Rupert seemed to buy it.

"Yes. And yes, we are." The dark-haired angel said it as if he wanted to shout it off the tallest building in Undertown.

"And what makes you say something as ridiculous as that?"

"It's a fact." Rupert's eyes smiled even if his lips stayed straight, the color of fresh liver. Jonas could see he was going to keep the conversation short, not volunteer anything, and maybe get him to beg for the answers to the huge question between them.

I've never begged. I never will.

Jonas looked around him again and laughed out loud. He was clearly outmatched in strength, and the element of surprise was lost. Now that he had something to go home to, he wasn't looking for a fight.

But I'm no coward.

No one else had joined him in the laugh. "God, you boys are so serious. You came all this way to entertain me with this. This all you got?"

All five of the men came to attention. Jonas saw they were well trained, and moved as one unit. The only thing Jonas liked about the situation was the fact that Rupert obviously didn't want to talk to him without some serious backup. It meant he was respected, and that was a comfortable feeling.

"Well, you don't act like the Red-X fiends running all over Undertown, yet you come here with your little pod, like bullies in the playground. Are we the entertainment here tonight, or did you have some other agenda?" Jonas wasn't going to come right out and ask. "I mean I'm scared, really fucking scared," he said as he grinned from ear to ear.

Rupert made a very slight twitch toward him, but at the last minute appeared to reel himself in. Jonas noted he did have a bit of the hotheadedness Peter had. He liked that he could get under this guy's skin and twist something.

"You gonna kill me, like you said you came here to do? Well then, go right ahead. I might be able to take three of you with me, but I doubt I could take the whole pod. Much as I like dancing and all."

Rupert looked down and his shoulders softened. "Jonas, I dream of killing you just about every day since I learned of Peter's death. I hold you responsible. You were bound to protect him, Jonas. As part of the guard, it was your duty." He bent down and picked up a glass of Apricot and tossed it back. He walked past Jonas, motioning to the two at the doorway to disperse and called back. "I can wait for now. Besides, there's someone I think you better meet. Come."

Outside the Pink Pussycat, the two dark angels walked down the wet cobblestoned streets of Undertown. Rupert's henchmen stayed a safe distance behind them. The smell of Red-X and blood running down the gutters at the sides was stronger tonight. This was the seedier district of the village, and none of it was safe, especially after dark. But for whoever wandered this ancient part, safety was the least of their concerns. This was where dark angels came to get lost and stay lost, sometimes forever.

The red mist lifted as they mounted the stairs out of the village, into the bustling city above. Only scooters and bicycles—things that could be transported from the human world in a limo—zipped by and tooted at the pedestrians wandering the heavily jammed streets. Jonas was greeted by every female they passed, looking secondarily at Rupert, who seemed to enjoy the added attention.

"You like it here?" he asked Jonas.

"Yeah."

"But you prefer the human world."

"I liked this one better until you showed up." Jonas looked around Rupert. "Where's your army?"

"My army? Why would I need an army?"

"Okay, then. Your pod of likeminded souls." Jonas chuckled to himself, thinking it was pretty damn funny.

"Look cuz, asshole extraordinaire, you're baiting me, trying to make me mad, am I right?"

"Could be." Jonas was alert to every little drip, scurrying animal or leaf that moved. His nerves were on edge, but he was ready, knew he'd be ready for whatever they were going to throw at him.

They walked along in silence until they got to a heavy locked gate. To the right was a black metal box with a lighted yellow button on it. Jonas knew the big shuttered mansion behind the gate housed the most gorgeous ladies in either world. Only powerful dark angels got to spend any time there. This was Josh's doing, his way of rewarding his new recruits and dealing favors.

Jonas missed Josh, who had been granted a pardon by the big man in the sky. This was something no one else had ever heard of: a chance to become human once again. If Joshua was good enough, he could become a Guardian himself after his human life was over. This act of grace, pardon and forgiveness, made a profound change in the Underworld. For although everyone who lived there expected their lives to be evil and self-indulgent, with Josh's pardon, the seed of redemption was planted. It was never talked about, but Jonas knew everyone thought about it whenever Josh's name came up.

Josh had turned and handpicked most of the ladies of the house himself. Before his pardon, Josh had even invited Jonas to accompany him here on occasion. He watched Rupert's finger depress the yellow buzzer. Jonas recognized the melodious voice of Helena coming through the little box.

"I'm here with Jonas. We're here to see…"

Before he could finish, the gate began to open with a loud clanging. Inside the large rose garden, frosted in moonlight, the delicate scent of the flowers usually relaxed him, but tonight Jonas was tense. He knew he wasn't going to like whomever he'd been brought here to meet.

"I've been told you've spent some serious time here," Rupert whispered.

"Want me to tell you who I preferred?"

"Would it surprise you to know I am a married man?" Rupert's chest extended with the bravado of his words. "Just wait. You'll see what I mean."

"I'm not a man easily surprised," Jonas lied. He was getting more itchy to be back outside with his men, ready to do battle, rather than trapped in a glorified cathouse.

Rupert laughed and Jonas saw he was trying not to. They mounted the wooden porch steps. Several couples were seated or lying outside in the night air on wicker furniture that squeaked as their bodies moved. Whispers enveloped the two men as Jonas asked the question he'd wanted to since they started their walk.

"So who are we seeing?"

"She's my wife, recently turned and staying here for a few days while I make suitable arrangements." Rupert smiled. "What?"

Jonas could see he was having way too much fun toying with him.

"Just how to you get that we're related, if I may ask?"

"Well, perhaps you and I being blood-related *was* a bit of a stretch."

Jonas was still reeling from Rupert's comment when they opened the front door and he looked at the beautiful black-haired woman who stood at the bottom of the stairs. Her face looked oddly familiar. Her dark eyes grilled him with a hatred spewing from deep within her soul.

"I finally meet you at last," she said with a slight accent. She did not offer her hand. Jonas looked over at Rupert, feeling a coldness creep up his loins, all the way along his spine to the bottom of his skull.

"Jonas Starling, I would like you to meet your twenty times great granddaughter, Catarina Blade."

Chapter 13

CARL LAY IN bed naked and alone. The smell of fresh coffee, that succulent wonderful smell, warmed his soul. He closed his eyes and willed for it to come to him, held by a red-haired nymph who was completely naked, blowing on the top to cool the mixture swirling with real cream. He opened his eyes and saw such a vision. Her green gaze raked the length of his naked body, modestly covered with a sheet, tenting around his mid section. Her eyebrows rose.

"Oh, Professor. Time for another lesson, n'est pas?" she said in mock French accent.

"I am so grateful you are such a slow learner. I just have to keep teaching you over and over again." He matched the grin on her pink lips, sitting up to accept the steaming mug of caramel-colored fresh brew. She snuggled in next to him, playing with the hairs on his chest and then reached below.

"Molly, you are not letting me have my coffee."

"I'll wait until you're finished."

He leaned back, sighed and smiled. His fingers laced through her flaming hair as she lay against his chest. "I think I have died and gone to heaven."

"Don't say that, Prof. Carl."

"Why?" He looked down at her. "That's not a bad thing. Could you imagine us living forever in heaven, waking up naked and drinking coffee in bed on a sunny Saturday morning?"

"Yes. But isn't there something wrong with that? I mean, angels don't have sex, do they?"

"If we were there, we would. I don't know nor do I care about anybody else."

She sat up on her knees, removed the mug from his fingers, setting it down on the bedside table. "I don't care about anybody else either. It's just you and me here, in this bed, all day." She straddled him and leaned her breasts into his chest, rubbing them back and forth. His hands gripped her little ass and then tickled up her spine, barely touching her flesh. He let her consume his lips, let her match her opening with the end of his stiff cock and angle her peach so he could slide in. Her sex was hot and slick. He felt her vibrate as the full length of him slowly separated her folds and stirred her insides.

She did have the look of an angel, an angel in lust, he thought. Her pink skin gave off a rosy aura, casting a golden shadow across his own. Her red hair glistened in the morning sunlight, framing her face like a halo. As if she was some ancient fairy queen and he the explorer who discovered her in the forest, he felt utterly enchanted. He was ageless. Time stopped.

I am completely, hopelessly in love.

Her green eyes focused down on her breasts and she squeezed them together, and then raised her gaze to look at him. He bent his knees and raised himself up to penetrate deeper. She arched backward in response, hands clasped over her head. He brushed her long curls aside, uncovering her nipples, pinching them. Her slim body writhed over him, letting him see the ecstasy on her face from multiple angles.

Carl could not believe what his life had become now that Molly was in it. He looked at her smooth creamy skin, the delicate shading inside her belly button as her lower part undulated, pleasuring him. He could watch her face forever. Her eyes would close and then open again with a sultry smile, the green reminding him of fields of fresh grasses in spring. She spun a web he was gladly caught in, something that fulfilled a lifetime of looking for someone he wasn't sure existed. His fantasy life took a back stage to the reality of the goddess riding his cock this morning in his big bed. And he knew, the more he filled her the more he wanted.

She was caught up in little spasms, her head bent back, showing the delicate muscles of her extended neck. He felt her orgasm come on as his cock swelled and responded. She stopped, shuddered and looked down on him again with rosy cheeks. He quickly flipped her onto her stomach, raising her tummy with one hand and re-seated himself firmly inside her pink opening. He pumped her little body as she moaned and shook. Her muscles twitched and he exploded inside her, holding her tight to him as he covered her neck and shoulders with kisses.

He collapsed on top of her and she giggled.

SHE MADE HIM scrambled eggs, adding some cheese and sour cream she found in the refrigerator. Sitting on his lap, wearing his discarded shirt from last night, she fed him. Each mouthful was followed by a kiss. By the time he was done, he was rock hard again.

Then he remembered his appointment this morning.

"Molly, I totally forgot. I have to meet someone downtown in less than an hour. The person who asked me to do the research on Jonas Starling."

Molly pouted. "How long will you be gone?"

"You could come with me. Wait until I'm done."

"I'd rather wait here in your bed."

"Well, I don't think it will take too long, maybe a half hour."

"You going to your office?"

"No, why?"

"I just thought maybe you were meeting him at your office, is all."

He traced the outline of her pink lower lip with his index finger. "I'm meeting *her* at Café Contada at ten o'clock."

"Her?"

"Yes."

"What's her name?"

"I...I...can't remember—a Linda something, She's doing some historical research for a book she's writing." he said with a chuckle. He could see Molly was getting concerned. "Love, she's already paid me—in cash. I didn't get anything in writing."

"Okay. I'm going then."

Carl held her face in his hands and kissed her again. "You are such a wonder. What would I ever do without you looking after me?"

"Well, Professor," she said as she kissed his eyes one at a time, then his cheeks and nibbled a way to his lips, "You would be uptight, still wearing bow ties," she kissed his neck under his jaw, "and trying to hide that wonderful body of yours from all the females around you who want to rip your clothes off."

That was something he never expected. "Really?" He was serious.

Molly nodded her head, smoothing over his face with her fingers. "Have you ever had a red-haired girlfriend?"

"No. I've only had two friends. I wouldn't even call them girl-friends."

"See? You were saving yourself for me."

In a way, it was true.

"Although I would have never known that," she whispered in his ear.

"What?"

"Professor, you are very good in bed. You seem very experienced."

His initial smile was wiped from his face when he thought about how much experience she had. She was his first love. Did it matter what order he was, as long as he was the last?

"That's because, my beautiful Molly, I'm totally inspired. You have brought me to life."

CARL PARKED THE car and put quarters into the meter. He let Molly go in ahead and order his cappuccino, since they were running five minutes late. The shower took way too long.

Inside Café Contada it was dark, but there was no mistaking the black-haired woman who looked up with hungry eyes just as he walked in the room. She smiled, acknowledging his recognition of her. He didn't see Molly at first, so he went over to the table, greeted his client and sat.

"Good morning," he said stiffly. He looked around the room.

"Your little friend is in the ladies room." The woman's eyes scanned his face and paused at a place under his left ear. "You might want to pull up your collar." She motioned with her forefinger to a similar spot on her own neck.

Carl did as he was told, remembering the hickey Molly had placed there in the shower this morning. His pants were a little tight and he felt his shoulders tense so he rolled his head and winced.

"Too much sleep always gives me a stiff neck," she said.

He felt like she was trying to draw something out of him. *Actually, I've had very little sleep the last two nights.* He smiled. "It's a common ailment for researchers and writers. Too much time in front of the computer, you know."

"Oh, that must be it, then." She looked him squarely in the eyes, showing off the odd violet hue that seemed to change colors as he stared. He wondered if she possessed some special power, and he felt dizzy.

Molly made her way from the ladies room, walked up to the counter, picking up Carl's cappuccino and an Italian soda for herself, and came over to the table.

"Here you go." She placed the mug in front of Carl, touching him on the shoulder afterwards.

"Thanks. Molly, I'd like to introduce you—and forgive me, but I don't remember your name."

"Glenda Sisted." She held out her hand and Molly gave a brief shake, quickly retracting it.

"Nice to meet you, Glenda." She looked at Carl. "I'll just be over there." She pointed to a dark corner across the room.

Carl wasn't sure why, but he felt the chemistry between these two women wasn't healthy.

"She's very lovely, Professor. Is she one of your students?"

He shuddered. "No. That is not something I would ever do."

Glenda gave him a sultry catlike smile, obviously pleased with herself.

"You'd be surprised what some people will do in the name of love."

Carl noticed her lip color matched her eyes, deep violet. He thought he'd remembered her eyes as blue or hazel. Her very pale skin was as translucent as Molly's. But her dark hair and her demeanor were completely different. Fear was having its way with his body. He shrugged it off and picked up his folder with the research he'd done for her.

"I'm sure you're anxious to see what I've come up with." He didn't look at her but poured over his notes and copies. He could tell she was eyeing the top of his head. "I found his bio very interesting. In my studies, I had not run across him before, and I'm a little surprised, frankly." He looked up at her. She had placed her chin in the cup of her hand, resting her elbow on the table, smiling.

"Go on."

"Well you wanted to know if there was any evidence that he lived beyond his years in the Caribbean, or if he had family, and I can't find any trace of it. The trail ends with his death on Antigua. Now," he looked up at Glenda and felt a pull, like she had willed him to move toward her face. He felt her hunger for his kiss.

Carl shook himself. Glenda sat up and peered out the window at the street and people passing by the coffee house. "As far as I can tell, he never married, or had a family, although he was betrothed."

"To Anne Mackenzie."

"Yes. So you know his story?"

"A little. But no evidence he became a father?"

Carl was unsure whether she knew the particulars of Jonas Starling's tale, so started to tell her with care. "Well, he was asked to help the king and queen father a child, hopefully a son. But the king died before the child could be born. It is said it was Jonas' child. But no one ever writes about it. Now, I would guess the child died as did all of her other thirteen offspring."

"Yes, the queen was cursed. Isn't that obvious?"

Carl laughed and drew an icy response from Glenda. "I don't believe in such things. Surely you don't either..." But Carl could see she did. He inhaled deeply and decided to ask the question that had been festering in his mind. "What exactly is your interest in this person, Jonas Starling?"

"I'll tell you after you answer my questions, but only if you have the answers." She looked at her violet nail polish. "Is Jonas Starling still alive?"

"No. Absolutely no. I mean, how could he be?"

"Are you sure?"

"Well, I haven't seen the body, if that's what you mean. But he is said to have died and been buried in the Caribbean nearly three hundred years ago. It would be impossible he would still be alive today. Perhaps a distant offspring—"

"Then perhaps you should do further research."

"Well, I think I've researched everything. I was very thorough."

"I'm sure you were, Professor." She turned around and smiled at Molly sitting at the bar.

Carl didn't like the feeling he was getting from the woman. He didn't like getting Molly involved as well. He looked over to her in the corner. She gave him a little wave, but her face looked concerned.

"Excuse me, but I must go." He stood. "Look, I will leave you all my notes here. We're done. I can't help you further. If you like, I will find someone else to help you and refund part of your generous fee. But I'm afraid I'm done here."

Glenda took a very long time to stand, and Carl saw her work to keep her composure in order. He stared at her, trying to figure out what it was he was feeling. The pull between them, like a magnetic field, became very strong, but he held himself back. And all of a sudden she released him.

"You are not done, Professor. Sit down. I insist. I don't want anybody else. I want *you*."

Chapter 14

JONAS WONDERED IF they would follow him to the human world for his scheduled rendezvous with Audray. He circled down back streets and visited a couple of watering holes, pretending to be settling in for the night. But his insides were burning to see Audray, and tell her about the danger they were in. He didn't dare trust the phones to relay this information. He needed to tell her in person. That meant he had to make it to the transport to the human world without being detected.

He thought about the black-haired woman who was his many times great granddaughter, and what she told him this afternoon.

"I am the direct descendent of your son, the Earl of Devonshire." She produced a locket with a hand-painted bust of a man Jonas did not recognize. But then he didn't want to get too physically close to her.

"I don't believe you. How can you know this?" Jonas returned. He stepped aside to allow a patron of Helena's house weave past him in the lobby and begin the staircase, with his chosen woman doing all the heavy lifting. *Staircase to Heaven, Josh had called it.* Jonas wondered why, of all times, he would think about that.

"Search your soul, grandfather…"

"I am not your grandfather!"

"True enough." She nodded, slipping her arm around Rupert's waist as he came to stand beside her. "But look deep inside and see if you don't recognize, don't smell the blood of the queen you pleasured, impregnated."

Jonas didn't want to look at her, but finally he did, and he saw it there. Catherine's face looked back at him with the same evil smile just as it looked three hundred years ago.

"So what is it I've been summoned for? You want something, that's obvious," he said.

"I want the throne that was mine, that was taken from my family."

"I cannot give that to you. You say I have fathered a son that should have been king, but that has nothing whatsoever to do with the Underworld or how succession is handled here. I have no standing. You know this. I've lived here for 300 years."

"Jonas, many generations of our family have heard of you and how you somehow survived your ordeals in the Caribbean. We have searched for you for over two hundred years. You led us to this place, Jonas. To the Underworld."

Jonas' stomach lurched as he sucked in a quick breath. He cursed his lack of care that caused his former safe haven in the Underworld to now become anything but safe. And now he'd exposed Audray to this danger through their very public relationship.

"You are the escort of the new Director. I believe you refer to her as your queen."

"But I have no authority. I am her paramour, surely you under-stand that."

"It's the same problem, Jonas. Back then, you delivered a child. You did not deliver the kingdom."

"But how could I have done this?

"By fighting for the monarchy in the uprising. Instead, you fled."

"After my family had been slaughtered. I had nothing to live for."

"But look at you, for having nothing to live for you manage quite well as a dark angel."

"It was the only option available to me."

"Yes! An now you are facing the same choice again, Jonas. Deliver the kingdom of the Underworld and earn your freedom."

"I am not sure even I can do this. It is not within my power to do so."

"Try," she had said coyly. "Or do you think you can live out your days peacefully in the human world and just run away? I have alliances up there too who will make your life a living hell on earth. Perhaps you need a little demonstration to convince you."

He worried for Audray's safety without him by her side. It also confirmed his suspicion that Catarina's plans went beyond a takeover of the Underworld.

In the end, she dismissed him, which was a surprise until she mentioned she wanted a face to face sit-down with Audray. He didn't swear an oath he'd help her achieve her goal, but the suggestion was laid thick: Audray might come to an untimely end if he didn't cooperate. They expected he'd help them convince Audray to give up the Directorship, just like he'd agreed to comply with the family's demand he deliver an heir to the king. And the fate of the woman he loved was once again in his hands.

Jonas shook his head to be rid of the memory of the meeting this afternoon. The smelly alley of Undertown at last broke through the fog of his thoughts. Standing alone under the dull light of a streetlamp, he ran sweaty fingers through his hair, retying his ponytail. His forehead was damp, and he wiped it down with his palm. He was grateful they let him go, but knew it was only to deliver their message. He felt like a dog on a leash. And someone was following him.

Jonas moved further down the steamy wet street with the awful odor gurgling through the cracks as it had for centuries. *How did I survive down here for all that time?* Coming to a more populated area, he searched around him yet did not see anyone who took special notice of him, except for the walkers. He could smell the layers of perfume and sex all over them, permeating their clothes, their hair, and their skin. Jonas could tell how old they were and who they had been with just by standing within ten feet of them.

"Hey there, angel. You look mighty lonesome," she said as she stepped out of the shadows and linked arms with Jonas, her short red hair blazing in the light of the streetlamp. She was beautiful, but overly made up and young. Probably not even twenty. Jonas felt sorry for her. He pushed her away and walked on but she persisted in following behind him, her little feet encased in stilettos, tapping on the stones like a bird as she tried to catch up.

"Come on. I know how to put a smile on that handsome face."

He kept walking.

"You got a hole in your soul? I can fill it, you know."

Jonas continued down the soggy street without turning.

"Hey, something wrong with you, big guy? You like boys? You don't like me?"

That made Jonas stop and look back at her, hands on his hips. His eyes swept up and down her body. She ran to him with little clawing steps, making all her luscious parts jiggle. He held her at arm's length and studied her innocent face.

"You could have another life, you know. Why do you do this?"

She leaned back and started to laugh.

He saw movement in the shadows to his left. *Good, let them think I'm interested.*

He squeezed the face of this dark angel, with one large hand, puckering her cheeks and red lips. She seemed drugged, oblivious to any danger. He saw the flawless face of a young girl who had given up on life, her human life. But then, she wasn't human any longer.

Audray, forgive me.

He tenderly lowered his mouth and claimed a kiss. He felt a jolt run through her body and she started to pull away. "Who are you?" Her eyes were large and round.

"That's a good sign, my dear," he whispered as he refused to loosen the grip on her arm, keeping her close, but not touching the length of her body. "You still notice the difference, don't you?" He leaned into the side of her face and added, "That means you are not completely evil. There is a kernel of hope they didn't rob you of when you turned."

"Hope? I hope you can fuck me silly, that's what I hope." She recovered and became the walker again. "You look like the kind of guy who can make a woman forget herself. I like to lose control…"

"Then let's go." He motioned down the street and dragged her behind him. Her little footsteps faltered, her four inch steel-tipped heels had no traction. She was no problem to hold up with one arm.

And in the old days, exactly his type.

He stopped a few times as if looking for a doorway, but took the advantage to search behind him. Not detecting his tail, he abruptly ran back down the road in the direction they had just come from, and took her into an unlit doorway.

"This is fine," she said as she began to hike up her short skirt.

"No. I have another place in mind." He blew on her face and saw her eyes flutter.

"Oh, God, you're one of those?"

"You will tell me the truth."

"Of course I will. Do it again, and I'll tell you anything you want to hear." She looked up at him with eyes of need.

He blew on her face again as she tipped her head back to inhale all of it. "You know how to get a girl primed and ready, my big new love." She gripped his package and he removed her hand quickly.

"Who do you work for?"

"No one. I'm an independent."

"Nobody down here is independent. Who is your maker?"

"Well, that is why I'm independent. My fucking sponsor went and got himself humanized, and now all of his girls have to fend for themselves."

"Say his name."

"Joshua Brandon."

Jonas was thrilled his former boss and friend was her sponsor. That also meant he might be able to trust her, just a little bit.

"I'm going to take you out of Undertown, up top. How would you like to conclude our business in the human world?"

Her eyes surveyed him carefully as she leaned in, and pressed her lithe body against his chest. She wound both arms around his neck, pressing her sex against his thigh, and whispered, "You can take me anywhere, dark lover. I am yours for whatever you want to do with me, for as long as you want. I got all of eternity, and so do you."

Works for me.

He grabbed her upper arm firmly and almost carried her down the street and up the stairs, out of Undertown. The night bustle was getting underway. Neon lights lit the eccentric array of showy dress, people parading in bright silks and feathers, some with just feathers, and some with nothing at all. Excesses of every sort assaulted his eyes. He mounted the steps of the transport station and took the next driverless black limo.

The girl snuggled next to his body in the back seat. He put his arm around her and kissed the top of her head. He had just met his twenty times great granddaughter. This one could have been one as well.

Damaged and hopelessly flawed, he would protect her nonetheless. He sighed.

Fuck, I miss Audray so much. Thank God they let me leave.

The girl looked out the windows of the limo when they arrived at the human transport side. "A warehouse? You live in a warehouse?"

"No. It's a run-down area humans wouldn't find interesting. It's easy to defend."

"Defend? Defend from what?"

"It's a very long story." He took her hand and helped her step from the limo. The instant her second stiletto hit the concrete pavement, the limo took off in a streak.

"Jeez. Remind me to be more careful. That one didn't even have a driver."

"Do you think they really care about you? You think they'd care if they ran over one of your legs? No, they'd send someone to come clean you up. It would be a minor problem. Only that."

The girl shuddered.

"Now, see that street over there?" She looked.

"See the bench right there?"

She nodded her head, eyeing the bus stop bench.

"I'm going to call you a taxi, have him take you to a store to get some decent clothes." He peeled off a wad of hundred dollar bills. He looked her straight in the eyes. "They don't do trades for sex up here, or if they do, it's definitely not a place you should be. They do money. So you have to have some. If you don't, you'll get into trouble."

She took the money, tucking it in her bra. Her face fell; her eyes swept down to his lips.

She can clean up. She'd be a pretty little thing. He wrote Joshua's address on the back of a note sheet and tore it off, extending it to her. Before she could grip it, he held it up in the air, out of reach. "You don't tell anybody about this, okay?"

She nodded.

"You sure? This is a one time offer, Missy."

"It's Judy."

"Okay, Judy. This is the address to Joshua Brandon's house here. But I'm going to warn you, he has a jealous woman." Jonas smiled. "You want to talk to Joshua first so he can break it to her. I don't want you dropping in and ruining something good he has made of his life. You understand?"

"Yes," she said softly. She studied him as Jonas pulled out his sat phone and called a cab.

"You have close to two thousand dollars there. That won't get you far, but it will get you properly dressed and to Joshua's. And you don't tell anybody until you find him, hear?"

"Why are you doing this?"

Jonas had to think about that. "Because I made a lot of mistakes in my life and now I've begun to see how I can change it. I didn't save my own child. So, I'm going to help save someone else's."

He watched as she sat her little body tentatively on the bench, swinging her legs, her tiny ankles crossed, like the young girl she was, as if she were waiting on a playground bench at school.

Chapter 15

J ONAS WAITED FOR the waif to speed off in the night air, red brake lights coming on just as they rounded the corner.

Perhaps I should have written him a note. But, in case she was caught, she'd be caught with a wad of cash and no name to pin it on. Joshua had turned hundreds of souls in his centuries as a dark angel before his conversion. Someone might even think a grateful patron sent her up top to snag him again.

Cute little redhead. Hope you start making better choices. Though Melanie was light brown haired, Josh's preference had always been redheaded Guardian angels, until he met Melanie. "This little one could tempt the pants off him in the old days," Jonas chuckled under his breath, "maybe even now." He hoped he was doing the right thing.

He scanned the area, making sure he was alone. Sounds of a small town, with the occasional siren, highlighted an ordinary evening on a Saturday night. He ran up the steps to Audray's home which was close to the transport entrance. He unlocked the door and made it upstairs to the bedroom. No one had disturbed a thing. He felt slightly relieved. He could smell his lover, and he wore it like an elixir. He opened her closet doors and inhaled the sweet scent of her body lingering on her clothes. He needed to feel her warm flesh undulating under him as he took her. His groin got hard thinking about it.

Best keep my wits about me. He checked the windows for signs of a tail, but he appeared to be alone.

Jonas put some things in a canvas bag, showered quickly to get rid of the Underworld stench, and changed into his black long-sleeved tee shirt and leathers for the ride to San Francisco.

His beast was the only vehicle in the garage, since Audray had the Maserati. Stuffing the bag into the carriage box he kick-started the bike, punched the garage door opener and took off down the gravel road in a trail of dust. Before rounding the corner he took one last look at the home they shared, waiting for the metal garage door to slowly close.

His heart was racing faster than the bike all the way to the City. Across the Golden Gate Bridge the lights of San Francisco glittered like jewels. The ocean air calmed him. He raised his head and tried to pick up her scent, imagine her tightly gripping him from behind. He was starved for her touch. He was starved for the feel of her flesh all over him, peeling off the layers of fear and regret. She could make him soft again. He chuckled. She was such a powerful dark angel, she could almost make him feel human again.

Down Van Ness he tooled, turning down Geary after going around the block. At last he made it to Union Square and the St. Francis. He pulled up to the entrance, two red-suited doormen standing guard. They were boys, really. Only armed with a whistle to summon a taxi. *They couldn't keep a dog out of the lobby if their life depended on it.* So funny, humans were. How they carried such a false sense of security. Only interested in appearances. For years he had appreciated the honesty of the Underworld. No pretenses; cheating and lying were expected. There wasn't any such thing as disappointment, character or honor.

And there is no hope.

He handed one of the red boys a twenty. "I'm going to go inside and make arrangements for this," he pointed to his bike. "There's another twenty you can share if I come back and find not a soul has touched it, understand?"

"Yessir," they said in unison. The taller one took the twenty.

The bell captain, Watts, was an old acquaintance. His chocolate skin and slicked back, curly hair made him look like a French dandy. He wore too much cologne, a little blush and sported a gold cravat with a diamond stickpin, which was unnecessary as far as the St. Francis was concerned, but very important when it came to Watts.

"Watts, my man. Good to see you."

"Hey, Holmes! Been a while." Watts looked out the glass doors and asked the question, "You bring the iron maiden?"

"Yes, sir. She's primed and ready to ride."

"Oh, she and I gon' get some one-on-one time, my man. When she done wid me she gonna purr real sweet and not let your hairy legs straddle her again."

"Yeah, she likes a good time. She's been a bit jealous of late."

"So I heard. So I heard." He leaned into Jonas and whispered in his ear, "My friend, you let me know if you needs any help with that one too, okay?"

Jonas chuckled and nodded before he lifted Watts up with one hand at his throat, careful not to hurt the man but left him dangling six inches off the floor. "No help needed." He set Watts down gently.

"I feel you. No problem." Watts straightened his jacket and cravat. He lengthened his sleeves with a healthy tug at each gold braided cuff. Jonas thought he looked absolutely ridiculous.

"Do you know if she's here?"

"Don't think so. Check with Estelle at the front desk. She'd know."

"Thanks." Jonas patted the lean black face of his friend and tucked a hundred dollar bill into his hand without anyone being able to see. "Gas money," he whispered and winked. And give the boys this." He handed Watts another twenty.

He walked across the thick gold and red carpet of the lobby, anxious to get upstairs.

Audray could still smell the smoke on her clothes and in her hair, the charred remains of her mother mingled with twisted metal and plywood. She also hadn't stopped crying, feeling a lump of coal in her soul at the thought she had planned and plotted the demise of the angel, her sister, who had saved her life. Did Claire know this? Somehow, she didn't think Claire did.

Then she thought about their mother's death. She hoped the woman was already dead by the time the flames hit her. Audray had grilled the policewoman who was first on the scene, informing her who she was.

"You have any idea how it happened?"

"No. We just got the fire out. We gotta wait for the arson investigator."

"You suspect arson?"

"It's routine."

Audray thought the cause of the fire had been her mother's cigarettes, but the fact that they were doing an investigation, though they said it was routine, made her worry. Everything was happening so quickly. If this was arson, someone had been one step ahead of her. Had that someone also found out about Burt?

She stormed up the freeway and made it to San Francisco close to ten o'clock. Jonas had not answered his cell, and she was annoyed and worried at the same time. She was in need of his strong arms. She needed to bury her head in his chest and let him take her away someplace.

Watts came out the glass doors when she pulled up to the entrance to the St. Francis.

She fished for some money, but Watts stopped her. "He already paid me well."

She handed him the keys. "How long's he been here?"

"About two hours." He picked up her scorched scent. "You been to a barbeque?"

"Hardly."

She ran through the lobby and then remembered she'd left her bag in the car. As she whirled around, Watts was standing behind her with a smile, holding the black leather satchel. He gave her a smirk. "Unless you were willing to stay naked during your stay, I'm thinking you'll need this."

Audray managed to eek out a smile and took the bag. "Thanks."

"Course, the look on his face, I think he'd be happy just the same if you didn't have any clothes. And the robes are nice, I hear."

She picked up her room key, although she was hoping she didn't need it.

The elevator took her up to the tenth floor. She sniffed the sleeves of her jacket and a lock of hair, then sighed. She felt like she'd been at the bottom of a coal mine.

Before she could turn the handle, the door flew open and Jonas stood there bare-chested wrapped in a towel hung low on his waste. He lifted her up off the ground, and carried her into the room. She wrapped her arms around his neck and smelled the soap and muskiness of her man. She held him, trying to eliminate all the memories of the last two days. He put her feet on the ground and let her slide down his frame until he could gaze into her eyes and claim her mouth. Audray knew he read everything inside her when he did this.

"What is this, Audray?" he brushed away her tears as he tilted his head and scanned her thoughts. "Is this about your mother or about

Claire?" She could feel him tense up.

"My mother is gone, Jonas. There was a fire." Audray buried her head in his bare chest.

"Oh, baby, so sorry. Why didn't you call me? I should have been there." he asked.

She untangled enough so that their faces could meet. Their lips touched and some of the burdens of the day were lifted from her.

"When did this happen, Audray?"

"Today. When I came back—" She concentrated on the gravesite so she wouldn't have to reveal her visit with Burt. She hoped he didn't pick up her ruse. "I saw her grave, Jonas. Hers and my father's graves. I visited them."

"I'm glad. I'm glad you know about Claire now."

Audray wasn't sure "The world is coming unraveled. The more I search into my past, the more I wish I'd never known these things. I almost destroyed my own sister who had saved my life. What kind of a despicable person does that make me?"

"You didn't know."

"But I *should* have known. I should have felt it."

He hugged her again, his powerful fingers massaging her scalp again. "You are way too hard on yourself, Audray. These special powers didn't come until you'd turned. You've been a pawn in a dangerous game."

"We still are pawns, Jonas. I don't want to lose you. Whatever I have done, I don't want to lose what we have together."

God, I hope this never ends. Let me stay here forever.

"Yes, my Queen." *Do not think of these things. The past is the past. Live here with me now, in our future. Bring your mind back to me and be with me here, what we have today.*

She felt her powerful need eclipse her pain and remorse. Their tongues played through the long kissing as he drew her into the white marble bathroom and, without slowing the sucking and pressing of their lips, began to peel off her clothes, some pieces coming easily and some needing to be shredded. At last, she stood before him naked, and he took her to the shower, turning on the double heads and the steam. He dropped his towel and joined her.

"I don't ever want to be gone from you that long again," she said.

"Me neither." His erection touched her, teasing and bobbing, full and expectant. Jonas put her head under the water and kissed her eyes, under her chin and then on her lips as the warm water cascaded over both of them. It was a safe place to cry, the warm liquid carrying away all the grief along with the tears.

He lathered her hair with his probing fingers, pushing up from the bottom of her skull, his thumbs pressing with strong deliberate strokes. He rubbed her temples and kissed her neck. She melted with the sound of his deep breathing in her ear, as he slipped soapy fingers behind and rubbed the back of her neck. His hands moved lower as he put her head under the water spray and turned her around. He swirled the lemon shower gel into her back and down to the crack between her butt cheeks. She put her palms on the snow-white wall and pressed her forehead into the cool wetness as he went to his knees to rub between her legs from behind, kissing her soapy cheeks. He formed a ring with his massive hands and worked the soap down her thighs, over her knees and down and over her ankles.

She turned to look into the face of the only man she had ever loved, kneeling before her.

"I have so much to say…" she started.

"Shhh. Not tonight, my love. Not tonight. Tonight we don't talk."

"Yes."

His eyes smiled but his full lips only parted in a half smile. He slipped his index finger between the lips of her pink peach, rubbing back and forth. Audray began to feel her body come alive again. She felt like she'd been buried in a shallow, dusty grave. Blood rushed to fill the delicate parts of her anatomy. She reveled in the pleasure of his ministrations, and let him tickle her soul.

She arched up, placing her face in the warm spray. The feel of his tongue on her sex was beautiful and perfect and exactly what she needed, but there were tears anyway. She looked down on him, his mouth savoring her juices, then laying his cheek flat against her lower belly to gently part her thighs and feed from her again. Audray played with the wet curls of his head and caressed the undersides of his ears. Her sex quivered and he swept his eyes up the full length of her body, slowly.

He loves pleasuring me more than taking the pleasure himself. She saw the man, the hero, the warrior, the protector.

The keeper of my flame.

Jonas rose and their bodies pressed against one another in the warm sluicing rain. She made room for his hardness, but pressed her mound against him, rubbing up and down. They both sighed, sending erotic steamy air over each other, inhaling the other's passion. Jonas turned her body and lightly bit the side of her neck, claiming her. Her shoulder needed his touch. He kissed the violated skin and gently grazed his teeth over her flesh.

He pulled back, Audray feeling the airspace between them for a second before he placed his cock at her backside and bent her gently at the waist. He let her wait there, his readiness primed, encroaching just barely on her wet opening. She pushed back to lean into him and he held her but kept his cock only part way inside, teasing.

She turned her head around to him and he covered her mouth from the side, lips sucking hers, tasting her with his tongue. One of his hands was firmly placed on her lower belly as his other migrated up over her breasts and splayed out at her chest and lower neck, holding her in position. She knew if she melted, and she was in danger of doing so, he would hold her up, and it would be no effort at all. Her thighs enjoyed the feel of the length of his against them. She swayed her lower body from side to side to feel him at her pink rim.

And then he held her tight and plunged in. She exploded. She saw the vision of every happy moment of her life play out before her, like her soul had released the dark holds and black smoky rags that had encapsulated it so it could run free. He ground into her and then pulled back, and then plunged in, each time deeper. Each time her eyes saw the tiny particles of light like stars in the midnight sky, little lanterns flashing underneath her eyelids.

I am rescued at last.

Chapter 16

AUDRAY AWOKE THE next morning to the chirping of her sat phone. All calls were blocked except for Underworld emergencies and other pre-programmed numbers, so it was important. She looked at Jonas over her shoulder as she reached for the phone but he pushed it away. She could tell he'd been awake, just letting her sleep or perhaps eavesdropping on her dreams. He raised his eyebrows as if he'd been caught doing something naughty.

Audray fell back into the down pillow and the thousand thread per inch buttery Egyptian cotton sheets, staring up at the ceiling, pulling the hair back off her forehead. The phone continued to chirp. Jonas had propped himself up on his elbow looking down at her. She rubbed his forearm with the backs of her fingers.

"I should get that."

"Later," he whispered. He smiled without parting his lips. With a forefinger, she traced the curved half circles framing his mouth, then let her palm rub flat against the sandpaper of his cheek. She was still fascinated that growing hair was something they could do as dark angels.

Jonas started kissing her neck. One large hand smoothed over her left breast and began to move down the center of her torso so slowly it was making it difficult for her to concentrate.

"Jonas," she whispered.

Jonas nodded silently as he stuck his tongue into the little cave of her belly button and sucked it. With a swishing motion he moved his tongue lower. He had reached the area just to the top of her slit and was snaking a tongue, barely breeching her lips. Jonas' large paw reached for the phone on the bedside table and threw it under the bed.

"Jonas! You are positively wicked. You'll get me into trouble."

Jonas licked the length of her quivering peach in response. Without looking at her, he did it again. "I intend to get you into real trouble, my Queen."

She sighed and then allowed herself to melt as Jonas continued laving her, and doing quite an expert job of it. His singleness of focus in his lovemaking was something that drove her wild. His tongue took all the cares and the aches of her heart away.

She had only been a dark angel for less than a year. Jonas had a few centuries to perfect the art of ignoring the human world. She envied that in him.

He had separated her lips, lapping, sucking, inserting two fingers inside her. She watched his forehead with the vein that coursed right down the middle, the rough stubbled surface under his nose where his thin clipped line of hair and the skin around it was shiny with her juices. When he put his lips on her sex that damn crease at the side of his mouth showed up and she was lost.

Audray arched back, raising her arms above her head and floated away. She gave into to him, a slave to his tongue.

I'd give up my kingdom for an afternoon with your tongue!

This made Jonas chuckle. His tanned face beamed as he looked into her eyes.

Yes, my love. It is that good this morning, and I never want it to end. But I also need to feel your cock inside me.

It was too perfect that he could read her mind. Just too perfect.

LATER, SHE WAS wrapped in a velvet soft white robe with matching slippers adorned with the distinctive St. Francis logo on them. When she was human, her last lover had taken her here, and she stole a pair of the slippers, wearing them around his house afterwards. But today she had enough wealth and power to buy the whole hotel, so the slippers were viewed from a different perspective.

Jonas had ordered them breakfast, and the room service cart clattered with the tinkle of silver and glasses of ice water. She was looking forward to the cappuccino she could smell. She tiptoed to the bathroom, brushing her hair and applying just a little lipstick. It still surprised her to see her dark eyes, not the emerald green she had grown up with. Her turning had been easy, surrounded by people who cared for her. Jonas was even there that day, but he stood in the back as one of Josh's lesser helpers. He watched her, always watched her, and said not a word until at last they were alone together the afternoon the former Director was eliminated.

Opening the door from the bedroom suite, she walked barefoot on the cool marble floor, standing in front of the huge gentleman she knew was naked under his white robe, who offered her the frothing coffee with a heart pattern drawn into it.

The foam covered her upper lip and Jonas immediately tipped his head down to clean it off for her, ending with a deep penetrating kiss. His handsome face in the morning light was such a source of joy to her, made her almost feel like everything was perfect just the way it was, and they would have forever and forever without a disruption in their joy.

But the pain of losing her sister and her mother came back, and she knew this was not the case.

Jonas must have read her thoughts, for he put his finger to his lips and bade her be silent.

"Not now, Audray. I have no answers for you. We'll find the answers in time. But not now. Now you are mine. Focus here, with me. The rest will take care of itself."

She nodded her agreement.

He lifted the silver covers on the black and gold-rimmed china to reveal a brilliant yellow vegetable omelet made with fresh eggs, new potatoes and slices of bacon he would eat for her. An iced compote held an enormous silver bowl of strawberries next to a pitcher of cream.

They ate silently, basking in the morning sunlight. When she tasted her first strawberry for dessert she remembered something.

"Just a minute," she said as she stood up. She tried not to think about it so it would be a surprise. She jogged to the bedroom and drew out the can of whipped cream she'd packed in her overnight bag.

Jonas nodded to her and arched his eyebrows.

"I like it. I like this very much."

Audray shook the can and squirted a three inch high mound of the white cream over the bowl of strawberries. Audray dipped her finger in it and presented it to Jonas, who sucked it and licked it in long strokes. She dipped a strawberry in the topping and fed him. He did the same for her. She fed him another one. He fed her again. Then he washed the residue of cream from the corner of her mouth with a long lingering kiss.

He pushed her back onto the loveseat, allowing their robes to fall open and there he covered her flesh with the warm strong muscles of his body. He kissed her nipples, first one and then the other. With a wolfish grin he grabbed the can of whipped cream and covered her pink areolas and then licked them clean again with the sandpaper of his tongue.

Audray's arousal came on strong. She felt the muscles in her sex tickle, hungry with anticipation, feeling the need in her passage to be filled with the maleness of him, ached to feel whole and complete.

She grabbed the can from his hands and placed a trail along his penis. She bent over and licked and sucked his dick. He repositioned them so she was on top of him as he brought his head under her sex and squirted the cream along the slit of her peach, extending beyond past her anus. She opened her legs to him and he took his time nibbling and sucking until she was sparkling clean. She massaged his balls with both hands and had him deep into her mouth, rolling her tongue over the velvet surface of his cock. She nibbled the large vein that zigzagged down the length of him as he sucked her folds and lapped her juices.

He moved to sitting position and brought her body back against him to sit on his lap with her back pressed to his chest. There he raised her body and impaled her on his shaft. Audray felt the dull delicious splitting of her insides and drew him up with her muscles clenched, squeezing as hard as she could until she got a satisfying growl from Jonas behind her. She repeated the movements again, full of the need of his hot thick cock buried deep within her. He would squeeze her breasts, then remove his hands and let the joining of their sex be their only point of contact. Her feet found traction on the floor so she stood, leaning over as he rose pummeling her from behind, pulling her into his groin.

One more pulse from her sex and her orgasm came in gentle waves, forcing her back onto him deeply as she felt his shudder and explosion of seed inside.

He was going to get up and get her a warm towel, but she put a hand to his ass and asked him to stay inside her. They fell asleep on the loveseat, Jonas cradling her back, the can of whipped cream rolling free on the floor, remnants of a breakfast only half eaten, their bodies still connected.

Chapter 17

CARL CHASTISED HIMSELF all the way home for bringing Molly, getting her involved with his dangerous client. He was sure he was dealing with an insane individual, someone who believed in curses and people living for hundreds of years after they were "dead," whatever that meant. Reason and logic were replaced with fear. The strange woman had an emotional fixation on this Jonas Starling unlike anything he'd heard of before. He wasn't an expert in psychology. He was just a history professor. But he knew what depths this obsession could take. He was going to have to make a choice, and soon.

Molly had picked up on it too. She sat beside him during the short car ride to his cottage, without saying a thing. Carl had tried not to let Molly see his alarm from her perch across the café as Glenda said those fateful words:

"I know you won't give two thoughts for yourself. But I believe there are those you would protect. You cannot deny me without suffering the consequences."

Consequences? I'm being blackmailed. He replayed those words over and over again as he drove toward his home. Though it was disgusting, he knew he would do whatever it took to keep Molly safe.

"Carl…" she began, taking his right hand off the steering wheel and placing it in her lap between her palms, "I don't like that woman. Something off about her."

"I agree." He bit his lower lip and scanned the road.

"So, tell me what she said about your research." Molly's eyes swept up to his and he saw the bigger question there.

She's already involved. He was weighing her innocence versus arming her with knowledge. He chose to trust her.

"I think the woman is unstable. She has an unhealthy fixation on this Starling character."

"And?"

How do I say this?

"She believes he is still living…" Carl stole a quick glance at Molly's face. She was staring down at his hand, nestled between hers. He continued, "And she wants me to find him, or, rather, verify that it's him. She gave me an address and asked that I do a kind of stakeout, take pictures and such. I'm to deliver him a message." He sighed as he aimed the car down the driveway to his cottage. At the front door, he stopped, and then turned off the ignition. The leather seats creaked as he turned toward her in the cramped space, his knees tightly jammed together.

She was nodding slowly. He could see moisture in her eyes.

"Please," he said as he leaned over and smoothed the tear away with his thumb. "I'm begging for your forgiveness, but I have to work with her. I don't want to, but I have to. She threatened me."

Molly looked up at him, her green eyes full, about to burst. He expected to see something more than sadness there. He expected to be mocked, or worse, that she would be angry with his crazy suspicions. She placed her delicate pink palms on either side of his face. The heat radiating from her hands sent an erotic tingle down his spine and awakened his groin. He cursed himself for the inappropriateness of his reaction to her touch. But there was no way around it.

I am enchanted.

They made their way into the cottage, and suddenly Molly turned to him.

"Promise me you'll tell me everything later on. Right now, Carl, I need you to wash away the blackness. Bring me the heat and the glow I crave. I want to feel our fire together."

He studied her flawless skin with the red aura like a halo surrounding her. Carl found the worries of the morning did melt away. All his favorite places were waiting for him as he kissed her skin over the tiny blue veins in her neck, her upper chest and the insides of her thighs. He buried his head in her femaleness and let her scent cover him. Her young, supple body gave itself so freely, it was difficult to control himself. She would do one little thing, and it would eliminate the many minutes of control he tried to exert over himself and his cock. His member would march to the band of her passion, a willing participant, despite the fact that he was trying to prolong the session, the feel of her insides sheathed over him.

And it seemed to Carl that the more they made love, the more he wanted her.

Am I becoming obsessed, or is this real love?

Later, as she stirred in her sleep, her back pressed into his chest, he didn't care any longer. It was wonderful sleeping in the protective nest of her flaming hair and having her warm, smooth, willing skin rub the length of his thighs and pull out of him the best that he could be. Every pore craved her essence.

SHE MADE GRILLED cheese sandwiches and green salad for a late lunch.

"Professor, you need your strength."

Her half smile, her head cocked at that angle always told him she loved pleasing him.

"Protein. Maybe oysters?" He chuckled. What would his teacher-friends on the academic committee think if they knew what he had been doing all last night and all morning? Molly's boss, the head librarian, certainly knew, and so did the Dean.

She bent over to serve the sandwiches, leaning just a little too much so that the dress shirt she'd borrowed hiked up over her ass, and he was undone with the look of her two perfectly formed cheeks, and the ripe fruit between them.

I'm going insane with need.

As if she heard him, she turned and gave him that little smile again. "You should eat first." The smile left her face as she came up to press into his chest. "Then we talk. Then you can do with me whatever you want, Professor."

And of course it was impossible to concentrate on eating the cheese sandwiches or crunching down on the salad. Everything reminded him of what he wanted to do with her. Now that they had been so intimate so many times, his imagination ran wild with new thoughts, mixed with the pleasures they had already shared. He forced the food down.

She made him a drink, a combination of bottled lime juice and mineral water. At the last minute, she squeezed a sliced blood orange into the mixture. "Come, we need to talk."

He started to clean the plates between them, but she would have none of it. She led him to the living room, and they sat together on the couch. She crisscrossed her ankles, raising her knees and faced him, so of course he could see everything in front of him. He was beginning to get hard again.

"Molly, I have never felt this way. I just can't get your...your...aura, essence. I don't know what it is, but I feel it all over."

"Is it too much?" Her eyes were serious.

"As if you could control it!" He smirked, but her eyes didn't smile. He tilted his head but didn't ask the question on the tip of his tongue. With furrowed brow, he glanced down, but then he could smell her sex and so he had to inspect her pink petals again. There. *Jeez! I'm like a teenager. Better handle yourself correctly, Carl. You're about to get so carried away you won't know the difference between reality and fantasy.*

"Carl, now we talk. Tell me what's going on." She still wasn't smiling. But she wasn't making fun of him either.

"I have no idea." He leaned into her and gave her a quick kiss. "And I don't care."

I love the way you distract me. I need to be immersed in your femaleness.

He was rewarded with a beaming smile that lit up the room, something he could feel emanating from her body without touching her.

"You need to tell me about the woman. How did she find you?"

Pulled back to reality, Carl began the strange story. "Well, she called me at my office at the college, said she had a research project she wondered if I'd be interested in tackling. She said she would pay me four thousand dollars to dig up what I could on a particular character. I mean, how could I say no?"

"Okay." Molly nodded.

"We met at the coffee shop last Saturday, just a week ago. She paid me and said she wanted information on this Jonas Starling guy."

"How did she find you?"

"She said someone recommended me. She couldn't remember the person."

"Did she tell you why she wanted the research done?"

"No. I didn't ask." Carl turned his head and gazed out the window at a fast-moving white cloud in an otherwise blue sky. "I don't know why I didn't ask. She kind of spooked me a little, probably."

Molly gave him an appreciative glance. "I'm sure you have pretty good radar when it comes to character, Carl. I wouldn't blame yourself."

"First of all, young lady, it's probably just my imagination, which could be damaged. Perhaps my radar is bent due to all the use my antennae," he pointed to his groin, "is getting."

They shared a laugh.

"Honey, there's nothing wrong with your antennae," she whispered.

Carl saw her half-lidded eyes drawing him in again. *Damn! It feels so good to be wanted so much.* He had never heard of a man getting so hard so many times in one day. And night. And how well he could function on less than four hours sleep!

"Is this the part where I get to do anything to you I want?"

"Almost, but first we have to get the big stuff over with." Her eyes became serious.

"Excuse me?"

"I've made a decision about your Glenda. I agree you must help her. Then perhaps she'll leave you alone and focus on this Starling character."

"Molly, it's ridiculous to think he's still alive. No offense, but maybe it's me she wants. She did say so, you know."

"Yes, I figured that. But I think she just needs your resources. You should play along if you're going to get away from her."

"You're not making sense, Molly." He watched her glance down to her hands folded in her lap. Her knees had spread and her bent right leg extended off the couch so she sat with ankles crisscrossed in front of her. But her delicate pink folds were discretely covered by the tails of his shirt. He was certain some of her juices would remain there.

If you wear that shirt you won't get anything done all day.

Molly smiled. "Carl, this is the big stuff." She stopped, raised her eyes and took his hands in hers.

Maybe it was reflex, but the pit in his stomach lurched down through the couch, through the hardwood floor of the cottage and deep into the earth a few hundred feet. His throat was parched, and he felt the pulse at the sides of his neck hammer like a drum. He couldn't hear anything over the loud thrump-thrump of his beating heart. He inhaled and held his breath.

"Glenda is a witch, Carl. A powerful black witch."

Carl exhaled. *Well, maybe that wasn't so bad.* But he knew she wasn't finished.

"She's also very old, possibly as old as Jonas Starling."

"You…you think he's still alive?"

"Yes."

"And she's a black witch."

"Yes."

"And just how do you know all this?" He thought there was a tiny chance she was messing with him again, like she liked to do before sex. He desperately clung to an explanation that was logical, not supernatural, something he would be able to accept.

Molly smiled, squeezed his fingers and rubbed the backs of his hands with her thumbs, like mothers rub the hands of their children before they go into surgery.

"Because, my love, I'm a witch as well."

Chapter 18

AUDRAY AND JONAS walked in the windy noontime rush impacting Union Square, looking into shop windows. The Tiffany display cases had flawless diamond wedding sets nestled in white satin. Jonas was silent, standing behind her with his hands on her hips, watching her golden hair play with the wind, feeling her scent feeding every pore of his body. He read her thoughts, her excitement. She was imagining a big wedding with lots of flowers.

She's imagining a human wedding.

Jonas searched his memories, and couldn't think of a single dark angel union in his three hundred years. He'd been to his share of family weddings as a child and human young man. And he'd been forced to attend weddings at court. But Audray wanted to be bound to him forever, in a ceremony he wasn't sure was possible.

For the first time since discovering his gift of reading her thoughts, he found he no longer wanted to hear them. He was only glad she wasn't able to read his.

She turned to face him, her eyebrows raised, her sweet mouth in that moist red smile which always made him lean in to press his lips against hers. He held back this time and heard the question in her thoughts. He would try to answer.

"My gift to you would not be one of these. I can only give you my heart and a silver band, as was the custom with my people for genera- tions. I'll not be having you buying a fancy ring yourself and then showing it off as being from me. That I won't do."

He felt her recognition spread, like tumblers in a large bank vault adjusting to unlock. She was scolding herself and her lack of understanding of him and his ways.

"No matter, Audray. You are young in dark years. I am very old. I've had lots of time to think about these things."

"But you will marry me, Jonas, won't you?"

"Of course, but mostly because I see how happy the thought makes you." He peeled her away from the window. "But you must let me ask you formally. Even in your time that is usually the way it's done, right?"

"Yes, although the lines have been blurred a bit over the years. Women are so much more direct and forceful."

"I'd have to agree there." He chuckled. "But some things stay the same. The woman chooses the man. But the man asks for her to bind herself to him, asks for her hand. Only a man can do that."

"I used to lead when I danced ballroom."

"I can see how that would happen. And if I were a skinny lad of fifteen, I'd let you do whatever the hell you wanted to do with me too." He tucked her arm into his chest as they walked down the windy sidewalk. "But we're talking about eternity, and a life's decision is a man's decision and a man's question."

They walked to the next block and crossed the red light with a horde of tourists. He pretended he could get lost in the crowd. He began the discussion he knew it was time to have.

"I don't need a ceremony to declare to anyone I would defend your life with my own, that your life is more important than mine."

"Because I'm the Director."

Jonas stopped them mid stride and placed his hands on either side of her face. She seemed so delicate and small to him now. "Being

Director's got nothing to do with it." He felt a twinge of anger well up, and it annoyed him.

"Sorry."

"Part of the beauty of finding something you've always wanted is that, for us, we can have this for all eternity. But the difficult part is knowing if we were lost to each other, we would spend eternity alone. It is the double-edged sword, is it not?"

"Yes. But I want to focus on the future."

And my past puts that in peril.

Jonas hailed a cab and took Audray to the pier with the thirty-foot red metal arrow sculpture that pierced the earth. He had always liked this piece of urban art. Before he met Audray, he had thought it symbolized how he would feel if he ever really did fall in love. Staked to the ground with a hard-to-miss enormous red arrow through his heart. And he'd been right. It was exactly the way he felt now.

They took a seat on a wooden park bench overlooking the bay dusted with whitecaps and white sails of the swarm of boats navigating the waters. He felt her watching him, knowing there was something on his mind. She wasn't worried, not nearly as worried as she would be after he told her.

"We sit here like we're a couple of humans in love. It's a nice fantasy, and it's the one thing I cannot give you. Our world as we know it is about to come apart at the seams. I'd like to think we'll be able to escape the consequences, but I'm too old, and I know too much."

"What are you talking about?"

"Turns out, I fathered a son. Remember what I told you about the Court? That family has reached out to me from the past to claim what they think is their birthright." He could tell she was struggling with the idea.

"Are you already committed, then? Does this mean we can't get married?"

He knocked his head back and barked a laugh. Then he grabbed her, squeezing her supple frame, feeling the excitement of her breasts against his chest. He felt her arousal and it made him glad.

"No. I had a child. That doesn't mean I have a wife." He smoothed the hair from her face and gave her a deep penetrating kiss. "You are the only woman I will bed, the only woman I will marry, I swear it."

"So then, what is the problem?"

"They want me to give them a kingdom I didn't deliver before. I gave them the child, but I didn't give them the kingdom."

"Your son was to be king?"

"Yes. But the old king died before my son could be declared the legitimate heir."

"That's not your fault."

"In a way it is. They asked me to help with the uprising when the country was tossed into turmoil by the death of Charles. I refused. That cost me the lives of my father, my brothers and…and…my betrothed and her family."

"You were engaged?"

"Yes. When they were all killed, I fled to the seas, and became a wanted man. Someone came to me and offered me a life of immortality. I thought becoming a dark angel was payback for the crime I'd committed against my family. And I was a coward. I thought I could disappear."

"You didn't commit a crime. You refused on principle. That's not criminal."

"I caused the death of everyone I held dear. My death was just a little step further, that's all. I already was dead inside."

"So what has this to do with the here and now?"

"They've come back to claim their kingdom. They've been looking for me for three hundred years. They want me to give it to them, and they've threatened to do you harm if I don't."

"I don't understand. What kingdom do they want?"

"They want your job, Audray. They want to control the Underworld."

"Then why shouldn't I let them take it?"

"Because they'll never let us go, my love. They'll use the Underworld to find us no matter where we try to hide. If they found me after three hundred years, they'd find us eventually, and they'll make me watch while they destroy you."

He read that she would willingly give up the Directorship. Though it came out of her love for him, he had to correct her thinking.

"We'll only exist as long as you are the powerful Director and can call on allies. If you relinquish that, they'll use the Underworld as a steppingstone to dominate the entire human world as well. They want it all this time, and they'll destroy anyone who tries to stop them. This time, there's nowhere else to hide."

Chapter 19

ALL AFTERNOON AUDRAY thought they had been watched. She felt it as she and Jonas sat at the pier. She felt it as they toured the Egyptian exhibit at the DeYoung Museum. Jonas had been fascinated with the weapons display, even reading about a primitive mechanism to release multiple spears invented by one of the Pharaohs, a young scientific genius.

Audray saw a strange man dressed in black reflected off the glass case covering a sarcophagus. When she turned around, he had disappeared. This alerted Jonas.

"You've seen someone." Jonas' jaw muscles tensed.

"Yes, I feel like we're being followed."

"We are. I saw his face."

He grabbed her elbow and led her out of the exhibit hall so fast, she almost mistook his swiftness for anger. They hopped into a cab. Jonas gave the Middle Eastern driver instructions down to the Mission district, far away from their hotel and the tourist area. The dark blue cab lurched and sliced through traffic like a chariot.

When they arrived, Jonas searched the street through the rear view window before he exited the cab and then extricated her. They quickly ran into a narrow red building with blaring mariachi music piped from two huge speakers by the front door. Inside, it was dark and smelled of fried tortillas.

"Why don't you let me just disappear, Jonas. I can take you with me. I have that power."

"I'm not sure I want them to know that just now." Jonas pulled her to a corner table, hunkering down next to her, surveying the street through the painted window.

"Who do you think it is?"

"Someone from here. Not the Underworld."

"How do you know that?" she asked.

A heavyset teenage girl in a brightly embroidered white smock dress appeared with two waters, interrupting Jonas' comment.

"We have especials here." She handed them a plastic menu covered with smudges, tapping on the handwritten note clipped to the top. "You want something to drink first?"

Jonas ordered them each a Dos Equis.

"Honestly, Jonas, don't you know by now I don't drink beer?"

He looked at her and she melted. This man could make her eat or drink anything. Her knees quivered as the spot between her legs swelled. He smiled. She knew he felt it too.

Jonas leaned into her and after brushing her lips with his he said, "Humor me, just a little, my Queen."

It was everything she could do not to jump on him right there in the restaurant in front of their little audience. Delicious thoughts were running through her head. It had only been a few hours since their last encounter. She missed the sex already.

Every day she got more of a glimpse of the man she thought she knew, and every day she was surprised with some new revelation. *Maybe this is what happens when you live over three hundred years.* Like he had said, life was complicated.

Their beers arrived. Audray pushed hers to sit touching his with a little clink. He ordered one *grande* tostada and two forks. His large paw dove into the chips and the red salsa the waitress brought with the beer. Audray watched the eating machine in front of her and wanted to lick the salt and corn meal remnants out of the corner of his mouth.

He smiled, in an open invitation, so she did. "Um, you taste so good. You always taste so good." She let her tongue work over the salty goodness of her lower lip.

"Do that again and you'll have me unable to walk in a few seconds."

"I could relieve the pressure, if you like." Her hands went to the zipper in his dark pants. She pushed up the long rod she felt underneath the smooth bulging leather. As the heel of her hand pressed against him, he grew even larger.

The welcome sandpaper of his cheek brushed against hers as he whispered, "I can't wait, my love, but I brought you here to talk. We'll do this later."

Disappointed, she sighed and removed her hand. "Right. So you were saying about the man not being from the Underworld?"

"He had blue eyes, did you see them?"

"No. Saw his reflection, but not a look at his face. So he can't be a dark angel, then."

"Right again."

"So what do you think?"

"My newly-found relatives," he paused as he rolled his eyes at the ridiculous predicament he was in, "must have human accomplices. I'm not sure why they would have a human following us, but apparently they do."

"What if they're following me?"

"Not sure I understand."

Their tostada was delivered and Jonas took no time to dig in. Audray took a sip of her water. He put a forkful of beans and lettuce in front of her mouth and gestured for her to open.

"I have need for all your strength later," he whispered, covering her with plenty of his erotic breath. They both laughed. The beans tasted remarkably good, though Audray's stomach was acting up. "Another?" he asked.

"No, thanks. I am not hungry. I'm having the first stomachache of my immortal life, can you imagine it?"

He smiled. "Ugh. I'd forgotten how I used to feel as a young lad after a night of drinking and chasing the lasses."

"Maybe the whipped cream was bad." She was serious.

"Oh, no. The whipped cream was good. Very, very good."

She basked in the glow of his gaze, blushing at the memories of their morning together. She could still feel the slick texture of his red cock as she licked the whipped cream from him, leaving him glistening and ready for her.

But then an awkward pause returned. She scanned the room and the street outside to check for the dark man, but saw nothing. She remembered what she'd found in Bakersfield. "I still can't get the vision of my mom out of my head. And my sister, Claire."

"Yes, I felt some of that." He kissed her lightly. "I worried, but didn't feel your fear or I would have come. Your thoughts were a bit masked to me, though. Like there was a short or some kind of static connection and I couldn't feel everything like I normally can."

"Has that happened before?"

"Not to me. Used to happen to my dad. He used to blame it on evil spirits. Of course, he wasn't a dark angel and knew nothing of the Underworld."

"See, that's what I mean. Something strange is going on. I can feel it."

"I do too. And remember, we have to be careful. I do feel it's more safe for you up top with everything going on in the Underworld. There at least we know who our enemies are."

"Agreed." She stared at her food and could not bring herself to eat. Her nerves were frazzled. She was turning her head and scanning everyone and everything around her. Perhaps she was worrying too much.

"Come on, sweetheart, have a little more."

Audray shook her head.

"What if it was arson? What if someone deliberately killed her?"

"What do you think?"

"She was in pretty bad shape. She even passed out on the bed with a cigarette when I was there..."

"There, you see? Don't go worrying yourself over things that aren't real."

"After what we've both lived through, how could we doubt anything being real? Would you have believed anyone if they said you could live forever, or would be able to go back and forth between the human world and the Underworld?"

"Or find true love?" He whispered through his teeth.

"That too." Audray brushed the backs of her fingers against his cheek, glad he had mentioned it. "Do you suppose there are forces of evil here in the human world, not connected to the Underworld? And what if they're after me, not you?"

"I don't know, love. Possible, I guess."

"I look at what happened to my mother. She clearly had interventions, perhaps Guardian angel interventions. But she also had other influences, evil influences that don't have a dark angel's thumbprint on them. Our little family of dark angels is all about the claiming, getting the job done efficiently, culling the human population for its weak links. It would have been no problem for a dark angel to send her off the deep end and make her end her miserable life. But it's almost like something or someone wanted to prolong her pain, at least until I got to see her again. And then she was done away with." Audray searched his face. "Do you think this is crazy?"

Jonas shook his head. "Crazy? No, I don't think so. But I must admit I haven't seen or felt anything like that." He took her fingers in his large hand and kissed her palm.

"Haven't you ever felt the presence of evil, real evil? Not in the Underworld, in the human world?" Audray asked.

"Evil on earth? I suppose so." He chomped down on another chip laden with salsa, dripping a large dollop onto the Formica tabletop. "So, you're talking humans, not immortals, who walk the line between good and evil, try to straddle the fence and work their magic for their own purposes?"

"What kind of creatures would do that?" Audray asked.

"Well, witches for one. But they don't exist."

WITCHES? HAD SHE seen witches? Had she felt them around her? She thought not. But it would explain one of the things that bothered her about the timing of her mother's death, the situation with Burt and the discovery of Claire's grave. It was like someone was one step ahead of everything she tried to do in the human world. Though her experience was limited, it didn't feel like something from the Underworld. This was something new. Someone had inserted themselves in her life. It felt like a festering wound. Her stomach lurched and she almost vomited.

They were waiting for another cab to take them back to the St. Francis. Audray was watching Jonas finish a private phone conversation with one of his men when her sat phone rang. It was from below.

"Audray here."

"Geez, Director," her Chief of Staff whined. "I was about to get the minions out to look for you." Luke was beside himself, although Audray knew he could handle anything, even an attack from aliens or space monsters. He would make a much better Director than she, but like the friend who sponsored him, Joshua, he never had a desire to run for office. And that's why he made such a good Chief.

"I told you I was spending a few personal days up top with Jonas."

"Yeah, well we've been calling his phone too. I'm not going to tell you what he told us this morning, or what everyone's thinking down here."

"Thinking?" She smiled at the thought.

"Not funny. The boys on staff have been having a field day making up what you guys are doin' 24/7. May I remind you that there's a world to run? Decisions have to be made. We haven't finished the housecleaning. People need to be fired, Director. It's a mess."

"I know. Look, I'm coming back in a couple of days. In the meantime, what's so urgent you couldn't wait?"

"Okay, well there's a challenge to your Directorship. You know we are supposed to have free and honest elections next month to confirm your appointed position?"

"Right." Audray saw Jonas' arms going out in all directions, having some sort of heated conversation on his cell she desperately wanted to listen in on.

"There's this guy, Rupert Blade, who is saying you fried his little brother, Peter, and took over. He wants a full investigation." Audray smiled at the image of Peter being torn apart by the wrath of Father, who had descended from heaven just to take care of the former Director and his dark winged angels. *Hard to think of Peter as anyone's little brother.* But there wasn't much left of him.

"So, let them investigate. I have nothing to hide." It amused her, the thought of them trying to subpoena Father. *How would they properly serve the most powerful being in the universe?*

"Well, with Rupert here and you up there, he's done a good job getting a few people riled up. I'm sorry to say, the winged ones that witnessed Peter's death and had their wings stripped off, those miserable burnt dudes, well they're changing their story."

"No doubt someone promised them wings."

"Something. You know how everyone is down here. We don't like all this upset and controversy. Makes everyone nervous."

"God forbid, it would interfere with the consumption of Red-X and the local lovelies."

"It isn't what we promised the people we turned. We told them their worries would be over forever. Sort of makes us look like a pack of liars."

"We are a pack of liars, Luke. We stretch the truth every day to get what we want. Otherwise, no one would come."

"You need to get back here and start scorching people, clear the decks. Put the place in order. Make it run like it used to, before Peter even."

"It was shit before. Chaos, really."

"Yeah, but nobody got hurt, unless that's what they wanted."

"Nobody wanted to run for office."

"So we always elected somebody who couldn't read and didn't care."

"The good old days, huh?" Audray smiled.

"We need our freedoms back. Everyone's looking over their shoulders all the time now." He sighed in resignation, and caused the phone to go static. "Guess it can wait a few, but I just wanted you to know. Things are strange down here. Have a good trip."

"Will do. Thanks for the call. I'll think on it, Luke. I really will. I think we're done here. You think I should get back tomorrow?"

"I think that'd be wise, Ma'am."

"Sounds like I should be prepared for a battle."

"Well, you should be. They say the Director shouldn't have a paramour. Said it's too distracting, your current love holiday being proof of that. They say Jonas has to go."

Now this got her mad. "Who said this?"

"These…these rabble rousers."

"Rupert?"

"Nah, he's too smart for that. Lackeys. The guy has an army of lackeys they've been turning day and night. Everyone at the arrival center is way overworked and about to quit. You know what happened the last time…"

"I'll be there tomorrow, and we'll take care of business."

"Good. I'll start making my list."

"Excellent."

IT WAS A shock when they returned to the suite at the St. Francis. The room had been completely tossed. The sheets on the bed had been shredded, stuffing pulled out from the mattress as if a jealous female animal with claws had had her way. Nothing was missing, except some of Audray's underwear. Her makeup was smashed, lipsticks ground into the carpet.

Even the hotel staff was nonplussed. They apologized profusely at the obvious breach of their security and offered them a room at a nearby hotel, complimentary, of course. They offered to pay for front row seats at the Curran Theater and dinner afterwards at Harris's. Jonas didn't appear to care much about the spoiled things, the room at the Stanford Court, or the theater, but he was excited at the prospect of dining at the best steakhouse on the peninsula.

My lover is indeed an eating machine.

Then her stomach heaved and she barely made it to the bathroom, where she threw up the single forkful of beans and lettuce Jonas had fed her earlier.

"You wish for me to send for a doctor?" the hotel manager blurted out, clearly scared. His brown eyes were the size of hardboiled eggs, Audray thought. And that led her back to the bathroom for a dry retching.

I've been poisoned. What have they done to me?

She recalled what she ate at the greasy spoon in Bakersfield. But that was too long ago. *Something in our breakfast?* But when she thought about it, her tummy had been sensitive throughout their mad sex last night. Just that the sex covered it up.

"No, thank you. I think we should get her out of here though. Could you please pick up all our things and have them delivered?" Jonas spit out the instructions with his centuries-old experience leading men into battle. He drew her to him, wiped her mouth with a wet washcloth. "There. All better. Do you need anything here?"

"No. Everything that's important is in my satchel." She pointed to her red leather bag, which had not left her side. "Just maybe some clothes."

"You don't need any clothes, my love," he whispered in her ear. "Until you are ready to wake up and have a cappuccino. I think we'll turn in early and stay in bed late, hmm?" The playful creases at the sides of his mouth deepened as his lips curled upward. He tipped her chin with his thumb and forefinger and placed a soothing kiss there. Their lips parted and he blew in her face so she could feel his erotic power wash over her, and, although she became a little dizzy, she felt absolutely wonderful.

The room was a beehive of activity. Several staffers in maroon smocks began cleaning, picking up their things and speaking in hushed tones.

"Again, let me express my sincere apologies on behalf of the St. Francis Hotel. We have never had anything like this, ever." The manager's hands were flapping in the breeze as he ran slightly ahead of them, pushing the elevator button so they wouldn't have to wait more than a second. The doors opened two floors down, but there was no one there. Audray felt Jonas' muscles spring to full readiness. He pulled an arm in front of the manager and peered up and down the hallway, and then leaned back in.

"Can you override the calls with your key?"

"Yes." Shaking fingers produced a large brass key he slipped into a keylock bordered with a maroon plastic ring. One quarter turn and the elevator began its descent to the lobby.

"No. Make it stop at the parking lot underneath."

"S…s…sure." He kept his fingers on the turned key until at last they stopped. The sensor above the door read P2. "This is the second parking level. You have to take another elevator up, or the stairs to the right, one flight and out the emergency exit. We don't keep it armed in the daytime since many of the staff use it themselves. Disregard what it says."

"Thank you."

"I'll call the Stanford Court…" his voice trailed off as the doors closed in front of him, sending him up to the lobby. Audray and Jonas stood in the middle of the parking garage. Alone.

Taking her hand, Jonas led her to the stairwell and up one flight. A car motor revved, so Jonas pulled her back inside the enclosure to wait until the sound of the vehicle and screeching tires faded. The overhead fluorescent lights buzzed. Mixed with the gasoline smell, Audray felt sick again, but she willed the nausea away and was surprised she could do that.

The red Maserati waited a few steps away. Audray began rummaging through her bag for her keys, but Jonas put his finger to his lips.

"We must leave it."

She nodded.

A large red set of double doors plastered with warning signs was around the corner, on the other side of a concrete column. Jonas inhaled and pushed the doors open to the glare of the dying afternoon sun. Sounds of passing cars echoed off the walls of the hotel, getting louder as they made it to the street.

Jonas motioned to a taxi waiting nearly tenth in line at the entrance. He opened the rear door and handed the cabbie a fifty dollar bill. "You get another fifty when we get to the ferry terminal."

Discreetly, the cab pulled out of line, switched on his yellow light and spun in the opposite direction.

"Where are we going now?" Audray asked. She was scared, her stomachache long forgotten.

"Ferry terminal," he whispered so the driver couldn't hear. "We'll buy tickets and board, then you'll transport us home. We'll need to find some place private where no one will see. You need to get us back north to your home where we'll be closer to the transport station."

"What about the rest of our things?"

"I did that so they'd think we're taking the room. We're not staying there tonight. Too many people know about it."

Once on-board the ferry, they stood at the brass rail and watched as the city began to shrink. Audray loved the feel of Jonas' strong arms around her, holding her warm and secure on the windy deck. She could almost believe nothing would be able to touch her. She could almost imagine a forever without danger, where the only concern of the day was when she would next be able to lie naked with him and feel the pulse of his life force pumping into her soul.

Chapter 20

AUDRAY PUT HER arms around Jonas' neck and hiked her knee up over his hip. She was about to put her other leg on the toilet seat of the ferry's unisex bathroom, but Jonas stopped her.

"Not here."

"Why not?"

"Because we're trying to get away clean, remember?"

"But you don't know how it works." She steeled some of her thoughts from him, yet painted a vivid picture of them being transported, with a large appendage of his inserted deep inside her.

Jonas drew back, looking at her in askance. She willed herself to speak to him through her thoughts. *Oh yes, that's the way it's done. We must be connected, physically.*

"No holding of hands?" he asked with a puzzled expression.

"Perhaps. But I wouldn't want to take a chance and leave part of you in the bay." She tried to paint a picture of that one too, and was rewarded with a shudder on his part. The thought that he would arrive at her home emasculated was no doubt troubling.

"Now, as your Director, I order you to impale me on your rod. See if you can make me come before we land." His mouth covered hers and his tongue penetrated deep. He fumbled with his zipper but at last she felt the familiar skin slide against her white panties under her skirt, seeking plunder. She used one hand to pull the elastic to one side to give him entry. She heard the panties rip as his huge cock dove in and split her lips open.

"Deeper. It must be very deep."

Jonas obliged.

"Ah, yes." Audray leaned back and felt the delicious pleasure of him pumping into her core, while Jonas busied himself holding her back and kissing her neck. "Now we are ready, my love," she said looking at him and the need in his eyes. And yes, he saw that she had played a little trick on him, just as she closed her eyes and sent the winds of transport swirling around them. She heard his attempt to speak.

"I can't wait to get even with you." His voice was distant and scratchy, coming through the static of the transport current.

The instant their feet touched ground she knew something was wrong. She had brought them to her bedroom, but the room was fully ablaze. Jonas sprung into action, grabbing a blanket from the bed. Covering her, Jonas carried her out into the night air through the front door. She watched in horror as her home, the one the former Director had constructed, went up in flames. Jonas was brushing down her clothes, swatting and patting away bits of smoke and soot.

"Are you alright?" he hurriedly called out, bringing her back to his side.

"The house. Just like my mother's. Who is doing this?"

Jonas stood beside her and stared up at the second floor that was now caving in upon the first. "Someone who wants us dead," he said softly. "Anything in there worth saving?"

"Only you," she said.

He put his big arm around her waist and whispered into her ear, "And that you have, lass, mind, body and soul."

CARL AND MOLLY arrived at the house just in time to watch a dark figure slinking off to the bushes. Unsure what to do, they decided to wait.

"I'm going to get out and walk around the place," Carl stated. Before he could open the car door, the house in front of them exploded into flames. When he saw a couple run out of the burning building, he wasn't sure if he was relieved or scared.

The big man might be the man Glenda mistakenly thought was Jonas Starling, but Carl knew it was more likely he was a distant relative. With his woman in tow, the man headed right for Carl, who instinctively held onto Molly while standing his ground. The man looked at him and Molly as if Carl were the devil himself. He pushed the blonde woman behind his massive frame and growled, straight at Carl.

"I—I saw someone come out of the house just before it exploded. He ran into the bushes, r...r...right over there." Carl pointed again but he found it hard to raise his arm. The big man looked in the direction he pointed. He seemed to relax just a bit. Carl could feel Molly shivering behind him.

"Who are *you*?" The big man asked.

"My name is Carl Carrington. I'm a Professor over at Meriwether and Grant College."

The man looked confused, then added, "I am Jonas Starling."

Carl couldn't believe what he'd just been told.

"Not *the* Jonas Starling?"

"Is there another?"

Carl realized if this was true, he was staring into the eyes of a three hundred year old ghost. "I was sent to find you, given this address," Carl insisted, trying to diffuse some of the tension between them. He could see Starling was lowering some of his guard, assessing the threat and apparently had judged him safe. That relieved him.

"Look, I don't mean you any harm. I was given a research project, and I've studied a lot about you."

Both Jonas and the woman were scanning the area, and Carl sensed they'd be leaving shortly for safer ground, practically ignoring his statement.

"Look, I have a car. I could take you to the hospital if you are injured." Carl couldn't believe the size of this man, the tanned skin covered in arm tattoos, the silvering hair tied back in a ponytail with a leather strap. His eyes were jet black, as were the woman's, and his jaw was firm. The muscles twitched as he appeared to be grinding his teeth.

Carl could feel where Molly had taken position behind him, peeking around his right elbow. When Jonas saw her, he seemed to relax.

"I'd be in your debt if I could borrow your car," Jonas said.

"Ah, no. I won't do that, but I will take you anywhere you want to go." Carl rethought the logic of that remark and cursed himself. "You can trust me. I am a friend."

Jonas looked down at his companion and frowned. "You pick up anything from the bushes?" he said to her.

"No. But, Jonas, I need to rest. I don't feel well at all."

"Damn." Jonas looked over at the two of them.

Molly was shaking, still cowering against his back.

"She needs to lie down where she can relax a bit."

"Then come with me," Carl insisted.

Carl's Mini Cooper groaned as Starling took a seat beside the blonde woman in the back. Starling practically filled the entire space and his large head blocked the rear view mirror. Carl rolled down his window to look back and did not see anyone lurking in the shadows, but he heard the sound of sirens. No doubt the fire had gotten the attention of the local authorities. Molly's frozen stare out the front windshield further chilled him. He quickly started the motor and left the scene in a cloud of dust and gravel.

No one said anything all the way to Carl's campus lodging. The air was thick with the scent of smoke and sweat. The blonde was breathing heavily. Every once in a while she moaned. He could see Starling was concerned. He kept kissing the top of her head, rubbing up and down the length of her arm as she leaned into him, clutching her belly.

Molly turned around, gave Starling's companion a long look, her eyes following down to the woman's lap and then whipped around to face front again. Carl noticed she didn't want to look at him.

You know something. Please tell me.

Molly looked up at him and whispered, "Later."

The sight of his own front door was welcoming. After turning off the ignition, he immediately went to Audray's door and opened it, but allowed Starling to push him away as the big man picked her up and carried her with little effort towards the cottage. Carl ran ahead and just barely opened the door before Starling kicked it open.

"In here," Carl called out, heading towards the only bedroom.

Jonas laid Audray on the bed and whispered to her softly, kneeling at her side, kissing her, brushing the hair from her face and blowing on it, as if cooling her down.

"Is she running a fever?" Carl asked.

Molly jerked his arm in an indication to leave them alone.

"Tell me," Carl pleaded.

"I will. Wait just a little." Molly gave him that half smile of hers that told him not to worry. But when she walked to the window in the living room, he saw the fear resident there.

"They can't stay here, Carl. It isn't safe. It might not be safe for you either."

"Why? What is going on? Molly, I need some answers." Carl was going to insist, but he heard Starling in the doorway, and turned around to face him.

"She's right. Our being here puts you two in jeopardy. Do you have relatives you can stay with?"

"There's my place," Molly spoke up.

"But I thought…" Jonas' eyes sparkled, as if realizing they were a couple, but not yet living together as man and wife. "So be it. I will let her rest a bit, and then I think it's best to take off. You should pack some things. Not sure when it will be safe to come back here."

"What is this all about?" Carl said, his eyes moving back and forth between Starling and Molly. Somehow he knew that the two of them had the answers, or would be able to put it all together, if they could talk unfettered.

"Well, I've got some questions before I can answer that," Jonas started. "I thank you for your assistance, but I need to know how come you two happened to be there just when the house went up in flames?" Jonas looked at the both of them, but fixed himself on Molly in the end.

Carl began as best he could. "She gave me…"

"She. She who?" Jonas asked.

"Glenda. The woman who hired me to get information about you, or your ancestor Jonas Starling."

"But I am Jonas Starling,"

Carl shrugged his shoulders. "Yes, and I believe you, but I was researching the Jonas Starling who was born in 1667 and died on Antigua."

"I am the only Jonas Starling, and I assure you—" He looked over his shoulder at his resting companion before continuing in a whisper. "I am he, the man you are searching for."

"Explain how can that be. That would make you over three hundred years old."

Molly touched Carl's arm. "Wait, let him finish. He'll tell you." She gazed back at the large man and Carl wasn't sure he was going to like what the man told him next.

"I am—" He looked back to the woman again. "*We* are dark angels and we come from the Underworld. We are immortal. I am over three hundred years of age."

Carl was ready to pee his pants. "Angels?" First he'd been told Molly was a witch, and now this reveal. Had he been living in some kind of human bubble, oblivious of these creatures breathing the same air as he did? And now there was an Underworld. He sat down quickly on the couch as if willed so by some invisible hand. Starling advanced, but for some reason, Carl wasn't afraid.

"I need information, and then I won't trouble you any longer. Who is this person who asked about me and what does she want?"

"That's a good question. I don't like her. Don't trust her. *Molly* says she's—"

"I told him Glenda is a witch. She's a dark witch," Molly finished for him.

Starling seemed to let this settle before he asked his next question. "So, how did she pick you, and what was she interested in?"

"I'm a Professor of English History at the college. My specialty is 17th and 18th century England, and I've done extensive studies on the monarchy." Carl sat up straight, hoping to impress the man.

"Go on."

"I gave her your background, and she told me you were still alive, which I disputed, of course. She ordered me to do some followup or…well, she threatened me and Molly." Carl saw no reason not to be honest with Jonas Starling. He had great respect for the man, after researching his past.

"So how did you find Audray's house?"

"Audray? Oh, yes, I see. Well, Glenda told me where you lived. She said that you would make an appearance there, and she wanted me to report back to let her know if in fact it was you."

"So how the hell would you confirm that if we were destroyed?" Jonas asked.

"Because I think she knew you would survive," Molly said flatly. "And I think she plans to read Carl's memories. Anything that is said here is not safe information as long as Carl is present."

"So she is the one responsible for this fire?" Jonas asked.

"I'd bet on it," Molly returned. "Tell us what happened before you came here."

"We're being chased by someone, and we don't know who. Her mother's home was burned. They killed her. Now today we've been followed, and when we escaped and came here, her home was destroyed." Jonas sat down after checking the view from the living room window. "Besides that, it's complicated. I'm not sure I can explain it clearly. Almost like they were trying to force us to Audray's place for some reason. Where they knew we'd go. I can't explain it."

"I know who they are," Molly said to Jonas. "They are witches. Jealous, hate-filled witches and they want something from you and from her."

"Witches?" Jonas looked like he'd been run through with a spear. "I don't understand. What would witches want with us?"

"This dark witch, Glenda, you know her from your human life?" Molly asked.

"No. We've seen only a man following us. Someone dressed in dark clothing, and he has blue eyes. Deep blue eyes."

"Because you would recognize or somehow be able to sense her.

I'm sure of it," Molly continued.

Jonas searched the toes of his boots. He shook his head. "I know no such person. I've had no knowledge of witches, until today."

"Today?" Carl asked.

"Audray said she felt like there was an evil presence that had inserted itself into her mother's life. I was making fun. I told her it must be witches. But, to the best of my knowledge, I've never met one, never been under one's spell. And I have to say right here and now, I do not believe in them."

Carl looked at Molly to see how she would answer him. "You need to, because even though you are both immortal, they can hurt you both."

"I'm just not following," Jonas said.

"The only reason you both are alive is because they need something from you." Molly walked over and took Carl's hand as she spoke. "They want one thing from you, and they want something else from her."

Carl's stomach was filled with dread. Molly stood up to deliver the message he knew he wouldn't like.

"Search your past. I think she wants your progeny. I think they've searched for hundreds of years to obtain this goal."

"But I can't father a child. I'm a dark angel now, and we don't father children." Jonas' brows furrowed and his fists balled at his sides. He spoke so loudly Audray was awakened. Her pale figure appeared in the doorway behind him, yet he was so furious he did not sense her.

"Yes, you can," Molly answered. "The child growing in her belly," she pointed to Audray, "is what they want to take from her."

Chapter 21

J ONAS' BODY WAS riddled with a wide variety of emotions, all of them vying for dominance. On one hand, he was elated with the notion that Audray was carrying his child. On the other, he knew this fact put all of them, but especially Audray, in grave danger from those who would either want the child or want to terminate the pregnancy.

And then the gnawing question came forth: how could Audray, an immortal, have a living being inside her? Will the child be immortal or human? How could it properly grow, how could Audray possibly carry the babe to full term? What was full term? Or would she stay pregnant throughout her immortal life? As he looked into her ashen face, he wasn't entirely sure this new life growing inside of her wouldn't cause her own death. It obviously wasn't agreeing with her biological makeup, whatever that was.

And there's no one who has the answers.

But then he reconsidered this question. And a name came to mind. He needed to protect this name, so would not utter it in front of the others. He even put it out of his mind in case the witch could hear him. Molly didn't react, so he hoped his secret was safe. For now.

Audray was so weak she needed to sit while they quickly stowed some things they might need. Jonas made a quick call to his men. He asked that the Underworld Council be told that the Director's home had been destroyed by fire, and that there had perhaps been some injury to the Director. They might be delayed a day. He didn't want to make the call himself to the council, raising too many questions he didn't want to answer yet. He knew his men would do their job. He hated not telling them the good news, but it was best for all concerned.

They exchanged Molly's address at the car rental. Jonas told them he needed to take Audray someplace for an exam, and then would meet up with them afterwards. Watching Carl take off in his Mini, Jonas knew he never intended to follow them, so after renting the black Hummer, he made a reservation at a local out-of-the-way inn. They would be closer to the transport station in case they needed a quick escape. But first, Jonas had to find out what was safe. Could Audray travel between worlds now? Or was this travel what was making her sick? Would the pregnancy affect her other powers? Or would those activities affect the baby?

He looked over at the face of the woman he would gladly die for. Her peachy complexion was now sweaty and sallow. Her color had turned such a flat pale shade, she almost looked dead. He held one of her hands as they drove toward the old part of town.

"Are you hungry at all, love?"

"No." Audray barely spoke.

"Are you worse?"

"No. I feel weak, so frail. But it isn't getting worse."

Jonas had difficulty reading her thoughts, as if her life force was ebbing and wasn't strong enough for him to pick up. It worried him, but he decided to keep it to himself.

"I am thrilled we made a baby." She smiled and even in spite of her color and the beads of sweat forming on her forehead, she looked happy. "I never thought I would be a mother…"

She looked over to him with her big doe eyes, asking the question he heard inside.

"Yes, my love, I am delighted you carry my child." But he also had concerns about her previous liaisons with Peter, the former Director. Audray had seduced him as part of the strategy to delay him interfering with Josh's plans. There were only a couple of months since that event. He knew in his soul the child was his, but what if it turned out to be Peter's?

"Where are we going?" she asked.

"To see a familiar face." Jonas knew his former boss, indeed, Audray's former boss, Joshua Brandon, now a human, was the only person with the information they needed. He turned down the wide tree-lined street that signified the old district. Historic houses lined up like grand old ladies, many of whom were painted to their Sunday best. Immaculate gardens, gazebos and flowers—all the things a human family with means would covet, displayed in their finery. He watched the humans out in their yards, oblivious to the war going on around them.

At a dark-shingled Victorian with dark green trim, Jonas slowed down, then turned up the driveway to a locked gate. He kissed Audray, and was about to get out and run to the front door when the massive iron gates began to open. Jonas started up the Hummer and parked in back of the house as the gates closed behind him.

Jonas went around to Audray's side and helped her step out of the vehicle. She stumbled, so he picked her up, quickly traversing the yard to the back porch. Joshua Brandon stood just inside the screened in porch, and he wasn't smiling.

"I had nowhere else to go, sir. I need to ask a favor of you, if you don't mind." Jonas deferred to his days when he did Joshua's bidding.

"Of course not. Why else would you come here and put me in jeopardy?" Josh's smile was curt. "And thanks for the little waif. Because of you, I've had to sleep in the spare bedroom ever since." He opened the screen door. "Perhaps you could explain it to Melanie, for my sake?"

"No problem." Jonas brought the near-unconscious Audray through the kitchen area into the living room, depositing her in one of Josh's red leather chairs by the unlit fireplace.

Audray tried to right herself and took a swing at Josh, missing him completely.

"Whoa. Wait a minute. What the heck are you all uptight about?" Josh returned.

"My sister," Audray hissed. "Claire is my sister!" She was standing, but Jonas was making it possible.

Josh stepped back like he'd been struck. "What the fuck are you talking about, Audray? How could that be?"

"She became Guardian because she saved my life, you asshole." Jonas continued holding her by the waist, and tried to calm her with soothing mental suggestions. She turned on him and spewed out, "Shut up!"

"What's this?" Melanie was running down the stairs barefoot. Josh rolled his eyes and looked at Jonas, who deposited Audray this time on the couch and elevated her feet.

"Help." Josh whispered.

"Another surprise I see. Seems like all your old buddies from the Underworld are coming back to become part of our lives." Jonas could see Melanie wasn't happy with this new event.

"Ma'am. I am Jonas Starling. I worked for your…your…"

"Boyfriend." Josh winced at the sound of his description.

"You have to understand about the girl." Jonas began.

"Oh, I understand about the girl quite well and I wish you'd never sent her, to be honest." Melanie had her arms wrapped around her upper torso and was tapping her left foot.

"What girl?" Audray's anger flared again, as if now she was distrusting Jonas.

Jonas and Josh exchanged a look between them. Jonas went over to her reclining form, knelt down and brushed the hair back from her face. "I used a walker as a distraction to get up through the transport station. I needed to get to you without them knowing where you were. When I got up top, I released her, and suggested she contact Joshua, here."

"Yes, and she dutifully came right over," Josh said rocking on the backs of his heels, his tongue poking out the side of his cheek.

"I saw in her the possibility she wanted to reform herself. I thought Josh could help," Jonas tried again.

Audray shook her head. "I don't know who to believe anymore. You take a walker up top and want me to believe it was to distract—who? Who were you trying to distract?"

"The guys following me."

"All this is too much for me to take." She leaned back into the couch and sighed. Jonas' heart ached to be alone with Audray, to explain everything further, answer all her questions.

Josh smiled, but then looked with concern at his former favorite trainee. "You are ill, Audray?"

"Yes and no. You're going to love this," she said as she tried to flash him one of her legendary smiles. She attempted to stand again. Jonas once again stopped her.

"No. I'm going to do this standing, thank you." Audray held onto Jonas' thick forearm for support, pushed the hair from her face, wiped her forehead with her other sleeve and stood erect. She inhaled and then blurted out, "I'm pregnant."

Josh looked stunned and uncharacteristically at a loss for words. He backed up two quick steps to keep from falling over. Melanie looked from Jonas to Audray, back to Josh and then Jonas. Jonas could see she was thoroughly confused.

Audray relayed all the events of the past couple of days, her quest to find her mother, the fires.

"Josh," Jonas began, "she isn't well. The pregnancy isn't agreeing with her. I've never heard of this. Perhaps you know something that would help us? This is why we came here. What do we do?" he unloaded.

"I've never seen it before, but I've heard of it. A long time ago something like this happened."

"How did it end?" Melanie asked the question no one wanted to ask.

Josh pensively crossed the room, slowly placing both his hands on his friend's shoulders. "The child lived, but the mother did not." The two men stared at each other a few seconds, and then Josh dropped his hands. Jonas felt like he wanted to hit something. His whole world was crushed. He couldn't bear losing Audray.

"Okay," Audray began. "Now that we've established what's so. Figures, just when I thought I had everything I'd always wanted, turns out I won't be there to enjoy it. My own mother would have thought this only fair. Maybe it is what I deserve after all." Audray sat herself down and put her face in one hand. She began to cry softly.

Jonas' heart was melting. "There has to be someone who can help us, Josh. Is there anything in any of the manuals at the Directorship? Anything there that would give us a clue?"

"Possibly, but there isn't any way I'm going back down there, not even for you or Audray. Father gave me a reprieve. I'll not get a second chance."

"Well, while you guys get all mushy, why don't I get this woman upstairs to a bed so she can rest. She looks like she needs some quiet time alone," Melanie said as she helped Audray up. Jonas took the other side, and the three of them ascended the staircase to a guest room. There Audray lay down on a big bed with a dark blue coverlet. Jonas positioned pillows around her and lay next to her for a bit, holding her hand, kissing her fingers. Melanie closed the door and went downstairs.

CARL WAS DISTURBED Jonas and Audray had not returned to Molly's apartment. The longer the minutes dragged on, the more concerned he got about his situation and the fact that he would have to make that call to Glenda.

"You should call her," Molly said. She read his reluctance. "No other way around it now. I don't think they are coming."

Carl agreed and punched in the phone number. Glenda picked up before the ring had finished.

"I want good news. But I'll take what you've got," she said.

"Did you...did you set fire to their house? What have you gotten me involved in?"

"Shut up. Did or did they not survive the fire?"

"They did. But you probably know that already. Was it your man who did this horrible thing?"

"Yes. He wasn't supposed to destroy it, but seems he doesn't know how to do anything half way." She sighed. "So?"

"So what?" Carl answered.

"So where did they go if you didn't help them?"

"We gave them a ride to a rental car agency. They agreed to meet up with us later, but apparently that was a lie."

"Yes, well, I can tell you stories about Jonas Starling. He'll lie if the stakes are high enough. And I think he's just begun to realize that. So, where do you think they've gone?"

"I have no idea. They didn't say. I think he purposely didn't tell me so I could tell you the truth."

"How sweet of him."

"Well, I think that ends my obligation. I've confirmed it is Starling. You have my research. You know they are here somewhere. I'm sure with the minions you have at your disposal, you can find him. I doubt he'll want anything to do with me from now on. And that is just fine with me too."

"Carl, just where did you get the idea I have "minions"? I have resources, but honestly, you give me too much credit. Who do you take me for?"

Carl knew it would be a mistake to let her know about Molly's suspicions. "You seem to be everywhere at once. You have me doing your bidding while you have someone else do something else. Kind of diabolical, don't you think?"

"Funny you should say that. Has your little redheaded friend been filling your head with strange ideas? Perhaps I misjudged her."

Carl was tense. "I'm of no use to you. Please leave us alone."

"On the contrary, Carl. You've proven your usefulness to me in greater ways than you imagine. Stay tuned. But don't try to run away, dear. It won't go well for you or for her."

Carl paused, wanting to be angry but afraid to incur her further ire.

"Your house is safe, by the way. We know where you are, but no one will bother you there or at hers. Feel free to roam, as they say. Goodbye."

Glenda hung up.

Chapter 22

THE GARDENS IN Josh's yard hissed with late night watering. Jonas left Audray to sleep and went downstairs, making himself an ice water. He wanted something stronger but didn't want to indulge his desires without permission.

Never in his three hundred years had he felt so uneasy and conflicted. At a time when he should be the happiest, he was filled with regret. He didn't want Audray or his unborn child to pay for the mistakes he had made with his human life. The familiar feelings he had when he caused the deaths of his father and brothers, as well as Anne and her family, surfaced. They weren't any easier to deal with this time around. And, as he had told Audray the afternoon before, there wasn't anywhere else they could go. They would have to make some sort of a stand. But where? The Underworld? The human world?

He sat in Josh's opulent living room, staring at the large splashy oil paintings. Audray and Jonas had played important parts in the showdown with Peter, and they were still part of Josh's support network. Now they would need Josh's help, and perhaps Audray's sister, as well, who was now human, an ex-Guardian. He was hoping Josh would be up to the task at hand, even after he learned of the stakes.

Josh made his way from the back of a downstairs bedroom, dressed in a tee shirt and a pair of red silk boxers. His hair was mussed in all angles, indicating he just woke up.

"You want something to drink?" Josh asked his former helper.

"Thought you'd never ask." Jonas' temptation to drown himself in liquor was a shadow of its former hold on him.

"You like it neat?"

"Ice, please. I'm grinding my teeth tonight. Maybe it will help me with it."

"Think I'll join you." He walked into the dining area and poured plenty of the amber liquid into thick crystal tumblers over two big chunks of ice. He downed his first, then poured another, adding one more cube of ice and a little more Scotch to Jonas' glass. The tinkle of the ice in the clear liquid was a welcome sound to Jonas. He took the glass and watched Josh deposit himself in a heap on the other red chair with a sigh. He noted how Josh's obvious lack of sleep and worry was taking its toll on his human body.

"You still sleeping downstairs?" Jonas looked at his former boss with a smirk. "Never knew a woman to be able to resist your seductive powers."

"Ah, my friend," Josh said as he held the cool glass up to his forehead. "Be very careful when someone offers you everything you've ever wanted." He smiled at Jonas. "Life is good, but I find myself getting impatient. Sometimes I want to take shortcuts, and then I remember, oh yes, I'm not a dark angel any longer. I'm only human."

Both of them chuckled.

"But it is worth it?"

"An interesting question."

"I thought you'd have a quick answer for me. You were rewarded for your service by the gift of being made human again, with all its limitations." Jonas had missed his former boss. The relationship between them had always been more of friendship than loyalty. And now that Josh was human, and Jonas was a much more powerful dark angel, the friendship survived, blossoming into something deeper still.

Josh smiled and stared into the top of his tumbler. "If she leaves me, the answer to that will be a resounding no." Josh swirled the mixture and then finished his glass off, depositing it on the table nearby. "So, are we going to have this man-talk now, or when the women are up, curious and freaked out?"

Jonas smirked again at Josh's words. He was glad his former boss hadn't lost some of his odd sense of humor. In a time where so much had changed, this, at least, had not.

"Jonas, I must say, you've really outdone yourself this time. From what I knew of your background, I'm thinking history really does repeat itself. One might even say it was divine intervention, making you go through all this stuff again until you get it right."

"I never intended to involve you, but I honestly can't just sit by and watch her be destroyed—either by this baby growing inside her or the forces around us."

"Well, let's just start at the beginning. I've heard from a couple of the old crowd that there's unrest down below, and Audray is a bit of a no-show and some don't like it."

"I'm to blame for that too."

"So, even if her pregnancy were normal, and, my friend, I am not at all sure this is good for either you or Audray, you have a problem. Though I know you would wish it otherwise, her infirm condition will not make them feel any more confident in her. She could loose the election."

"Screw the election. At this point, I think she'd willingly vacate it. But it's not that simple."

"Tell me, then."

"Turns out Peter has a very nasty older brother."

Josh shrugged. "You're a fairly nasty dark angel yourself. I don't see the problem."

"He introduced me to someone I thought I would never meet, his wife." Jonas finished off his drink and set down his glass. "She is a direct descendent of my son, who lived and became quite a wealthy man after I left for the Caribbean."

"Forgive me, Jonas," Josh said as he reached for his glass and picked up Jonas'. He walked to the bar and poured them each another. "I'm not feeling the problem. Back then, you and I, we probably fathered all sorts of children, right? As modern men, we wouldn't do that now, but at the time, this wasn't considered anything bad—Hell, the king had thirteen illegitimate offspring and, what, twenty mistresses? What would make any of these families come after us after three hundred years, or am I missing something?"

"They want the kingdom of the Underworld. For their own domain. They've turned hundreds of their kin into dark angels to grab it."

"So, let them have it. They'll muck it up. The place is a mess, has been for centuries. No one, and I don't care how many they put on it, no one will ever straighten it out. It's a bureaucracy that makes Washington, D.C. look like a high school picnic."

"I don't think they'll just give us a pass if they take over. I think they have designs on the human world as well. I think they want it all. None of us are safe, now that they are dark angels and have their special powers of turning. For all I know, they even have the power to vaporize others."

Josh frowned. "Not good. Not good at all."

"We might feel safe today, but, truth is, they have a plan they've been forming, passing down from generation to generation, until they discovered how to enter the Underworld. Now that they are immortal, they will never stop until they conquer and payback everyone who ever stopped them before. Even if I help them now, which is what they are demanding, they won't let us go. I just know it."

"Sounds like some kind of religious zeal."

"That's a good way to put it. They intend to make lackeys of all of us. ALL of us, Josh."

"And who is the head of this cadre of lost souls?"

"My twenty times great granddaughter, Catarina."

"Fucking women."

Jonas gave Josh a glare.

"Well, it's true. The power trip they go on these days. There were definite advantages to a male-dominated Underworld where women were needed for pleasure. Now they want to run things. What sick times we live in, my friend."

"Face it, Josh. The Underworld mirrors the human world in many respects. I don't think it is really about women running things. It's about the treachery used in this war. I honestly haven't seen this level of cunning for centuries. Hell, I even ran with women pirates who were born leaders, and their men loved serving under them. I fought with women warriors and heard stories of captured slaves where the women were the defenders of a whole race of people. No, Josh, it isn't women, it's pure evil, left festering for hundreds of years. My grandmother used to tell me stories about the Circle of Evil cults in her day. They believe in the restoration of their kingdom, and nothing less will do."

"You say this woman, your distant granddaughter, is married to a brother of Peter's?"

"Yes."

"Now there's a relationship I'd love to explore. That's your weak link, Jonas. Can you imagine being immortally tied to that woman? And what do you suppose would happen if she tired of him?"

"He'd have an oily charred spot somewhere."

"Exactly. Forget reasoning with the woman. Go for Peter's brother. What's his name?"

"Rupert Blade."

"Now that's a good name for a lap dog. You need to remind him of the possibility of his own true death. He's immortal, but he can still be fried, just like his brother was."

JONAS AND JOSH talked until dawn began to break. Josh agreed with Molly's assessment of Glenda as a dark witch.

"I've known some of them, in a purely pleasurable sense. The light ones are exquisite with their red hair. Very satisfying partners in all respects. The dark ones I've stayed away from. Of course, they're never redheads. Only the light ones are redheads, and you know my fondness for any woman with flaming hair."

"Yes. I suppose that's part of the reason Melanie didn't like the girl."

"Oh, how right you are. But this is going to surprise you, Jonas. Little Judy was a turned Guardian."

"You're kidding."

"Nope. My handiwork. She had been a most enjoyable conquest, I might add. I had Doris notify Father." Josh leveled a twinkling eye at Jonas. "You know, Father asked me to get his Guardians back that day when he turned me human? Father was delighted. So you see, you've done the right thing."

"So where's the girl?"

"I have no fucking idea. I'm afraid to go look for her. I don't dare bring up her name. Still trying to get myself back in Melanie's bedroom upstairs, if you know what I mean. No, Judy's probably way better off that way."

Jonas nodded. "Well, you've racked up some points with Father. Good for you."

"Now if I could only convince Melanie…" Josh was lost in his personal thoughts.

"Where am I going to find out about Audray's pregnancy?"

"I'd go back to the witch, Molly. She probably knows someone who can help with that. Witches have been known to use their healing powers and spells where mere good and evil is insufficient. Sometimes magic is needed. And if she's right, the dark witch wants something. Molly or her kin may know where her vulnerabilities lie. Give her a chance, if she's willing to help."

WHEN JONAS AND Audray left early the next morning, Joshua thought about his loyal friend. Time to perhaps pay back the old warrior for his help. In the past, Jonas had helped save Melanie. Maybe helping Jonas would be the last real thing he could do for her. She deserved more than a human husband who was constantly having to reel himself in, trying to convince himself he could live a just and honest life without his special powers, without the pleasures he had indulged in for centuries.

Am I bored? Or, is it that I'm just unsatisfied?

His human life had taken on a civil tone. But now that he understood the war continued to rage on, he was surprised to find he rather relished the fight. Going up against witches and evil cults going back hundreds of years, dark angels wanting dominion over the Underworld as a first step to taking over the human world?

Now this was what he was created for.

But he'd have to clear it with Father first. He wondered how much the old man would let him dabble on the dark side. If he had to be honest with himself, he did miss it just a tad.

Chapter 23

CARL AWOKE TO the feel of Molly's arms around his bare chest, her head resting, as she liked to do, just under his chin. Her left breast was pressed into him, and her right one voluptuously tickled him as she raised and lowered her ribcage in deep sleep. He traced the smooth curve under her right arm, finding the pink pillow of her breast, loving the slow arousal she brought him at the touch of her skin. She stirred and stretched, looking up with a smile.

Her bedroom walls were covered in a warm primrose patterned wallpaper. The curtains were peach, made of silk material, that shimmered in the early morning sun, undulating in the air coming through the open window.

Carl felt time was suspended. As Molly became more interested in his enlarging body part, he felt like he was floating in the calm before the storm. He only hoped the two of them would be able to weather it. *So many unknowns. So few tools at our disposal. So few allies. How will we be able to make it?*

Molly's lips on his cock brought him back quickly to the pleasures of the moment. He hoped he could do this forever, but for this morning, it was pure heaven. He lay back on the pillow, letting her pleasure him without touching her, a new sensation for him. He was filled with joy as he watched her take him deep into her mouth and then lick the undersides of his engorged member and let it twitch at the end as she dug into the little crease at the end, probing for a drop of his seed.

How he loved that pink tongue that made him quiver all over every time he thought about the spell it cast over his body. How he loved the feel of her moist cherry lips that sucked his balls and kissed the head of his cock.

She straddled him, so he put his hands on her ribs, holding her thin body upright while she searched, and then placed him at her opening. She rubbed her lubrication over him before setting her luscious lips over his sex and slowly sliding down his shaft. It had become a routine; their first lovemaking of the day was always slow and deliberate. They always looked at each other as his cock penetrated her inch by inch. Each new day started with a new commitment to the pleasures they shared, the unearthly connection between their bodies. The aftermath left him craving for more.

Molly's skin almost went ablaze, as if every fine hair on her pink body stood out like a tiny flame. Her fiery curls cascaded down over her breasts as he raised himself up to kiss the rosy nipples that hardened as he suckled them. He gently pulled her hair towards him, pulling her face to his, so he could drink from her lips. Her fingers moved over his temples, sifted through the errant hairs there as she kissed him and whispered little incantations he couldn't understand but he loved hearing. She kissed him under his chin, and then along his neck to just under his ear. The scent of her body warmed him from the inside out. She wore that vanilla and cinnamon fragrance that wafted from the place between her breasts. Behind her ears it smelled of lemons.

She raised herself up and peered into his eyes. The green pools pulled on something deep inside of him. He felt his cock enlarge, instantly filling her with his seed, as if acting on cue. Her muscles milked him, as her green eyes remained steadily fixed on his. Her forehead beaded with sweat as she pulled every drop from him. At last she sighed and rested against his chest and, somehow, released his soul.

Carl was left with the feeling that Molly had just dropped a veil, revealing something previously hidden from him. He wondered if perhaps she had been given to him for some reason, by some outside force or entity. There was no question of her desire for him. And yes, he couldn't help but desire her. He wondered if she were sent by someone to do this, to enamor him, distract him, make him lose control.

But is this love?

He wondered why he was even thinking about this. He tried to put it out of his head, but found he couldn't. The thought stayed stubbornly fixed in his brain.

Carl, you're going insane. What is wrong with you?

Molly raised her head and looked deep into his eyes. She did not smile.

She's read my thoughts. He wished she didn't have this power over him. He had no explanation for the way he was feeling, but now he felt wary.

Molly frowned, and nodded her head. She climbed off his spent body. Where she had touched him his skin was suddenly cold as the remains of their mingled sweat attracted the morning air. She pulled her silk bathrobe off the back of her bedroom door, put it on and tied it around her tiny waist, seating herself in a chair in the corner, watching him. Her legs were tucked underneath her and she was silent, her face in the shadows.

He raised himself off the bed on one elbow. "Molly, I don't know what to say. I saw something, felt something. Can you explain it to me?"

Molly didn't respond, but checked out the bedroom window. She stood. "Your dark angels have arrived at last, Carl. Better throw on some clothes."

He got up and saw the black Hummer parking. Carl grabbed Molly and hugged her. "Don't misunderstand me, Molly. I haven't experienced this before, like this. It just takes some getting used to."

"I know," she said, dismissing him and wiggling out of his grasp. "Get your clothes on, unless you're wanting to show off." She closed the door without giving him a reassuring smile or even looking back at him at all. Carl's heart felt like it had been scored and lay bleeding.

What is going on?

MOLLY HAD ANSWERED the door and let Jonas and Audray in. She looked up as Carl arrived in a pair of drawstring pants and a tee shirt. There was still no smile there for him. But he did feel the electricity of their mutual desire.

"I'll make some coffee. Do you...?"

"I do, Audray doesn't," Jonas answered before she finished.

Molly went around the corner to the kitchen. Carl noticed Audray looked much better this morning. "I was worried about you when you didn't show up last night," he began. He noticed Jonas was leaning away from him, looking for Molly. The massive dark angel adjusted his muscled body so he could watch her in the kitchen.

Was he distrustful of her for some reason?

Molly dropped her shoulders and gave Carl a glare. Then she went back making coffee and returned to the living room with a glass of orange juice for Audray. She sat across the floor from him.

"We didn't want to get you further involved," Jonas started. "But now I think that is out of the question. We all are involved. Just a matter of how much and when."

Understatement of the century. Carl wasn't sure just what kind of involvement he had gotten himself into, but he wasn't feeling good about it.

Face it, Carl. You're fucked. Any way you look at it, you're royally fucked.

He earned another glare from Molly. This one didn't hurt so bad. He was rather getting used to it.

"Well, is it me, or does anybody else think we don't have a prayer?" Carl shocked himself with the comment. While he looked at the somber faces in front of him, he was glad he didn't have their level of knowledge about things dark and things magical. This time, he decided, it was better to be somewhat ignorant. He was the only pure human in the room, and he was glad of it.

Jonas leaned forward, clasping his hands together, forearms resting over his knees. "Molly, I need some information on how we deal with Audray's condition." He leaned around and touched Audray's knee and smiled. "About her pregnancy," he said as he turned and bored his black eyes into Molly's.

Molly raised herself a bit, as if Jonas stirred something inside her. Carl at first took it for some sort of sexual electricity, but then he saw a genuine care and concern for the huge dark angel and his consort. It looked like she had been called, despite probable danger to herself and those she loved.

That would be me. Please let it be me she cares about.

Molly nodded her head without looking at him, with a hint of a pouty smile. It was a gesture only the two of them understood. He was relieved to understand Jonas could not read her thoughts. It looked like she couldn't read his as well.

"It is true, Jonas, I am a light witch. But I am young, only barely finished my apprenticeship. I have not had all the schooling I am to have before I am fully functional, and the peak of my power won't occur for a few years." She bit her lower lip, glancing up to Carl before she completed her thought. "I was sent to watch over Carl."

No! This is not what I wanted to hear! Please! He stood up, searching around the room as if he couldn't find the front door.

Jonas was quick to grab him and force him to take a seat. "We have to have our wits about us, man. Where the hell are you going to go with that kind of information? It isn't safe, don't you understand?"

Molly stayed seated, gazing at the floor with her head cocked, as if she saw something there that interested her. Carl pushed down his frustration and part of his fear. He wasn't sure whom he could really trust. And he didn't care if Molly heard the thought.

"You can trust me, Carl." Molly said it without a smile. "I don't lie. Ever." She gestured for Jonas to take his position next to Audray, and she resumed her story. "At first, the assignment was just to glimmer him a bit. That's what we call it, "glimmering," using our powers to cast an erotic spell. It won't work unless the person is already halfway interested. It was to be a practice run." She got up and crossed the room, looking out the windows to the street. "I soon learned my mentor suspected something was going on with Carl involving a dark witch, and she was testing me to see if I picked it up as well. When I told her about the interchange with Glenda and my suspicions, she confirmed my thoughts. But she was furious with me for revealing my powers to Carl, so furious that she forbade me to see him again."

Carl felt pain with these words just as if he'd stuck his finger in a light socket.

"I've fallen in love with Carl." She said it as she looked at him, and Carl saw all the softness and sincerity return to her face. "And I've disobeyed her, which could be a huge problem for me, for all of us. But I think I have a way to fix this. I need to bring you and Audray to see her, seek her counsel."

She went to the kitchen, bringing both Carl and Jonas a steaming mug of coffee with cream.

"You think it's safe, Molly?" Carl asked as he blew on his mug.

Jonas looked at his coffee and paused before he took a sip. Then he gulped it down.

"I wouldn't suggest it otherwise," Molly answered.

"When could we do this?" Jonas asked.

"I don't see why we should delay any more than we already have. I need to tell all of you, regardless of what you have heard about us, we don't like to see any of our kind interfering with immortals. It is expressly forbidden. The darks are supposed to honor the same code. It would take a lot even for a dark to cross that line. I'm guessing Glenda is not the real one in charge, that she is doing someone else's bidding. Someone from the Underworld."

"Catarina," Jonas muttered.

"My mentor will not like this violation and wickedness, this diabolical plan. She'll want to stop it, if she can."

"And so you think your mentor might help us?" Audray whispered. Her eyes lit up, and Carl could see she had picked up hope.

Molly nodded her head. "She is very temperamental and elderly, not in the best of health. Let's hope we find her on one of her good days."

"Meaning she could do something to us. Would she harm the baby?" Jonas asked. "I want a straight answer or we're not going."

Molly chuckled, musing on an internal thought Carl wished he could read. "No, you and Audray and the baby have nothing to fear. The worst she will do for you is send you away."

She paused before she looked up at Carl and smiled. Carl's stomach dropped to his ankles. "If she's grumpy, Carl might wind up spending the rest of his days as a frog, and I don't mean a Frenchman."

Chapter 24

THE LITTLE CABIN was obscured, covered in the largest grapevine Audray had ever seen. It gripped the boxlike dwelling with green tendrils, crisscrossing over windows that could barely be seen through the thick foliage. Audray knew if the house somehow exploded, its contents might be scrambled inside, but the structure would hold firm due to the vines. The plant appeared to have more strength than anything else around it, including forces of nature.

Still, she wasn't afraid, her need for information was so great. Audray knew she would have to go back to the Underworld, if only to escape the clutches of the dark witch who had set her sights on Jonas. The thought of anyone else lying in his arms, whether he be forced or not, was so abhorrent Audray knew she would gladly kill or die to stop it. But now she carried his child, at least she felt it was his child, wondering if she would ever know for sure. She would not risk harm to her precious package, regardless, and knew she would have to make careful, calculated choices, controlling her hunger for revenge. She'd had a meal of it when she visited Burt just a few days ago so her urge was somewhat satisfied.

Glad I got that one out of the way.

Jonas rubbed the small of her back in response, as all four of them walked down the mossy brick path to the old witch's front door. Even Audray would have to stoop to enter the low doorframe. The woman answering had a shock of white hair and was very frail, but her emerald green eyes were those of a young woman's and sparkled with an unearthly enthusiasm.

"Drucilla, these are my friends," Molly started. The old woman looked each one in the eyes as Molly introduced them, as if deciding whom she would allow to enter. "This is Carl."

He reached over, bowing with respect, looking down as he extended his hand. "Nice to meet you," he said to his feet.

Drucilla stepped forward at once and was not careful as she gripped his chin with her bony fingers, requiring him to make eye contact. "You spineless human males are all the same. Afraid to show her granny the face of the man who has kissed her granddaughter in places even she hasn't seen."

Audray felt Jonas' chest rumble, stifling a chuckle. Knowing he found this funny lightened her mood and relaxed her.

"Sorry." Carl looked at Molly and shrugged. But no one moved. Audray was sure a threshold had to be crossed, a test had to be passed. Carl's acceptance in the circle was at stake. Fumbling, he knelt on one knee, which also released the hold Drucilla had on his chin. "I am in love with Molly. With all my heart." The last part he said with both palms pressed to his chest.

Molly looked close to tears. The old woman sized Carl up and down warily, and was about to say something when Carl interrupted.

"And this comes from deep inside my soul. It is not from the glimmer." His eyes bored into the old woman's and at long last, she smiled, revealing that several of her teeth were missing.

"It matters not. It's been a long time since someone with so much sexual energy knelt at my feet, and for that, I thank you." She patted the top of his head, and Carl stood back up.

Drucilla turned her gaze onto Jonas. "And you are the hunk dark angel."

Audray squeezed Jonas' hand. She didn't like the tone, the liberty the old woman took, being too loose with her comments. Jonas squeezed her hand back, but did not look into Audray's eyes. He kept his gaze on the old witch.

"This is Jonas Starling, Grandmother."

Drucilla stepped very close to Jonas, having to look up with difficulty into his dark eyes. Audray could feel an electrical connection between the two of them, as if Drucilla were measuring something.

"Lovely. Simply lovely." Drucilla smiled at Audray, "He even warms my bones, and God knows it's been decades." She took the hand Jonas had been holding with Audray, separating them. She put his palm to her cheek and smiled. "In the old days, I'd have taken him for my own, if I could get him. Welcome, Blackbird."

Audray felt Jonas flinch at the name she called him. She knew it had some significance.

Drucilla placed Jonas' hand back with Audray's and squeezed. "So your union is fruitful, I see." She smiled as she stepped in front of Audray, putting both her hands on Audray's cheeks.

Drucilla closed her eyes and inhaled. "Ah, the smell of fresh life. It grows strong and healthy." When she opened her eyes and removed her palms, a little jolt went through her body. "Oh my!"

"What is it grandmother?" Molly said, suddenly alarmed.

"The babe talks to me."

Audray was dumbstruck. She and Jonas gazed in shocked silence at each other. Deciding it was probably a good sign, they both smiled and then hugged. Jonas whispered, "Thank God, the child is healthy."

Audray was dying to ask a question. "What did the baby tell you?"

"Well, this is just splendid. I'd thought I'd seen, or felt, it all. The babe asked me whether it should be a boy or a girl. It hasn't made up its mind. It can choose!"

"That's incredible," Molly offered. Carl was speechless. Jonas was tense.

"And what advice did you give my child?" His brow furrowed, his voice deepened. His breathing was irregular and raspy. Audray's hand was caught in a vice grip with his, cutting off circulation.

Our child. Our child, Jonas.

Jonas relaxed but his focus was intent on getting an answer from the old witch.

"Never fear, sir. I don't meddle with the affairs of immortals."

"My child will be immortal?" Jonas asked.

"Not sure," Drucilla said as she shrugged. "This I cannot tell." She stepped back and addressed the whole group. "But I told it to let nature take its course. I said it wasn't a decision any of us should make. I said to let Father decide." She scanned her audience. "You all seem surprised with this." She smiled and inhaled. "You have to know about the rules before you decide which ones to bend. But I don't break them. Your child simply asked a question that was above my pay grade. Unusual for one so small to have such power, though, isn't it? A really very exciting development, don't you all agree?"

Audray rubbed her belly, giving silent love thoughts, showering the baby with the goodness in her soul, which was growing each day, mirroring the growth of the baby.

I am changing too, young one. I never thought I could love another as much as I love your father, and my heart is expanding to love you both. But you are flesh and blood. You are the best part of both of us. Be strong, and know you are adored.

Jonas squeezed her, pulling her body into the delicious muscles of his. Audray felt safe and protected in his arms. His strength allowed her softness to take root and grow unbridled. It had never been anything she had wanted before. But now it was something she could not live without.

"Come, come. Let's go inside and have a spot of tea!" Drucilla clapped her hands in mirth, waddling into the tiny cabin as her guests ducked and followed her.

Inside, it was lighter than Audray would have expected. Skylights that opened let in plenty of fresh air and wonderful late morning light, filtered through the green grape leaves that seemed to turn and grow as she watched them.

Everything around her seemed alive. Drucilla had a pair of small green parrots. A mouse ran across the floor, Drucilla chasing it with a gnarled broom. "Know your place, Tabitha. You will get your introduction soon enough," she spoke to the mouse, who squeaked a response before making it to the safety of a wall hole. A large fluffy white cat was lounging on a brightly flowered overstuffed couch. He was unceremoniously shooed from the warm pillow with a stern incantation Audray didn't understand.

Molly's face was lit up like a Christmas tree. Audray noted how comfortable the young woman appeared, as if she had spent hours and hours here as part of her training. Stepping into the old woman's home was like being introduced to a deeply intimate part of Molly's past.

Carl stared at every bunch of dried flowers hanging from the ceiling, every cupboard, dish, chair, rug or animal. Audray remembered the first time she had visited a Farmer's Market and saw all the variety of beautiful fruits, vegetables and flowers. She had never known something so opulent. She'd always thought food came from packages and cans. Carl's face looked just like what hers must have looked like those ten plus years ago.

"Sit, sit. Please." Drucilla scurried to the kitchen and turned on her electric teakettle. With a groan, she pulled over a small stepstool and reached up to the top shelf of one cabinet to retrieve several teacups. Jonas was at her elbow in a flash, as she handed down to him five sets of delicately handpainted flowered cups and saucers. None of them matched.

Drucilla made a point to hold her hand out in front of Jonas' face with her little pinky in the air, indicating she needed help down off the stool. Instead of taking her hand, the big dark angel picked her up by the waist and swung her around, setting her down as she squealed in delight.

"Now, Carl, there's a real man for you!" Drucilla giggled. Audray saw Jonas blush and look down at her.

Yes, there is a real man. And he's mine.

Audray was rewarded with an air kiss.

The unlikely serving pair prepared the tea, placed cream in a clear glass pitcher, and added sugar cubes to a small cut crystal bowl. Jonas presented the whole array carefully on a silver tray, placing it on the coffee table in the middle of the small living room. Drucilla seemed to beam with enjoyment, asking for orders and pouring the tea as if she were a duchess at a State dinner.

As the tea settled in, Audray did feel relaxed, warmed heart and soul.

"Now. You came for information. I'm of a frame of mind to help you. Ask me quick, because these moods don't last too long these days. Molly can attest to this."

Molly almost spit her tea out.

"Frogs? You think I'd turn them into frogs?" Drucilla asked her.

"No. Not them, me," Carl piped up.

"The verdict is out on you," she said, pointing a bony finger at his chest. "But I can see your use to my granddaughter, and for the moment, I approve." She turned to Audray and Jonas, whispering,

"I'd have him housecleaning, rubbing my feet, scrubbing my back in the tub, perhaps gardening...and see where it leads from there."

Audray found this delightfully hilarious. She covered her mouth and looked up at Carl, who knew he was being talked about and had a puzzled expression on his face.

"Glimmering is so much fun, and," the witch leaned in and lowered her voice further, "he is very susceptible. So much more fun when they are." She winked.

Even Jonas thought this was worthy of a chuckle.

Carl looked around the room, clearly uneasy with his situation. Molly leaned over and took his hand. With a sweet smile, she tried to reassure him. "Sweetheart, you're going to have to get used to my family. We are a bit eccentric."

Carl was going to say something, but the big white fluffy cat jumped into his lap and he spilled his teacup, which had been balanced on his knees.

"Off! You are the devil himself!" Drucilla screeched at the cat, who found a patch of rug in the sunlight to hunker down on. The cat looked back as if unmoved by the event.

Carl stood, exposing a dark stain of spilled tea, front and center on his jeans in the groin area. He cursed.

"Not in my house!" Drucilla screamed. "You will not defile this holy place with obscenities." Drucilla glanced at Jonas and Audray adding, "There are times for those kinds of words, and times when they are not appropriate." She turned around and addressed Carl again. "Since we're not having sex, I don't want to hear you say the f-word, understood?"

Everyone but Carl laughed. Carl put his hands on his hips and hung his head.

"If you can't stand the heat, boy, better get out of the kitchen,"

Drucilla needled him further. Audray began to feel sorry for the young professor.

"Look, you old bag," Carl began, drawing strength as he continued, "I think your manners are horrible. I was raised to have more respect for others." Carl's breathing was ragged, his face red. He looked like he was could punch Drucilla if she said something else he didn't like.

"Ah, there's hope!" Drucilla sauntered up to Carl, extricating the tea cup from his hands, wiggling her eyebrows up and down. "It's been a whole twenty-four hours since I've been called that." She rushed to the kitchen and brought back a jar containing another mouse. The top was covered with netting, secured by a blue ribbon tied in a bow. The little mouse inside stood on his hind legs, paws pressed against the glass, sniffing and looking at Carl. "Molly," she began, but she remained focused on Carl's face, "Your cousin Tremaine called me the very same thing yesterday, so I've given him a time out."

Carl's eyes got big as saucers.

"Now, son," the old witch said as she thrust the jar into Carl's quivering hands, "call me that name again." Audray noticed through her sickly smile that all of her teeth had returned to her head. But this time, instead of sparkling white, they were pearlescent yellow.

Carl looked at Tremaine through the glass jar and began, "Holy sh...Holy succotash." He stopped and took a deep breath. Composing himself carefully, he spat back, "Not only are you an old bag, but you are a heartless old bag." He held the jar up in the air. Tremaine shit a green liquid that started to pool at the bottom of the jar. "You vile woman, hurting members of your own family. You should be ashamed of yourself." As an afterthought, Carl held out the jar. "You should apologize to this little fellow here, and set him free. Or should

I?"

Drucilla smiled from ear to ear. "Ah, I do love a man in uniform."

Silence descended on the room. Audray didn't know what was going to happen next.

"Go ahead, release him. If the cat doesn't get him, he's free." Drucilla had folded her arms in front of her.

Everyone watched as Carl loosened the top and poured Tremaine out onto the rug. The little figure made a beeline for the mouse hole Tabitha had disappeared into.

"When are you going to release him?" Carl asked.

"You just did, my boy. He's gone home to Tabby. They have a nest of little squeakers that keep me up all night long." She smiled again and patted his shoulder. "Good job, son. You don't think I would really turn a member of my family into a mouse, do you? Although, I must say, I don't mind that you think so."

With a loud cackle she retreated to the kitchen in search of another cup of tea for Carl.

Carl exhaled and sat back down next to Molly, who pulled her chair up and snuggled next to him. His half smile told Audray she had said something about how brave he was, and Audray agreed.

Jonas looked at his watch. It was getting past noon. Audray could tell he was impatient.

"Okay, fun's over," Drucilla started as she brought in Carl's replacement cup. "Let's get down to business so we can begin our battle plans."

"One thing I'm going to need to know right away is whether or not it is safe for Audray to go between the worlds, between the Underworld and the human world," Jonas said.

"It will be more difficult the further along she is. I think her body has accepted its fate, and as long as you don't go back and forth too many times it will be okay. But I wouldn't push it."

"So, you think if I have to go back down there a couple, maybe three times, it will not hurt the baby?" Audray asked.

"I think the baby will be fine. What is changing is your body, Audray. You were brought back to life as a dark angel. I think it's possible your body is having to convert partially to a living human woman to accept this child and grow it inside you. You will not be able to tolerate the trip back and forth the more your body changes. And if you can't tolerate it any longer, it will affect the baby."

Audray was somewhat relieved with this information. Perhaps there was a way afterall. Her primary goal was for the safety of the child. But her ability to help clean up the Underworld affected her future, which included Jonas and the baby. She was glad to know she might still be able to do so.

"So what happens after the baby is born? Will Audray stay changed, as in part human? Or..." Jonas couldn't finish his sentence.

"She probably will die, sorry to say. I have only seen it work this way. The child will live at the sacrifice of the mother."

It was what she expected. The bitter words pricked her to the heart. She was hoping she'd either heard wrong or misunderstood. "Are you positive?" Audray asked.

"No. I have a couple of my sisters I need to consult. They won't be reachable for another couple of days. I'll school you on what I know this morning, and then day after tomorrow perhaps I'll have more answers for you."

"Thank you," Jonas said.

"Don't thank me yet. And don't get your hopes up. We're gonna need a miracle. Maybe a little divine intervention too." Drucilla's cackle left Audray's hairs on edge.

Chapter 25

JONAS URGED AUDRAY to stay a few more nights in the human world, where they could discuss things in relative freedom, hoping Drucilla and her friends would have more information for them. But Audray didn't want to put the trip to the Underworld off any longer. So they compromised and stayed at a local inn near the college, checking in early and delaying their trip back to the Underworld by a day.

"I have a bad feeling about this trip, but the longer I stay away, the harder it's going to get."

"I think you're right, love." Jonas had turned on some music and lit a fire.

She allowed in a little bit of sadness, wondering what their life would have been like if they'd met, both as humans. It was an impossible fantasy, but she wondered how it would feel to be human again, away from all the trappings of power and privilege. After dealing with Burt, her anger and lust for revenge had tempered. It was more pleasurable to want things for Jonas and for the child she was carrying, than for herself. For the first time in her life she knew she cared more about Jonas and the baby than she cared about her own life. It made her smile.

"Penny for your thoughts." He stood behind her, rubbing up and down the length of her arms. His strong manly scent was always there. She wondered what he would smell like, what he would feel like as a human man.

I was just pretending we were human. We were just ordinary beings." She turned around to face him, reaching to his face, searching his eyes. "I have never loved so deeply nor felt so loved, Jonas. Thank you."

"Nor I, Audray. I've had centuries to think about it, too. You are the only one I have truly loved."

"Let's just pretend, for tonight, that everything is the way it should be. I never wanted to do this before because I was always so disappointed—with everyone who should have cared. But let's just pretend you and I don't have pasts, don't have families from Hell or enemies after us. That we're just two humans who love each other, who want a simple life away from all this death and destruction. Okay? Can we do that?" She saw in his dark eyes the moisture building. She'd touched a nerve.

He nodded and swallowed hard. She was moved by the emotions, the thoughts and images he was sending her telepathically. Their breathing slowed and became tandem.

She lay her palms down over his heart. "I love this part about you. Not your smile or that ridiculous crescent crease at the left of your mouth that drives me insane. Not your strong arms," she continued as one palm smoothed up from his inner elbow and up over his bicep. "It's this," she said as she patted his chest with her other hand, over his heart. "It's what's in there, the way you are, the trueness of your spirit, how you're all in for me, unconditionally. That's what I love the most, Jonas."

"Nothing very special there. Just the way I'm wired up."

"But it's rare. You've taught me this. You've taught me to trust. I think all my experiences growing up made it hard to trust people, especially men."

"No wonder there. I'm just glad I was there. I'll always be here for you, Audray."

She knew this to be true, but she loved hearing it anyway. She still felt she didn't feel worthy of the love that he was giving her so freely.

He kissed her chest between her breasts and bit at the clasp of her bra under her cotton shirt. The bra split open and Jonas placed his palms over the mounds of flesh that ached to be touched, and squeezed.

He quickly slipped his hands underneath the top, then he lifted it and slipped everything over her head, leaving her bare to him. She instinctively covered herself up.

"Take your hands away."

"You are commanding your queen to submit to you?"

His hearty chuckle warmed her. She loved teasing him.

"Yes. Remove them at once or I will destroy your new pants, and then you'll have nothing to wear."

Audray looked up into the heavens, feigning the choice to take. "Who needs pants?" she said as she leaned back in his arms. Her breasts remained covered.

"Very well, then. You will be punished for this indiscretion. But first, your hands. Remove your hands so I can examine you."

Audray tilted her head and let her lips quirk up on one side. With genteel compliance she slowly removed her arms from her chest.

Jonas stared at her like he'd never seen her breasts before. Her nipples had hardened, but their color had changed as well, growing dark pink. "God almighty, love. You're huge." He felt the heaviness of her flesh, a handful in his large paw. He stood her up, knelt before her and slowly slipped off her pants, but left her panties on. "Listen little one," he said to her tummy. "You've got to lay low for awhile so your mum and me can have some fun. Don't be giving her a rough time of it."

Audray moaned as she rubbed his temples with her fingers.

He continued with his message to their child, "Now, I want you to close your eyes and ears for a bit whilst I pleasure your mum three ways to Sunday. If you're a boy, I'll teach you how it's done much later. And if you're a girl and you care about the lives of the men who come courting, you'll stay away from them. You don't need to know anything about what I'm about to do to your mum."

Good as his word, Jonas took his time. He seemed to forget the game of domination he'd intended to play. His long gentle strokes were decorated with bedtime whispers and promises, telling her how she made him feel, telling her stories of what their life would be like in the coming years. She'd never heard him say such things. It felt like he was convincing himself that the more he described their glowing future, the more they were creating it, actually making it a reality.

His mouth could bring pleasure either by words or by the hot touch of his tongue. She saw how intent and careful he was, how he loved to watch as his cock dove into her from behind. She felt the lips of her peach split open, massaged and kneaded to the side with gentle pressure from his fingers. He pressed on the knob at her front and encircled it, sending her into spasms. She gripped his thighs with her own and leaned back for deeper penetration. At last she gasped, resting her head against his shoulder as he kissed the sides of her face and neck, his other hand finishing the ministrations between her legs. He brought his wet finger up and had her taste her own desire.

Jonas turned Audray to her back, laying her down gently, raising her knees over his shoulders. His tongue lapped at her moist nether lips. She grimaced as her need shattered her composure and her pleasure peaked again, just before he sunk his cock in deep again, pulling out and then plundering her over and over.

She couldn't get enough. He would start to come and then would stop utterly still, waiting for her to rise up and demand more. He studied her attentively, began to stroke her again, letting her body go into a low rumble, raising her up higher and then giving her the full force of his cock inside until at last he exploded with seed. His body shuddered. His deep guttural groan made her feel like he thought this would be their last encounter.

LATER THAT AFTERNOON, Audray scolded him in the shower. "Some punishment you mete out. And here you call yourself a warrior." She had pulled him into the warm steam, glazing his body all over with lavender shower gel.

"Well, if you insist on keeping me covered with your body and the scent of flowers, what do you expect?"

"I expect that you use the silk ties in our spare bedroom. Keep me your prisoner, bound to your bed."

"You mean your bed. You could vaporize them in a flash, my love. Josh's old ties are no use to you, except as props. I couldn't detain you if I tried with all my immortal strength."

"See. I told you the female of the species is the strongest. You've just proven my point, my dear."

"Yes, you are my strong female, and you carry my child. That does change things. But it makes me mad with desire for you." He kissed her gently. "I want to take care of you now."

THEY DRIED OFF and dressed without words. Jonas checked out of the inn, telling the front desk their work had called them away and they wouldn't be spending the night. He drove the black Hummer to the transport station, parking it in the street, away from the warehouse entrance, but also a good distance from Audray's former home. He'd arranged to have the rental agency pick it up later in the day and have it ready later, if and when he returned.

The flames had left their violent mark on the landscape. Pieces of the Director's home were scattered throughout the abandoned construction yard. Jonas figured there'd been another explosion.

In a way, it was a blessing they hadn't spent much time there. Their attachments to the place were at best minimal, except it was the first place he had claimed her. Jonas decided he'd start looking for a new home on the next trip back. He'd feel safer closer to Joshua Brandon. Being close to the transport was no longer important to them.

THE TRANSPORT WAS efficient and faster than either one of them had remembered, and for the first time in many trips, a young female driver was at the wheel. She turned in her seat and greeted him. It wasn't against any protocol, but having a driver was a new development. She barely gave Audray any notice at all. Instead, her large overly made up dark eyes explored every part of Jonas, making him blush in front of his queen. This was also something new. Women never made him feel embarrassed before. He usually liked the ones that weren't afraid to show their feelings, their desires.

Jonas was sure the driver didn't recognize Audray and guessed she was a recent convert.

Probably one of Rupert's minions.

When the transport came to an abrupt stop in front of the station in the Underworld, Jonas kissed Audray's palm, whispering, "Showtime!" under his breath. She had been tense. Her skin was cool to the touch and her fingers had lost some of their pliability since the afternoon lovemaking sessions. She was distracted, he thought.

And for good reason. She's not sure what she's running headlong into.

"How are you feeling? Everything okay?" he asked. She looked healthy, a little cold and tense, but there was a warm glow to her face he was glad to see.

"I'm fine."

The female driver opened their door and, although fully clothed above the waist, she wore only a thong down below, matching the color of her black spiked heels. Her body was hard not to admire, due to the perfection of her well-muscled form.

"Excuse me, Miss," Jonas began.

The driver beamed back in his direction, eyes half-lidded, red lips moist and plumped.

"If you get summoned to pick up the Director again, you will dress properly? Or did you perhaps get us confused with a bachelor party coming later?

The smile left her young face as she glanced between Jonas and Audray, finally landing on Audray.

"I hope you will forgive my lack of taste. Obviously I made the wrong assumption." She turned around and sauntered the full length of the limo away from them, exaggeration prominent in the swing of her ass.

"Unbelievable," Audray began. "Obviously she's not very afraid for her job. Someone is making some promises they won't be able to keep." she added, "Or at least I hope not."

"She's a throwaway, just doesn't know it yet. Feeling powerful in her new immortal dark angel body. Her time for suffering will come." The limo sped off in search of another passenger. Jonas hooked Audray's arm and helped her up the steps to the Director's office.

The lobby had changed little. A woman they did not recognize sat at the reception desk. Both of them nodded to the young angel as they walked around her.

"Excuse me, you have not logged in," the girl called out.

Audray stopped dead in her tracks, dallied back to the desk as if unconcerned about the insult just thrown at her. "Who hired you?" she asked and flipped her blonde hair behind her shoulders.

"Mr. Blade."

"Good. You're fired. Now leave the premises," Audray said as coolly as ordering a drink at her favorite bar.

The pretty young angel was going to protest. Jonas came forward, gripped her elbow and shoved her out the glass front doors. "You've been fired by the Director herself. If you want to live on, I'd suggest you go and not return."

When Jonas came back, Audray was on her red phone. "Get someone down here right away. And I want a full report after you're done." She flipped the phone closed.

They passed several dark angels on their way to the bank of elevators. Audray's fingerprint on the red button labeled with a "D" opened the doors to the Director's private elevator. In an instant, they were transported to the top floor.

The area was quiet, too quiet. Audray looked around the pillars of the huge anteroom and then looked at Jonas' face. "Not a soul here. There should be staffers…" she began.

Just then, the doors to her private office opened. Jonas recognized the smell of him before he saw him. Rupert Blade walked through the doors like he owned the place. With a curt bow, he extended his hand.

"How very lovely to finally meet you, Miss Steele. I'm Rupert Blade, your paramour's cousin," he waved his eyebrows up and down as he thinly smiled, "through marriage, of course."

Jonas could feel Audray's body shaking. Aware of the proximity of their child to this cretin, he encircled her waist and stood behind her, pressing his chest against her back.

"*Thank you,*" he heard her mentally.

"Mr. Blade," she started, refusing to shake his hand or touch him in any way, "I'm not accustomed to having to explain to the souls living in the Underworld how things work. You have violated my space."

"I'm truly sorry." He bowed again, but upon rising, smiled at Jonas. "She's stunning. A real heartbreaker."

"That's two strikes, Mr. Blade. Your lack of respect could cost you an appendage, or do you have a death wish?" Audray delivered the sentence and then stepped to within inches of the intruder. "I haven't vaporized someone for a few days. Get out of my sight," she spat out.

Jonas took hold of Blade, jerking him toward the wooden doors of the office. He felt Rupert's body tense, like he wanted to react differently but hadn't expected the attitude from Audray. Jonas shoved the dark angel into the regular elevator but straddled the entrance, immobilizing the doors. "How did you get up here? Who let you in?"

"I have my ways."

Holding the dark angel at his throat as if to raise him off the ground, Jonas fished through Rupert's pockets and found an access override card. "Whomever helped you get this is a dead man," he said.

"Or woman," Rupert's dark eyes sparkled back in Jonas' face as he was released.

Jonas grabbed the front of Rupert's shirt and hauled him back into the anteroom; the elevator doors closed. "Even if *Catarina* did it for you, she will suffer the consequences." Jonas released the angel with a push toward the doors.

Rupert rolled his shoulders and his neck, an action reminding Jonas of his friend, Joshua Brandon. The smaller angel straightened his shirt but said nothing.

"This isn't your fight," Jonas started.

"She killed my brother, Peter."

"Who was sent by your family."

"Your bloodline as well."

"But I don't believe in the prophecy. I want no part of this so-called family."

Rupert seemed to gather the rest of his dignity. "Have you forgotten about our discussion, Jonas? Is your pride so important that you would harm those you love?"

Jonas was startled by the man's statement and couldn't find the words to respond. The reality of his situation began to descend upon him again.

"Catarina—"

Jonas found himself, finally. "Has you doing her bidding like the lackey you are. Tell me, does she punish you when you go home at night with less than perfect results?" Jonas allowed this last comment to accompany a sneer.

"She has no complaints. You've done your part too, or need I remind you it was your job to bring Audray back?"

"She's the fucking Director of the Underworld. This is where she belongs." Jonas said, mustering all the bravado he could, belying his fear for her safety.

"Yes. Well, for now at least." Rupert walked to the elevator doors. "I must go report and receive the pleasure reward that was promised me. She is a very generous woman, Catarina. Passion runs high in her DNA, but then you know this first hand." He smiled and bowed to Jonas.

"How long do you think you'll last if she becomes the new Director? Or did you think she'd let you rule? What do you think will happen when that passion flames for another? A warrior type? How long do you think she will be content and occupied with the likes of you?"

There was a moment's hesitation in Rupert's step to the elevator. Jonas saw it. He wondered if the angel knew he'd seen it. "With rewards come risks," Rupert said over his shoulder.

"So what does she risk? Why would she send you instead of doing it herself? Do you really think she sees you as anything but expendable?" Jonas railed back.

Rupert did not turn around, but pushed the button and the elevator doors opened. He took one decisive step forward staring at the red carpet of the carriage floor. As the lumbering elevator closed, he abruptly turned and faced Jonas once again, raising his chin.

"I'd watch my back, if I were you," Jonas said to the dark angel's face just before the doors sequestered the man to safety.

Chapter 26

AUDRAY GAZED THROUGH the picture window overlooking the Underworld below, now basking in afternoon sunlight. It was never as bright as the human world, she thought. There was always a hazy dullness, like the days when she was a child growing up in the Central Valley when they burned off the fields. She smiled at the memory of how she loved the smell of smoke as she rode her bicycle to the dance studio.

So maybe even then I knew where I'd wind up.

But her life's journey to the Underworld also landed her in Jonas' bed, and that had healed her soul.

My shot at redemption. In the Underworld. Again, she smiled.

But getting a second chance also brought her closer to danger all over again, like when she was sixteen years old. She feared for the impending birth of this child. At least she hoped it would be a birth, even if she didn't survive.

Our child must live.

She smoothed her hands down over her clothes, from her tender breasts to her belly which felt slightly bloated. No doubt about it. This child was transforming her from the inside out, and she liked it.

Do I have the pregnancy aura? Or is it my imagination? No way she could be showing yet, but Jonas was so attuned to her body, he noticed the subtle differences right away. She felt things she hadn't before. Little things. Tender things.

Looking around the office, she realized it had not been personalized to her tastes yet. Most of her time was taken up giving new direction to her staffers and being alone with Jonas. She sat behind Peter's legendary black desk. In the center lay a pink box tooled in gold leaf. Jonas had bought her an inexpensive musical jewelry chest at the pier in San Francisco. He'd wanted to get her something expensive, something worthy of her lofty position, but Audray liked this one, as it matched the way she felt about her young uncomplicated dreams as a human girl. She had never wanted great things, just a life where she could be in control, where she was allowed to be master of her fate, safe from her mother's predator boyfriends.

When the pink leather case was opened, a tiny ballerina in a white tutu danced in front of the mirror to the twinkling tune. She had always wanted one as a child. Through watery eyes, she gazed fascinated at the doll twirling in front of her and smiled.

Lady in red is dancing with me. Hesitant to put it away, she pulled down the lid and placed the box on an empty bookshelf to her right. She brought back Peter's empty silver In Basket from the top drawer, the only object that would adorn the obsidian surface. He would have approved, she mused.

Audray sat back down in the leather chair. It was comfortable for now. No sense changing it, since she didn't expect to hold the office long if she could help it. She pulled out a yellow tablet and began making a list of things she would need to do. It was odd no one was calling her on her phone.

She made notes about the normal succession of the Directorship after a death of the Director. To her left, black notebooks, all dusted and organized, catalogued by her staff, made it easy to peruse the topics and find the right one. She grabbed the book now, sat down again, and began to read.

...A dying Director can make an interim appointment for sixty days. Then a full election must be held. If there is a challenge to this appointment, a meeting of the council shall be called for by one member, wherein a majority vote for or against the appointee can be made...

Audray looked up from the book. As far as she understood, the council was formed without authority, since neither Catarina nor Rupert were present members. Yet, they were being treated as such. Perhaps this could be the out she was seeking. Peter had told her no one knew there was supposed to be one, going back many years. He was the first Director in years who actually had studied this. Perhaps Jonas would be able to shed some light on her problem, however temporary.

And then Jonas entered the office, as if on cue.

"That was interesting," he said to his lover.

"The man has the ego of an ox, but the heart of a snake," she quipped.

"Well said." Jonas dumped his frame into one of the chairs Audray had found in storage, his large frame causing the chair to moan under his weight. He sighed. "I'm wondering where everyone is." He searched the room, as if to find an angel cowering under a bookshelf.

"Yes. Well, thank the spirits we won't need their assistance for too long. I think Rupert has everyone pretty much spooked at this point." She frowned, tapping her pen on the yellow tablet in front of her. "Jonas, I've been doing some research, and it appears there is supposed to be a council. Have you ever heard of this?"

Jonas leaned back, staring at the ceiling. "Ah. It was maybe a hundred years ago. There was an issue about someone making winged dark angels." He looked back at Audray and shook his head, "Love,

I've never paid too much attention to politics. Those that do can't be trusted."

"So there isn't a council now? It says here they can vote to overrule an appointment by a dying Director."

"No council that I've seen. And they're all appointed by the Director. I don't think Peter had time to do it."

"I agree," Audray began, "And he never was one to share his power with anyone."

"Except you." Jonas leveled a smirk at her.

Audray shuddered, but Jonas chuckled. She had been intimate with the former Director right on this very desk. She tried to put it out of her mind, but could see Jonas was enjoying watching her squirm. "You are not jealous?" she frowned.

"Of a pathetic dead angel? Of course not. And I don't believe in ghosts."

Audray was satisfied with his answer and decided not to dwell on it. Jonas continued, "But I know what my Queen loves, and I am confident I am the only one who has ever heard her cry out when she takes her pleasure."

His sexy dark eyes warmed her whole body as they claimed her, raking from her face down to her waist and back up again, lingering over her breasts. Her nipples fisted as the urge to have him run his tongue over them made her skin sizzle. Naked or fully clothed, sitting or lying under him, Jonas always brought energy and life force to her, as if it was the only thing in the universe she needed.

Until now. Now we will be three. Father, if you can, help us be three.

A rap at the office door interrupted her thoughts. Jonas was up in a flash and allowed Luke and three other dark angels to enter. Luke's face was somber.

"We've lost Jacob and Timothy."

"Lost?" Audray asked.

The four angels stood with their hands in front of them like a soccer team at a goal kick. Luke answered her after looking to the others as if asking permission to speak.

"Timothy's disappeared. Jacob was...was...dismembered. We found what was left of him behind the Pussycat."

Audray looked from the four angels to Jonas, who did not meet her gaze. "Who did this?"

Luke handed Audray a crumpled page from one of her yellow lined pads. "I've taken the liberty of creating this list of suspects and troublemakers."

"What's got into you guys?" Audray asked, scanning the paper. It worried her that they were so docile. "We've got to roll up our sleeves and get to work. You took on your jobs willingly. Anybody got a change of heart?"

She could tell they all did, even Luke.

"Things are different now. We have to stay together all the time. When we get separated, one of us gets, you know, taken, and..."

"My men will protect you," Jonas offered.

"Thanks, Jonas," Audray said. "His guys aren't afraid of anything. You're going to have to buck up, like they do," she said addressing the dark staffers.

"No offense, Jonas, but your guys are lying low as well," Luke offered, hanging his long face.

"Only because I've not been here. They just need direction. You go to my barracks. Take your things and go there until this is over. And any of you that have loved ones, take them too." Jonas looked to Audray. "I need to see to the men."

"Of course. Don't be long."

Jonas came round the desk and gave Audray a kiss on the cheek, fisting her blonde hair. He whispered in her ear, "It's going to be okay. Don't worry, love. I'll be back in an hour at the most."

She nodded and Jonas left. The room suddenly felt huge and cold. "You will tell me what has happened in the three days I've been gone."

"This Rupert guy has been speaking out on the street corners. One of the dark ones who had his wings ripped off, he's been saying things like you killed Peter and have taken over illegally. Of course, everyone isn't ready to fight over this. I mean, I see the crowds. I can tell Rupert is frustrated that nobody cares like he does."

"So maybe there isn't a problem after all."

"Oh no, there is. You see, angels have been disappearing. I thought maybe Timothy had holed up with one of Helena's girls for a few days and didn't worry about it, although we were supposed to meet up. But when we found Jacob, we knew they were both targeted."

"And now you feel it."

"Wouldn't you?" Luke answered.

Audray stood up. "Yes. I feel it. And I'm going to fight back, damn it. They can't just come in here and take over." She felt suddenly dizzy and leaned onto her fingertips at the desktop, then sat down.

"Are you well?" Luke asked.

"I'm very well. But you see, Jonas and I are the real targets, not you four. They are trying to get to us through you. I've just spent a few days getting myself adjusted for this fight, cleaning up details of my human life, so to speak. I need to know whom I can count on and who is going to get squishy on me. You clear on that?"

They all nodded.

"No hard feelings. Now, and for the last time, if you want out you can have it. But you're on your own, mind you. Anyone who wants to fight with me can stay at the barracks and Jonas will protect them.

Otherwise you're up to your own devices. Search your conscience."

The four angels looked to one another, nodding. Luke was the only one who remained. As the other three exited the doors, Audray called after them, "And don't think that if I see you defending Rupert or any of his cronies I won't vaporize you on the spot. I hope that warms you at night, cowards."

She got up, slamming the door behind them, and got the satisfaction of a loud boom as the windows rattled.

"I will retrieve their passes, their things," Luke offered.

"No. We need ethereal locks. Jonas has an expert on his way over now. Rupert was able to get in here without anyone to stop him. We will need some security that is not compromised. Let them think they have value, for now."

"Yes, ma'am."

"Now, let's look at this list." Audray sat again behind the desk and gripped the paper.

There were twenty-five names on it.

Some of these angels were friends of mine.

Chapter 27

CARL DISMISSED HIS class ten minutes early. It was getting difficult to focus on his teaching. Manuscripts were piling up, mid term grades were a week overdue, causing the administration to send him a reminder notice. The second one.

Jeremy approached him. Carl had not paid attention to the Goth clothing and dark eye makeup the young student began to wear. This change in appearance surprised Carl. Jeremy didn't look anything like the youth who used to sit in his front row with the sweater vest and starched white shirt.

Carl loosened his bow tie, cursing under his breath. He pocketed it and unbuttoned his shirt. The room seemed hotter than normal. The smell of youthful bodies practicing various methods of personal hygiene was present. He'd gotten used to it, but now the cloying perspiration and scent of unwashed bodies annoyed him. He didn't feel clean.

I want shower sex with Molly. He had no control over the thought that just popped into his head. His dick responded and his pants tented.

Jeremy's smile disarmed Carl. It was like the student knew about the churning inside his stomach, in his brain, and the stirring in his loins.

"Professor. We need another meeting." Jeremy looked him directly in the eyes.

"We? Who are you talking about?"

"Glenda is my aunt."

Fuck me two ways to sundown. Carl ran his fingers through his hair, searching the little crowd of students exiting his classroom. Their light-heartedness and laughter seemed out of place today. He heard their voices echoing down the otherwise vacant hallway.

Here comes another memo from Admin.

"Well, Jeremy. I suppose I should thank you for recommending me to your aunt, but, under the circumstances, I would have preferred you never mentioned my name to her." Carl stacked a pile of class writing assignments together, tapping their ends on the desk. He found an oversized brass binder clip, bundling them. With shaking fingers, he concentrated on stuffing the fistful of papers into his briefcase. He'd been doing this same routine for the last three days, and each morning he brought them back, ungraded, unread.

"I said I would help you with those, if you need it," Jeremy stated as he nodded toward the brown alligator briefcase with the brass lock.

"No thanks, Jeremy. It's my job. My *real* job, not chasing after—" He stopped, not wanting to reveal he knew anything further about Jonas and Audray. "That's what they pay me for, after all." He wondered how much longer before he'd get called to the dean's office. He knew the students wouldn't complain, but their parents, who were paying nearly thirty thousand dollars a year, always wanted their money's worth. He had a couple of parents' messages he'd not returned.

Carl completed his desk straightening and picked up his briefcase, leaning it on his right hip, addressing his dark student, "So what's your part in all this, if I may ask?"

"Well, I happen to know she really wants to get together with this Jonas Starling guy." Jeremy watched the look of alarm Carl knew his face revealed.

"Get together?" he asked.

"You know she's old. So's my mom." Jeremy's chin rose as he tilted his head back, and smiled back at Carl at an angle.

"Why, I've met your mom, and she's quite lovely," Carl offered, walking toward the doorway. "And she certainly doesn't look old." He wrinkled his nose and slipped a finger around his collar to give his neck air.

"You really think so?" Jeremy brightly answered, making Carl wince. "Good. I'll have to tell her. She thinks you're pretty cute yourself."

This wasn't going anywhere Carl wanted to go. "No, no. You don't understand. I was just being polite. Your mom's a very attractive woman. I didn't imply anything other than that." He had the urge to run to his car and take off, never coming back to the college. He didn't need the jealous husband of a black witch to come after him too. He walked with Jeremy down the creaky wooden floor of the abandoned hallway. He could hear lectures behind windowed classroom doors, the sounds of learning going on, people's futures being shaped. He felt seriously outside all that now.

Carl, get a grip.

"Uh, Jeremy. You were telling me your mother and your aunt are very old. H...how old are you?" Carl wondered if he really wanted to know the answer.

"Oh." Jeremy chuckled, books balanced on his hip, his head down. "I'm only twenty." He leaned over and punched Carl in the arm. "In real years. But thanks for the compliment."

Carl let it sink in as they exited the hallway into the afternoon sunlight. He needed to check his box in the lounge, but didn't want his ridealong when he did so. Just in case there was trouble. He knew there would be trouble very soon. So he stopped. Startling him, several doors in the hallway swung open. A covey of students, flush with ideas, swarmed their way around the pair, jabbering like crows on a telephone line.

"So your mother isn't your biological mother, then?" *Carl, you idiot!*

Jeremy indicated he knew full well what Carl's question implied by answering, "My father is human. My mother has outlived many husbands and lovers. I have lots of half brothers and sisters, some of them still living."

Thank God for small favors. He's a human, not a witch. Carl was at a complete loss for words, and rocked back and forth in his wingtips, his Argyle socks damp as he tried to wiggle his constricted toes.

"That must make for some interesting family reunions." It was all he could think to say.

Jeremy shrugged, shook his head and chuckled, "You have no idea."

Carl didn't have to use much imagination to see the picture. He pressed the tips of five fingers to his forehead, which was creased in a scowl. He squinted back at the young student, "Jeremy, can we just get to the point here? I feel like we're digressing all over your family tree. Frankly, I think this is your business, not mine. So, let's just finish and be on our separate ways, okay?" He dropped his hand and looked around him as the ocean of students subsided and they were left alone.

"Like I said," Jeremy began, "we want another meeting. Glenda wants me there. She needs to talk to you in person."

Carl started to object, but Jeremy interrupted him.

"She wants to meet in an hour at the Café Contada."

"I can't just drop everything and show up at some meeting off campus. I've got things to do here, and…and…"

"At the library? In the stacks?" Jeremy grinned. "You like the stacks," he said as he wiggled his eyebrows up and down.

Carl pulled at the unbuttoned collar of his shirt, stretching his neck up and out of it. He rolled his shoulders and transferred the weight of his briefcase to his right hand. He thought of Molly all alone at the library, waiting for him. He would not put her in danger. This was a meeting he would have to do on his own.

"Agreed. I will meet you two in…" he checked his watch, "…at one-thirty."

"Cool. See you then." Jeremy punched him again in the right arm. It actually hurt this time. The casual attitude of this young student belied something deep and sinister, he thought.

Carl needed to go to his house and change first. His clothes were soaking wet. He gave Molly a call and told her he'd be delayed.

GLENDA WAS ALREADY seated behind a large frothing cappuccino when Carl arrived. He was glad he had showered and changed, since he figured she probably had a supernatural sense of smell. She would be able to smell his fear.

Jeremy was over at the counter making an order.

"Go ahead and tell Jeremy what you want. It's on me today," she said with a smile. She was trying to be sweet, he noticed. But it wasn't working. Something thick, black and oily was bubbling just under the surface.

He declined and took a seat across from her.

"Okay. I'm here. I should be at school. I'm way behind on my grades. But I'm here. Can we make this quick?" Carl asked.

"Well, that depends on you." She sipped her coffee and peered over the white foam, her black eyes scanning his face and down his neck. Carl saw a splinter of lust shooting towards him and, in spite of himself, he had a vision of hot sex with this vixen plastered against the back of his eyes like it had intentionally been pinned there.

"Stop it," Carl said.

She tilted her head to the side and gave him a smirk. "You're one attractive professor. Wish I had someone like you when I was doing the University thing. But in those days I loved rogue warriors and mercenaries."

Should I be flattered?

"Anyway, it's more fun when the male doesn't know I've sent the telepathy. So, you're safe, for now."

"I'd like to get this done so I can get back to school."

"To Molly."

"And to her."

"You know you risk her life by being petulant and a little defiant in your attitude, not that I don't enjoy defiant men occasionally," she answered.

Carl stood. "Look, I've told you everything I know. I agreed to take your money and do the research. I've agreed to refund the money. In fact, I'll refund every cent." He reached for his wallet from his hip pocket and discovered he'd left it in his pants at his cottage. It was a fruitless gesture anyway, since he never carried that amount of cash on him. "I'll return it and let's just call it even."

"Not acceptable. I'm still in need of your talents."

"And if I refuse?" he said with his hands on his hips.

"You know this won't go well for Molly."

"Your henchman on standby?"

"No, he was too heavy-handed and had to be dealt with." Glenda studied her red nails. "I was thinking…" she looked over to Jeremy who was on his way to the table with a plate of food. "I was thinking

Molly could stay with Jeremy for a bit. They are, after all, closer in age than you and she. And Jeremy here says he rather likes the girl, don't you, Jeremy?"

Carl ripped his eyes from Glenda's face and stabbed a look at Jeremy, who was watching his aunt, blushing. Then he met Carl's gaze and swallowed.

"You thought I liked men. Well, I do," Jeremy said and tried to smile. He sat himself down and looked at his food. Carl leaned forward, gripping the back of his chair, his fingernails digging into the leather until it hurt. He was about to say something he would regret, so kept his mouth shut and listened, but his insides were fuming.

"He is still experimenting with his sexual identity," Glenda offered. "I think Molly could help him with that, what do you think, Carl? She immune from glamour, or do you think she could take to suggestion as well as you?" Glenda smiled up at Carl but her eyes were stone cold.

"This is pathetic," he said, sneering down at the witch. "You know I have no power in this evil game you are playing. Leave me out of it. I can't do anything but make it worse, for all of us," Carl added, knowing in his heart it was the awful truth.

"Not so, Professor. Not helping me would certainly make it worse, much worse for you and Molly." Glenda leaned across the table almost planting her chest in her cappuccino as she pointed to the chair. "Sit down and shut up. I am only going to ask you one more time and then I'm done with you, with both of you." When Carl didn't move, she added, "Permanently."

Carl deposited his large frame in the brown leather barrel chair across the table from the witch, glancing through the window at the throng of afternoon shoppers streaming along the sidewalk outside. He reviewed options in his head and couldn't find any. He sat tall and inhaled deeply. He remained silent, head slightly tilted, squinting into Glenda's dark eyes.

A faint smile had formed at the ends of her upturned red lips and at the corner of her eyes, as little laugh lines revealed themselves tenderly. He wondered if she knew how much he hated this, and whether or not she liked seeing that.

"Okay, then." She sat back, flicking her dark hair behind her shoulder and running a jeweled white hand with red fingernails through the air dismissively. "I want to arrange a private meeting with Mr. Starling."

"You know what he is."

"Yes, a dark angel."

"So I'm not sure how to contact him."

"You have his phone number, or at least you have the woman's."

"Audray."

"That's the one," she said as if she had temporarily forgotten her name.

"What makes you think he'll come if I call him?"

She smiled, as if he'd asked the one question she was looking forward to answering. "Because, you and I both know, Starling is a hero. Heroes will always show up to save the innocent with no thought to themselves."

"But he's going to protect Audray. He doesn't really care about me," Carl said nervously.

"I don't think Audray is the only woman he cares about. I think he owes you a favor, and Molly too. And then there's the witch in the woods. Do you really think he could stand to see all of them harmed, if he could help it?" She leaned over the table again and held her hand outstretched, motioning with her fingers for his. Carl placed his hand in hers slowly. He instantly felt the electric current of a sexual glam come over him, and in spite of himself, his dick got hard. He tried to pull away but she crushed his fingers with superhuman strength.

Damn it.

"Don't worry, Professor. All I want is a meeting with the handsome dark angel. You can tell him that. I have a question to ask him. If you arrange this meeting, you can tell him he will be free to go afterwards. And I will ask nothing further of you." She squeezed, then let go of Carl's hand which he shook in pain. Glenda smiled. Carl's hand throbbed, but not nearly like his groin did.

"Professor, it's only a small request."

"Why wouldn't you do it yourself? Why couldn't you send Jeremy?"

"Because Starling trusts you. And I can choose where to meet him this way. That part is important to me."

Carl knew that was the catch. "So you've lied about your innocent intentions," he said.

"Meaning I will harm him or try to keep him from being with his woman? Hardly. He's safe." She inhaled and raised both arms above her head as she showed off her ample bustline and slender waist, her hands and wrists writhing in the air above her head. "But my intentions? I assure you they are never innocent."

Starling was not available by phone, so Carl left him a message. He thought the message was so cryptic, he doubted the brave dark angel would respond. He knew he was doing it for Molly's safety, but he still knew at some point he would have to make a stand against this witch, and hoped Molly could give him some help in that department.

"I need to see you, Molly," he whispered into the phone. He could see her sitting on her stool behind the reference desk, her pink ass spread into the folds of her skirts. He wondered what color panties she wore or if perhaps she had gone without them again, something that tented his pants as he sat behind the wheel in his parked car. Was this her glamour, now coming through the phone? New powers? Or was it coming from his own imagination, from somewhere down in the pit of his soul that craved the young witch.

"I was worried when you didn't come by. I can leave early. Are you at home?"

"On my way there now."

"Okay, I'll tell them I'm sick and meet you there, say in thirty minutes? Have to stop by my place to get some things."

Molly, you won't need any things. I want you naked, in my arms.

As if she heard his thoughts, she added, "I bought some new oils I think you'll like."

"Hurry. I need you," was all he could think to say. He rubbed down his fly to calm his erection, but it only made it worse.

"Yes, I can feel that. It's what I love most about you," she said and hung up.

GOOD TO HER word, Carl heard her car drive up just as he stepped out of the shower, his second of the day. He applied the lemon cologne to his cheeks. With the towel wrapped around his slim waist, he opened the door to his redheaded white witch and immersed himself in her scent, the feel of her flesh molding around him.

She reached under the towel and took hold of his cock, squeezing the length of him, moving her hand up and down from his sack to the tip, where she plied her thumb over the smooth surface and spread the droplet that had formed. He pulled her inside and slammed the door, pushing her body against it, kissing her neck and then plowing into her mouth with his tongue. His hands pulled back her fiery hair and he kissed her cheeks, her eyes and then plundered her mouth again. She squeezed his balls and moaned as his cock searched for her flesh. She raised her knit top over her breasts with one pink hand, and kneeled. She unclipped her bra and held her two breasts together, letting his cock root between them as she pushed and squeezed her soft flesh around him. The sight of the tip of his penis protruding through the top of her perfect mounds almost made him come, and he jerked as another drop of moisture appeared.

Molly quickly put his cock in her mouth and sucked the whole shaft of him as he moved in and out of her pink lips. She dug her fingers into his buttocks, pulling him into her mouth. She licked his shaft underneath, encircling his engorged head with her little tongue, flicking into the crease in the middle, seeking more salty moisture.

He would have her right there on the floor, on the towel. He had to have her. She smiled, picking up his thoughts, kneeling in front of him and pausing her tasting. She removed the useless unclasped bra. She licked his bobbing member as she deftly slipped off her panties, but left her skirt on. Her sandals were still strapped around her delicate ankles as she turned around on all fours, lifting her skirt to present her perfectly formed peach of an ass to him. He could see her sex was glistening and wet.

Carl knelt behind her, extending his tongue to the moist slit, tasting the warm honey of her body. He sucked the lips of her as his tongue slipped down across her opening to her clitoris and flicked it back and forth.

"Oh, God, Professor," she gasped.

"You like this when I taste you?"

"Yes. I've wanted to sit on your face all day."

"Nice if I could sit under the counter. You could spread your legs and I could pleasure you for hours while you help people at the desk."

"Yes," she agreed. He didn't think it was such a bad idea, either.

He pulled back and looked at her little ass. He pressed a finger into her peach, noticing it came out wet with her juices. He inserted another finger and heard her howl with pleasure. She moved back to force her opening over his fingers, clamping down with her muscles, then sliding back. Carl's cock pressed into one check and slowly, as he withdrew his fingers, followed the wet trail to her opening. He watched the head of his cock embed itself in the folds of her lips, losing itself in the warmth of her. He spread her cheeks wide and withdrew, lapping around her opening. She quivered as he licked and swizzled his tongue inside her.

Carl placed his cock back inside her. He adjusted his thighs outside of hers as she bent down, her chest on the floor, her ass rising up to meet and accept him. He pushed through to the hilt and almost spilled his seed right there, but was able to stop himself. A few brief seconds they paused, breathing in unison, and then he began to pump her.

He rammed her deep. She spread her cheeks for him to see his entry, driving him to deepen his penetration. He moved her onto her shoulder and raised her leg over him as he pumped her from the side.

He pulled her back onto him as he squatted and she rode his cock with her legs squeezing his thighs as she arched her torso up. She rode him deep.

He leaned back and she continued riding him backwards, raising up and then moving her ass down on top of his groin, as he raised his buttocks to join with her. Her heart-shaped ass rippled and bounced on his thighs. He felt himself twitch as his balls tightened and he began to spill. She ground herself into him as he came. She milked him, squeezed him, devoured him.

He leaned forward and squeezed her breasts, whispering into her neck and back.

"Love you, Molly. Love you. Love you."

"Yes, my love. I love you too."

"Marry me," he said impulsively.

"Ask me again when you aren't deep inside me. I want to see you on your knees in front of me. I want to see your eyes."

"And what will you say?"

"What do you think?" She looked around the top of her shoulder and in her half-lidded eyes he saw his whole world. And the answer he would want to hear.

She climbed off him, rubbing his flaccid member with the towel they had been kneeling on. She drew the towel to her own sex as Carl helped her with his left hand, sliding around the terrycloth towel edge to slip a finger inside her dripping sex. He loved everything about her, how she felt before, during and after sex. He wanted to explore her for the rest of his life, and was sure he'd be as turned on for the thousandth time he claimed her as he was today.

God, that will only take a year. He had plans spanning eighty or more years, whatever she could give him.

"Come, Professor. I need a shower now. I want you to wash me clean. Then I have some special cream that will make you rock hard for about six hours. Does this sound like something you'd like to do?"

"Are you fucking nuts?"

She lent him a hand as he rose, standing in front of her.

"Yes," she said as she leaned into him, pressing her breasts to his chest, letting him feel the slickness still remaining in her opening as she rubbed herself along his thigh. "I am consumed by fucking you. I want to spend my whole day under your body."

"Or on top of it," he answered.

"Yes."

"Or in front of me."

"Yes."

"Or tied spread-eagled to my bed, unable to get up. A slave to my body."

"Yes." She kissed him, her tongue playing with his. Her hands laced down his back and squeezed his cheeks. "I am yours to do with whatever you like."

THE FIRST LIGHT of day shone in through the blinds in his bedroom just as he pumped and expelled his last drop. He had fucked her all night long, literally. He'd lost count at five times. The instant she drizzled the warm oil over his throbbing red member, it sprang to life and would not be denied. He'd caught her from behind as she leaned over to place the little green vial on the bedside table. He buried his head in the steam resident in the back of her neck, where her damp hair smelled of lavender from the shower gel. He bit her earlobe and she squealed, moving her smooth ass into him as he plunged into her again and again.

He'd carried her, impaled on his stiff cock, to the living room and helped himself to her body in front of the fire's dying embers. The golden and orange hues from the fire softly illuminating the cheeks of her succulent rump. Her breasts looked like liquid gold as he grasped them, spilling over his fingers. With each touch they seemed to grow, just as his dick swelled. She stopped him once, tasted him just to the point of climax, then pushed him over the edge as she hungrily swallowed his seed.

He wanted her as he watched her walk to the kitchen to retrieve a glass of ice water for the both of them. He pleasured her with a cold ice cube he placed in her cave with his tongue and lips, and then felt her cool sheath as he screwed her again.

Exhausted, his body writhed and shook with the remnants of his climax, her body arching and moaning below him as he felt her spasms of pleasure. He dropped down on top of her without removing himself, and instantly fell asleep, feeling her fingers lace through the tendrils of his hair. She was whispering a strange covenant in a foreign tongue, over and over again.

"What is that oil you bought?" He asked an hour later as he rose from her steamy body.

"Something Granny gave me. She normally gives it to couples who have trouble conceiving."

"I see." Carl frowned. "Granny is just being sure we are permanently joined I guess."

"No way you're going to get away, Professor." She helped him lay on his back. "Are you tired?"

"Yes." He exhaled and she got up, entering his tiny closet. She came back with several of his silk ties she had placed over her neck, the ends flapping wonderfully against the smooth nipples of her full breasts. He traced a forefinger over one nipple as it fisted into a knot. "What are these for?" he asked as he turned up a small end of one of the silk ties.

"A game." She moved his arm above his head and secured his wrist with one of the ties to the poster just to the side. Then she secured his other hand to the left. She slid down his body, and over the bulge of his still erect cock, then down one leg, where she tied another knot around that ankle and secured it to the bedpost there. She kissed the inside of his thigh, dangerously close to his bulging sack, and then with a hot tongue traced a line from his inner thigh, down behind his knee and down to his ankle, where she adjusted and secured the last tie.

She grabbed a tiny purple jar from the floor and opened it. She smeared a light pink paste over her nipples and he watched as they tightened into little nubs of pleasure. Carl licked his lips as he anticipated being able to suck them. Her sultry dark eyes lowered to her midsection as she rimmed her opening with more of the pink cream. Her body shuddered as a silvery white aura emanated from her flesh, encircling her like a halo.

When she opened her eyes, Carl saw Molly's silvery flesh glowing in the early morning sunlight. Her hair framed her heart-shaped face. The silvery tip of her forefinger dipped into the purple jar and came out with a dollop of the thick pink paste. She stepped off the bed and with her finger let the delicious mixture line a trail on the underside of his cock.

Carl felt a tingling he'd never felt before. His balls swelled, the size of his shaft expanded but the most amazing thing was that his penis took on a white-silvery aura. He felt his pulse all the way to the bottoms of his feet. He wanted so to be buried inside her. She straddled him around the waist and leaned forward so he could get a mouthful of her right breast.

The taste was like mint buttercream candy, and as he sucked and then swallowed, his entire mouth and throat tingled. His tongue became hypersensitive, like he could feel every little pink bump of her plump nipple. He swirled his tongue around in circular motions as he suckled from her. He sighed with satisfaction as she drew back and smiled.

"God, Molly. What is that stuff you've brought here."

"You like?" she said as she leaned in and gave him her other breast.

"Um hum," he said with his mouth filled with her flesh. He licked her peach. "You taste wonderful."

She bent her elbows together, squeezing her tits, then slid down his waist slowly until he could feel his cock at her opening.

"I hope it's glue. I hope you make me stick there all day."

She giggled. "You let me do all the work now. Your hands and feet are constricted. I'll have my way with you now and there isn't anything to stop me."

He saw her spread herself so he could watch his entry. His eyes transfixed on the way his cock spread her lips to the side. He felt her squeeze her opening tight. Every inch was a pleasure all its own. She rocked and vibrated on top of him. She pressed herself over him deep, then drew up slowly and then back down over him again. Her rocking motions and whispers echoed throughout the room, as if they were with an audience. He heard a whisper by his ear, and could feel the moist breath of another being. The bottoms of his feet rubbed against warm flesh. He felt hands on his chest and another set on one of his thighs.

"You have awakened the Eros muses, my love."

"Who are they?"

"They join in our love. Love seekers. Attracted to Eros." Molly whispered something in a strange dialect and heard a multiple whisper response. "It is rare. The first time for me, and many never experience this."

Carl saw a white shimmering hand rub Molly's neck and down her spine as she leaned into it. Another hand squeezed her breasts, first one, then the other, as Molly arched back and closed her eyes. When she opened them again, her green irises sent a light green mist down to his face. He inhaled the sweet identical scent of the paste. A silvery finger traced his lips just before Molly claimed them. His balls tingled as he lurched inside her. An invisible hand had touched and massaged him there. As Molly began to climax, the muses' voices got louder as well. They were the echo to Molly's moans of pleasure as she rocked back and forth, rolling herself forward and back, pressing the nub of her clitoris against root of his cock. As she said, "Yes," there was a hissing of yeses swarming all around him, breathing in both ears. He could feel kisses placed all over his body.

The silvery coating seemed to burn off Molly and at last, when her shuddering was over he exploded inside her. Her pink skin had returned, dotted with a silvery residue. The whispers were gone, and at last, they were alone. She pulled the covers up over them, leaning into his chest and quickly fell asleep.

Carl lay there stunned at what had just happened. He wasn't so sure he liked the idea of the muses in his bedroom, but he was a fan of the paste and the oil. He knew that Molly's granny was the source of it all, and could almost hear her cackling with glee in the distance somewhere.

There was so much to ask Molly. He decided that if he died today, he would have experienced a lifetime of sexual pleasure most men never even dreamed of. He would risk anything, even death, to keep her safe.

His cell phone rang. The distinctive ring told him not to miss this call.

It was Jonas Starling.

Chapter 28

"STARLING HERE," JONAS said to the hello from Carl.

"Um, just a minute, please…" Carl's voice trailed off with rustling sounds in the background. Jonas knew he'd caught the Professor in bed. Carl began mumbling but not into the mouthpiece.

"Sorry, Carl. What was that?"

"I've been asked to request a meeting with you."

"Who asked?" Jonas knew the answer even before Carl said it.

"The dark witch."

"I'm busy."

"Yes, that's what I told her."

The pause worried Jonas. "So what are you not telling me?"

"I've been—we've been threatened, Molly and I."

"Unfortunate." This wasn't something he needed right now.

"More than unfortunate, our lives are threatened if I don't arrange a meeting with you and the witch. She says she has a question to ask of you, and after that, you will be free to go, and my obligation will be over with her."

Jonas chuckled deep in his chest. "You actually believe that cunt?"

"Well, under the circumstances, I have no choice but to deliver the message. But no, I don't believe her."

Jonas could hear the fear resident in Carl's voice. He wanted to help, but his first obligation was to Audray, who had increasingly gotten weaker, after appearing to make the last transition to the

Underworld without any complications. They were running a race against time.

Someone's got to figure out the pregnancy.

"Give me a day to set things up. I need to get Audray out of here for good." Jonas wished he had the vaporization power that was now waning in his queen. That witch would fry, he thought. He inhaled. "Tell her I will let her know tomorrow."

"Right. I'll do that. Thanks, Jonas."

"No. Don't thank me. This whole thing is a mess. There just aren't any safe places anymore." Jonas thought about the many battles he'd been in over the centuries. He'd suffered pain and bled, but never died. Was this now his time? Would he be able to protect Audray and the babe?

Jonas looked down at his feet as a couple of walkers slithered by him, barely touching his hips, one on the right and one on the left, like they knew him. They were headed to his barracks, where Jonas had just come from. The state of his fighting force had never been so confused, but he knew he could count on his men. The girls could take their fun tonight. Tomorrow the battle started in earnest.

"Okay then? I'll talk to you tomorrow," Carl began to sign off.

"Carl. You a good fighter?"

"As in?"

"Have you ever killed anyone?"

"Of course not."

"I suggest you make your peace with Father. And I'd get a gun, too."

"I can't get a gun in one day."

"Yes, you can. Just stop by any high school in town."

Silence. Jonas heard him breathing into the phone. "You really think a gun will protect me?" Carl snarled.

"No. But that and your witch might make you feel a little more prepared," Jonas returned. He could feel the wheels turning in Carl's brain, trying to sort things out, make sense of his dire situation.

"Why me? Do you have any idea why they chose to involve me, of all people?" Carl asked him.

"That's a good question. And there's an answer somewhere, but I just don't have it today," Jonas returned. "Get a gun, my friend. And get ready. This is going to be real ugly."

Jonas flipped his device before he heard Carl's response. He was sure Carl would do his all. But was it going to be enough? Enough for all of them?

He knew there was one person who might be able to help. And he wanted to get Audray back up top anyway.

Jonas strode with purpose down the golden late afternoon streets of the Underworld. The energy of the place always changed as the light settled into darkness. The neon lights started to come on, torches were lit and people's dress began to change. The girls wore less clothing. The guys wore tighter clothing. The distinctive cinnamon scent of Red-X began to permeate the upper level, coming from the bowels of Undertown below. The sexual games were beginning, as they did every evening just as regular as the tides of the ocean in the human world.

He heard flapping above him in the dark orange sky. The outline of a trio of dark winged creatures was hovering above him, circling. They dipped their bodies as if riding an invisible current. Their cawing and squawking like oversized parrots echoed off the sides of the buildings, causing passersby to scurry to the shadows of doorways or dark overhangs. These creatures had been outlawed. Audray had given Father her word. Clearly someone was building them without their Director's permission, an act of open defiance.

Not a good sign.

He climbed the shallow steps to the Directorship building and went into the lobby. The clicking of his boots on the black marble floor buoyed his spirits. He felt the anticipation of battle, something he was born and bred for. He was a revenge machine, softened by the love of a good woman he had rescued from her own wrong turns, but a killing machine all the same. The glory of a good death, he thought while waiting for the elevator, was in knowing he saved someone else dear. And there wasn't anyone more dear to him than Audray and this little life growing inside her. A part of him that would live on after he was long gone. Someone else to carry the torch, protect the innocent, hold back the forces of evil. He wanted to be able to live to see it happen, but that was a need he forcefully pushed out of his mind. No time for that thought now. Now he needed to ready himself.

Audray's office was humming with activity. She had hired new staffers to join her ranks. These newbies weren't to be trusted, but they were necessary insulation. Luke told him she had an organizational chart with job descriptions all laid out. He was tasked with removing those who would not be loyal and hiring staff to fill the holes. There were lots of holes.

Jonas chuckled. *She's young in immortal years, but she's perfect for me.*

And that was the other thing he thought about. A perfect life. He never thought he would ever find it, and still doubted it.

But wouldn't that be something?

Jonas nodded his head to the two guards posted outside her office. These were his men, tested and bred immortally for lethal speed and force. He noticed they had donned war paint and had strips of colored rags tied about their biceps, indicating their family origin. He smiled back to their salutes.

"At ease, gentlemen." Jonas nodded and continued, "I see we are ready for anything. I like that."

The pair grinned. He wondered if part of their joy in commitment was the chance at some form of redemption. All dark angels came to the Underworld through suicide, many of them through risky life-styles, which were considered a form of suicide. Did any of them desire a world free from the evils of this land? Want to make up for the pain and tragedy they had caused others in their human lives?

"I thank you for your service and your sacrifice," he told them. "If we stand together, we will prevail."

"Yes, sir," they said in unison.

"If we go, we go together, like the team we are."

Jonas pushed himself through the double doors and inhaled at the vision in front of him. Audray's blonde hair snaked forward in long curls as her illuminated face poured over the notebook she was reading. She looked up, and he saw the sunlight there.

My love looks more like a Guardian than a dark angel.

Jonas knew there was a time Audray would have been upset with this. He came around the desk, pulling her to her feet and against his chest as he planted a deep kiss on her full lips. He felt her flesh melt into him.

"God, I worry every time you are gone from me," she said.

"You worry about *me*? That's my job, my Queen."

"Let's not argue. We have too much to do," she whispered to his chest.

Jonas took one large paw and held her face, his other arm wrapped around her waist, squeezing her into him tighter. "We are not argu-ing, love. My job is to protect you, not the other way around. That and your body are the only two things I ask you yield to me." He smiled as he saw her blush.

He dropped his hand to her belly. "How goes it, little one?" he said, looking down.

"He's strong, but I'm afraid he's making me weak."

Jonas helped her sit back down. He perched himself with one knee bent, on the edge of Audray's desk, scattered with ringed binders. Audray watched him cautiously.

"I'm reading up on all the rules. They are calling a meeting tomorrow. I can't get out of it."

"Well, you can if you're not here. I don't think you should attend such a meeting."

"Jonas, at some point we have to stand and fight. But let's try exhausting all our other options first. Let them have their say."

"I'm against it. They don't want to reason. It's a delay strategy. It's dangerous, and I think unwise."

"I have to go. It's my job."

He saw in her eyes the warrior heart matching his own. He wouldn't be able to deny her, and he hoped he didn't have to die to protect her, but he would do it in a heartbeat.

"Very well," he whispered back.

THEY CHOSE TO walk home as the night was rolling over them. The two guards would be posted just inside her residence and would wait for reinforcements before leaving in the morning. All four of them walked in silence, though Jonas held Audray close to him with an arm over her shoulder.

The five minute walk to the Director's residence was uneventful. But what bothered Jonas was the fact that each person they passed did not look back at them. He felt Audray sigh at every encounter. Jonas knew then that she was noticing the same thing.

He kissed the top of her head, just as they came to the house. "Not to worry, love. Not to worry," he whispered.

He turned quickly as he thought he heard a sound. The men had become alert as well, one with his hand on a saber he had strapped to his waist. Jonas had seen this warrior train. He could send a twenty pound saber to the center of a man's chest with unparalleled accuracy.

The pair of dark creatures flapped and squawked above them as all four of them entered the house.

"I'm going to ask for additional guards. You two need to stay inside tonight. I need two more at the doors, and another on the roof."

"Yes, sir. Shall I call myself, sir?" the taller, blonde one asked.

"Immediately, soldier. Get them over here while I get her situated upstairs. Then we'll meet."

"Done, sir."

The master suite was on the upstairs level. Jonas followed behind Audray as they scaled the spiral staircase.

"You will need to eat something, I think," he offered.

"Ugh, the thought of putting something in my stomach is totally abhorrent to me."

"I think the baby is depleting your body."

Audray stopped at the landing just outside the bedroom doors and steadied herself before answering. "I think maybe a little soup. Wish I could take a bath, but I'm not supposed to."

"I'll keep you warm." Jonas said as he kissed the side of her face. "Take a shower and get ready for bed. I'll bring up some soup."

AUDRAY DRIFTED OFF to sleep. Jonas had kissed her body softly every place he could reach, massaging her shoulders, neck and her feet. It was still lovemaking to him, though they didn't have sex. His need to bring her relaxation and pleasure outweighed his own need for release. He rose up on one elbow, looking down at her naked body in peaceful repose, noticing the little bulge at her tummy. He rubbed her there, bent and gave his new progeny a kiss.

"You be a good boy and don't mess with your Mum. I've got plans for you, son," he whispered.

He slid down under the covers, wrapping his arms around her waist and felt the heat of her body transfer to his. He willed back to her strength and courage.

He thought back to his discussion with his men. There had been a small attack at the barracks they said was caused by a Red-X junkie who broke through the gate and actually got past several guards before he was restrained.

But Jonas knew it wasn't some random drunk. It was a test to see how their defenses were holding up, and he was sure they didn't quite react as smartly as they should have. But that was fixed now with a swift phone call. With five of his best soldiers protecting them, Jonas was able to fall asleep at last. He needed his strength for tomorrow.

Chapter 29

AUDRAY PUT ON a white long-sleeved silk shirt over stretchy black velvet Capri pants. She'd brought a black low-heeled pair of pumps from the human world she adored. They fit her feet like a glove without squeezing her toes together. She had never had a fondness for stretch pants, leather being more her style, but in the heat of the Underworld and in her new condition, sweating in the skin of a dead animal no longer appealed to her. The shirt covered a hard-to-miss belly she had never, even as a small girl, had.

She put her hair up in a ponytail with a black satin scruncci, and then wiped her hands carefully, examining the tips of her fingers.

"Something wrong?" Jonas said as he slipped behind her and planted a warm kiss on the nape of her neck.

Audray held out her fingers. "They feel different. Like the flames will hurt." She turned around and looked at the tanned face of her lover, who was watching her cherry lipstick covered lips. "Do you think I should try it once before we go? Just in case?" she asked.

"And what if you get injured? Or what if you can't do it again and you need it?"

She wrapped her arms around his neck and pressed against his hardness, "Well, I have you, don't I?"

"That you do," Jonas said as his hands found their way quickly up Audray's back underneath her shirt. They slid around the front and massaged her breasts. "When I get you to the human world, I won't let you wear any clothes. You'll have to stay naked, in my bed, twenty-four seven."

She smiled, blushing. Her excitement at the prospect sent a ripple throughout her body, an electric current arcing between her nether lips. "I'd rather stay home here with you in our bed and skip this meeting." She kissed him, accepting his tongue, enjoying the heat between them.

When they parted after the long sensuous kiss, Jonas whispered, "This isn't home. And it won't even be a place we visit soon if I have anything to do with it."

Jonas led her to the shower and opened the door.

"Try it now, in here," he instructed.

"I have to have something to vaporize."

Jonas picked up a large mottled sponge beside the tub. "Try this."

He placed it on the marble slab shower floor and backed up. Audray stepped forward, holding the glass door with one hand. She held out her other hand like she was going to bounce a tennis ball and released the fire she'd learned to throw. A spattering and hissing sound echoed throughout the bathroom as sparks and tiny flames ricocheted around the shower enclosure, leaving little circles of grey on the glass. Smoke from the half-burned sponge poured up toward the ceiling in dark tendrils.

Audray put her other hand over her mouth and nose to block inhaling the smoke. Then she repeated calling forth the flames. This time there was nothing but a searing pain which overtook the underside of her hand like she'd set it down on a red-hot stovetop. She drew back and looked at the red blistering underside of her fingertips and palm.

Jonas was quick to run cold water over it, but the pain was close to unbearable. Tears streamed down her face as she leaned into Jonas' bulging biceps. He firmly held her wrist under the stream of water at the vanity, allowing the cool liquid to flow over her injured fingers. "What are we going to do? I have no powers left," she sobbed into his powerful arm.

"No, love. You have a little bit of power in your left hand. But only once. You should only do it once. You have to hit something vital to make the statement."

She nodded. He dried her hand gently and then kissed it.

"It should start to heal right away. Be good in an hour," he said.

Audray noticed the pain had already started to subside. "I don't want them to know."

Jonas was swiping away the grey smoke with a towel and didn't answer her.

"So, how long do you think my power will be off?"

He chuckled. "You mean like you didn't pay your bill?"

"Stop it. This isn't funny, Jonas. I'm serious."

"Only thing this changes is you can't indiscriminately fry people. The new you will have compassion." Jonas grinned. "You're the Director after all, and my Queen. You'll play the part of a lady."

Audray thought this was funny. If only some of her past enemies could see her now. Playing a lady. How absurd.

"There's my girl," he said, looking at her smile. He leaned over, planting a kiss on her needy lips. "And I love that now I have to be careful not to hurt you. And you can't hurt me back." He smirked and she stepped on his foot.

THE COUNCIL MEETING was held in a large auditorium built for pageants and theatrical productions. *How fitting.* The drama of the day had taken its toll, though. Audray threw up twice before they could leave the house. *If I have to hurl, let me hurl against that bitch Catari-*

na's face or all over Rupert. Jonas once again whispered in her ear, "Careful of the temper, love."

They entered the hall followed by four of Jonas' finest warriors.

The room was barely populated. A handful of Rupert's guards, including four large black winged angels stood at the back of the room with their arms crossed. Audray thought they looked like a bunch of crows waiting on a telephone pole wire.

Their eyes were half closed, squinting, as if making a point of showing their dislike for the pair.

I feel false bravado. I feel their fear. Jonas nodded his head in agreement.

She turned to one of Jonas' men.

"Get these animals out of here." She pointed to the winged angels who fluttered nervously. There was no objection to them being led out of the room. Jonas' men returned.

The lingering smell of the winged ones was like burned candy. Audray whisked away the pungent odor with her hand waving in the air. She paraded herself with long strides down the center aisle of the room. Her ponytail flapped at her back. She could feel the heat of her hulking lover not far behind. His manly scent soothed her soul.

Rupert and Catarina were seated at one end of a long table, the other end taken up with a dozen dark angels. Audray noted she knew none of them. The others quickly rose and then seated themselves, adjusting fine silks and chains of silver and gold. All of them avoided Audray's gaze, so she turned her sights on Catarina and forced a full smile. Neither Catarina nor Rupert had risen, refusing her the respect she usually commanded.

"How pleasant to meet you, finally," Audray said tersely.

"Likewise," Catarina's dark face tilted to the right as she bowed her eyes, but not her head. "Madam Director."

One of Audray's eyebrows raised. She grasped Jonas' hand behind her back as she turned slightly and addressed Rupert. "You have called this meeting, then, Mr. Blade? And I see you have appointed a council. On whose authority?"

Rupert shot to his feet in reflexive action, his mouth open, his eyes wide and wandering, looking between Jonas and Audray and behind them to the dark guards. Audray didn't want to look, but was certain they had closed ranks and had now blocked the doors.

I never needed a door before. Let them try. She warmed herself with the vision of one of them with a fiery hole in their abdomen as the others looked on. Jonas squeezed her hand, reading her thoughts. She heard a faint rumble in his chest.

"Actually, I am the one who has requested this meeting." Phillip, one of the council members and a former staffer for Peter, stood, holding his hands out to the sides under his red cape as if he was Pope. His unsmiling, pious face softly spat out the words, "I received the request, and since you were absent and I was the only remaining former staff member available, I have convened this meeting. I also represent Mr. and Mrs. Blade."

Audray saw a flicker of discontent in Catarina's face. Her right eye squinted in a flinch, matching a corresponding quiver at the right of the dark woman's upper lip. One hand twitched as her fingers splayed out and then lithely settled back to her lap. Rupert sat down, adjusted himself and placed his folded hands on the table in front of him. Audray thought he looked totally outmatched in a dangerous game of cat and mouse.

"Fine." Audray said, addressing Phillip. "Please," she gestured back to Phillip's chair, "have a seat and let's begin." Audray then sat down, keeping her back ramrod straight, feeling the power and warmth of Jonas standing behind her.

"Mr. Starling. I realize you are not a party to this proceeding. Would you care to stand with the other guards at the side...over..." Phillip began.

"He stays." Audray interrupted. "Let's stop this little game and get on with the bigger one."

Several of the council members then lifted their gaze to her face, one nodding. It was going to be a good show. Audray figured none of them would want to miss a second of it. Phillip remained standing. He opened his mouth to speak, drawing his arms out of the protection of his quivering red cape thoughtfully.

"You may continue, Phillip." Audray smiled.

Phillip's eyes flashed with hatred. The edges were tinged with fire. *He's been playing with the vaporization skill. Well, well, well. Look who wants to be leader?*

It took Phillip a minute to compose himself. Everyone else was focused on Audray. She was glad Jonas didn't extend a hand or do something to show support. It was important for her to exude confidence, strength.

"I have been interviewing the two angels who made it back to the Underworld during the war with Heaven," Phillip began.

"War with Heaven? Just when did that occur?" Audray snapped back at him. "I was present. There was no war. It was a wipeout." Audray sneered.

"According to our witnesses, the poor Director was left in an ambush. They were unable to properly defend him because you intervened," Phillip returned.

"I most certainly did not," Audray stood and shouted to the whole auditorium. "I saw those deformed angels come down on defenseless humans, breathing fire. It was a completely unprovoked attack, planned by the Director himself. I attempted to come to his aid, in fact

I was the one that warned him there could be a fight but he, of course, wouldn't listen. He was trying to slip the human girl to the transport. That's when he appointed me, and I'm sure he expected to survive the little altercation or he never would have done it…" she glared at Rupert and Catarina. "He couldn't wait to get his hands on that little human. He appointed me to replace him in the event he was unsuccessful, so I could seek revenge. I had recently acquired…" Audray shivered thinking about the training she had to go through with the Director, "…the vaporization skill, but had not used it in a real setting. I was a little slow, tried to come to his defense, but the Director was already fried before my fire could throw."

Audray took a deep breath and continued, now fully composed, "And besides, Father himself is the one who terminated the Director. I saw it with my own eyes. They did too. It wasn't prudent to get myself killed with no succession in place." She sat.

One of Jonas' fingers overhung the chair at her back, touching her without anyone seeing. But he was there. He was proud of her, she could tell.

Thank you, my love.

"And Mr. Starling, this is how it happened?" Phillip asked Jonas.

"Oh, you can't ask him. He's been banging her night and day!" Rupert blurted out, earning a scowl from everyone in the room. He looked around at all the angry faces and sat back down.

"Mr. Starling?" Phillip asked, rolling his eyes at Rupert's outburst.

"Yes, sir. I heard Peter give the appointment. Of course, I couldn't know about the other part." Audray could feel Jonas' lie and his blushing behind her. "The Director and myself were not…familiar…at that time." His voice wavered but Audray was sure no one else could tell.

"And did you—seek revenge?" Rupert shot at Audray with a sneer.

"I do not have a death wish, Mr. Blade. I spoke with Father. If he'd wanted to, he could have eliminated me as well," Audray returned. She worked at a cool outer demeanor, but she was gripping the arms of her chair as her red nails dug into the dark wood.

"With all due respect, Madam Director," Catarina began, her tone sugary and sinister, "it is your word against theirs." All eyes were on Audray again. Catarina sat back and waited for her response.

"With all due respect, indeed, Mrs. Blade," Audray strung it out and watched as the label did what a sword could not do, "I'm sure if I removed a body part or two I could get them to change their mind," Audray said.

There was a collective gasp from the other end of the table. Audray continued, "Or, if I promised them I'd give them back their wings, which it appears they have received," Audray pointed to the doors outside, where the winged creatures had gone, "I'm sure I could get them to say anything I desired them to."

One of the younger council members commented, "Phillip, I think that she has a point. No one has ever questioned a sitting Director. Mr. Starling here has verified that succession took place. I see no reason to question his word, but we can call for an election in sixty days." He looked around at everyone seated at the table. "And perhaps that is the only logical solution."

"Yes, well, everyone knows the election is always fraudulent. Just a matter of who wants to cheat enough to win," Rupert added. He looked for approval from his wife and got none.

"I'm for an orderly transition," Phillip chimed in. Audray saw he was scheming to get himself elected. He saw this as a way to challenge Catarina, probably his biggest rival. He was a smart fox, not very brave or dangerous, but a smart one, she thought.

"I, of course, have no objection." Audray agreed.

"Well then, I suggest you meet privately with Mr. and Mrs. Blade," Phillip nodded in their direction but was speaking to Audray, "and see if you can't settle your differences, which would make an election unnecessary. That, ladies and gentlemen of the Underworld, would be best for all concerned." Audray knew the councilman realized he stood a better chance negotiating the Directorship with Audray than he did with Catarina or Rupert.

"May I make a request?" Catarina asked, her dark eyebrows raised, pushing delicate folds into her deep forehead.

Phillip nodded. "Please."

"I think we can resolve this today, and I'd like to request a private meeting with the Director and Mr. Starling, just as soon as we adjourn."

Phillip looked at the other members of the council, most of whom were nodding their heads. A trickle of sweat ran down Audray's spine and into the top of her velvet pants.

Damn. Something's up.

Jonas whispered back, "Careful."

"I see no reason to deny this little request, but I also caution you, we need to call for an election immediately if this meeting doesn't come to a satisfactory resolution." Phillip said.

"I'm sure it will!" Catarina replied, looking at Audray, her eyes sparkling with anticipation like a child in a candy shop. Audray's stomach began to turn over and she choked down a vomit. Catarina had started to look away, but then sliced a glare into Audray's face, then lowered her eyes, raking down the big white shirt to Audray's lap.

She knows, Jonas. I can feel it.

The council waddled from the room. Audray noticed, in addition to the new red cape Phillip wore, two others sported new capes, one in purple and one in a deep copper color. They each had hand stitching and intricate embroidery similar to the Guardian gowns Audray had seen. She wondered if some of the turned Guardians had started a cottage industry.

Audray watched them leave. *Pompous buffoons.* Turning around, she saw the guards remained standing on either side of the doors, nodding greetings to the departing council members.

Rather like pigs through the turnstile at the auction yard in Bakersfield. Once again, she heard Jonas chuckle under his breath. She sighed and held his hand, motioning him to seat himself beside her.

"You are ill?" the wicked woman asked her.

"No. I have some residual effects from our travels through the human world. I spent a good deal of time there, recently," Audray announced. "My system hasn't yet adjusted."

"Yes. I understand you found your mother. How fortunate for you." Catarina smiled.

Jonas let out a loud "humph" and crossed his arms. "Suppose we just get down to what it is you want to say to us," he boomed.

The hatred Audray felt for this woman helped her strength, but then her nerves collapsed and Audray threw up on the table, little pieces of soup and chicken traveling across in a yellow finger of vomit, almost dripping in Rupert's lap.

Rupert stood immediately, wrinkling up his face like a prune. Catarina beamed.

"And so I thought," she said nodding her head. "I got the feeling you were with child. Congratulations." She looked at Jonas. "Sort of changes things, doesn't it?"

Audray squeezed Jonas' hand. *We need help. This isn't going well.*

Rupert looked to his wife and receiving no direction, sat down.

"Well, I think we can wrap things up rather quickly, now. This is better than I expected," Catarina mused, smiling for the first time at Rupert who remained seated, his nose dangerously close to the spreading vomit. His smile was more a reaction to his wife's, but his eyes focused on making sure the awful smelling liquid didn't soil his lap. Seeing the forward motion stop, he gave Jonas a vacant stare.

"I understand Rupert has intentions of running for the Director-ship. If you are asking for an appointment..." Audray was interrupted as Catarina stood, leaning into the table with her fingers pressed into the dull black surface.

"*I* will be the new Director," Catarina demanded. She floated down to her seat with grace.

Jonas was having a hard time keeping a straight face. Rupert looked so green, the vomit appeared to come from his own mouth. Audray noticed his chair was slightly lower than Catarina's. *Some advanced planning here.*

"So, if I pass the Directorship down to you, what will you do for us in return?" Audray asked.

"Allow you to live up top, of course. I won't interfere with the rest of your miserable lives. Jonas will have fulfilled his obligation to his family, you'll be free to go."

"I've heard that term recently and I didn't trust it when I heard it then and I don't now," Jonas retorted. "What guarantees do we have?"

"My word." Catarina smiled sweetly. Rupert, sitting quietly beside her, allowed his eyes to widen and stared back to the mess on the table.

"Not good enough," Jonas added.

Wait, love. Perhaps this is best. Let's get as far away from this place as possible. Rescue as many of your men as you can and let's just flee, be safe.

"Well, I could threaten to tell the council. They could require a physical examination to disprove my findings. How well do you think you'd fare? You'd be declared incompetent to hold the office and would lose by default, on medical grounds."

"So now you're willing to get creative with the rules?" Jonas shouted back.

"No, Grandfather, if I may call you this," Catarina smiled as she delivered the verbal blow, "I have read the rules and there is such a provision."

After a brief pause, Audray was suddenly overcome with nausea again. She sighed, resigned to try to salvage what she could of the afternoon. "Under the circumstances, we have no choice. I will make the appointment official. I'll go back to my office and write it up, attach my seal to it. I'll leave it on my desk, and then we'll depart. You will let us go, and you will promise not to harm our child or interfere with our lives, is that our arrangement?" Audray looked up into the face of the gloating evil woman.

"Almost, not quite." She stood up again. "He," she said pointing to Jonas, "will go and get your seal and the letterhead. You will remain here with me until after he returns."

What do you think? You should go get them. You know where they are.

"I am not comfortable leaving you alone here, unprotected," Jonas answered.

"We wish her no harm. Besides, she is now carrying our bloodline, Jonas. There are rules about that." Catarina paced behind her chair, arms folded into her chest, just like Jonas liked to do.

"Go, Jonas. Bring my things," Audray said as she turned to him. *And then we will get the hell out of here and never return, my love. Please do this for us.*

THEY ALLOWED JONAS leave. As Audray watched his hulking form sprint down the aisle and through the back doors, she ached that he did not turn to say goodbye.

Perhaps he doesn't feel it is as permanent as I do. She was tired of showing her false strength. *Rest, little one. Your father goes to help us. He won't let us down. He never does.*

"Come, my cousin," Catarina said as she drew a slender arm around Audray's waist, helping her stand. "We will retire to our residence, where you can put those feet up. From what I'm told, this is the difficult part of the pregnancy. Although I cannot figure out how in Heaven this ever happened." She twaddled on with words Audray didn't hear.

Audray stopped, separating herself from the dark angel, staring back at the woman who would forever be her mortal enemy.

"That's because this isn't Heaven." It was the only thing Audray was sure of at the moment.

Chapter 30

"I WANT YOU to break into the Director's office," Jonas repeated to his senior Captain of the guard. "She has a red box in the top right drawer that holds her official seals. Take the box and don't tell me where you've put it."

"Excuse me, Sir. This is an act of treason."

"Not if I give the order. Son." Jonas had sponsored Omar nearly a century ago. The young man had lost his entire family during the Great World War, and with them, lost his will to live. Jonas' opportunity was something the man didn't have to think very hard about before he made the decision to end his life and become a dark angel. "I won't let you take the fall, if it comes to that."

"And I won't allow it. I just want to know why this is so important."

"It doesn't matter except that I say it is. When I get to the Director's office, I need to find it broken into and the seals taken. You understand?"

"You are buying some time. Is the Director well?"

"Very. But Omar, we both are counting on you. A lot is riding on this."

"Consider it done."

JONAS GAVE OMAR as much time as he dared to set his little ruse. Nearly a half hour later, when he ran up the shallow steps of the

Directorate, past the reception area, he was not stopped until he got to the elevator. One glare at the guard who came for him and he was left untouched. He traveled to the top floor, opened the doors and immediately saw the anteroom empty, but the door to Audray's offices ajar. The surveillance video camera was ripped from the wall. Inside her office, papers were thrown in all directions, drawers of the black desk pulled out and emptied. Omar had done a good job making it look like a small time thief had outsmarted them all. Jonas knew the story wouldn't hold up for long, but it might give him enough time to get Audray away.

AUDRAY PICKED UP Jonas' call on the first ring.

"Jonas, are you all right?" she asked. She was seated on a bright red flowered couch, legs propped up on a pillow. A young Chinese woman was giving her a foot massage. Catarina supervised.

"Yes, but we have a problem."

Audray sighed and sent him a message. *Jonas, I don't want to be here one more second. Things are not what they seem.* "Problem? Please explain the problem," she said as she looked into Catarina's scowling black eyes.

"Your office has been broken into. It has been cleared out. Everything is gone."

"What? Do you know who did this?" *Please, love, tell me you are not responsible.*

"No, but I have some clues. I've been followed recently, and I think they were looking for an opportunity when they knew we both would be gone."

Audray spoke to Catarina, who stood and held out her hand to receive the phone. "Jonas says someone broke into my office and removed..." she spoke back into the phone, "Jonas, they removed everything. My music box?"

"Give me the fucking phone." Catarina grabbed the device from Audray's hand. She screeched into the phone. "You better not be responsible for this. Whoever did this will be vaporized immediately, even if it's you, Jonas."

Audray could hear Jonas' response. "I completely understand and agree. But I am not to blame. I'm going to need more time. I'll come to pick up Audray so she can get some rest in her own bed while I go look for the criminals. One of my men has a good lead."

"Audray shall stay here. She can just as well sleep under the protection of my home, my guards. No one can touch her here."

Including me, Audray heard his thoughts.

"Take a day or two, but not longer. Audray will be safe here. I'll catch her up on all the family history. Would you like that?"

"Not necessary."

"On the contrary. She needs to know what kind of a family she's getting involved with."

"She knows."

"Very well. You need any of my guards to help? They are very good with interviewing suspects, although sometimes it is a bit messy."

Audray envisioned a child pulling the wings off flies.

"No thanks. But I could use Rupert's help."

"Whatever for? Rupert is completely helpless."

"One of his men is responsible, I fear. I think he would be an aid in the investigation."

There was a long pause before Catarina answered. "I'll have him meet you at your barracks with two of my guards who will keep an eye out for both of you."

"Can I talk to Audray, please?"

Catarina handed the phone back to Audray and stormed up the stairs in search of Rupert, pushing the Chinese girl ahead of her.

"Your music box is safe." Jonas whispered. Audray's breathing was shallow and irregular. She exhaled through her mouth. Jonas asked, "Are you crying, love?'

"No."

"It's going to turn out. Have a little faith."

"I have all the faith in you. I have so little in me." She sniffled. "What can I do to help? Is there anything I can do, Jonas?"

"Make sure Rupert comes to see me. Ask him if he can help us somehow."

"The guy is a snake."

"On a very short leash. And he knows he's about to be cut loose. She's a nasty one, Audray. Not to be trusted. Sorry to say we share the same blood."

"I don't believe it."

"Well, the important thing is, she does. As long as you carry my child, she won't harm you."

"I'm not so sure of that."

"Are you feeling well?"

"I've been lying down, having a foot massage. I'm surprised Catarina's left me alone."

"That's good. She's beginning to trust you. She knows you were going to give her what she wants and had nothing to do with the break in."

"Did *you*?"

"I didn't break in, no."

"That's not what I asked."

Jonas paused and then answered. "I was nowhere near the office when it happened. I don't know who did it, but I have some good guesses. That's all I'll say." Jonas let his words sink in. "Love, I need to go. Try to meet with Rupert, if you can. Alone."

"Will do. Take care of yourself."

"Take care of the little one, and this will all be over soon."

JONAS FLIPPED THE phone shut. Omar and his men approached, armed to the teeth.

"Sir, we heard about the robbery."

Jonas, grateful Omar hadn't let the others in on their little plan, told them, "Catarina is holding the Director hostage until we can recover her seals. These are not replaceable."

Omar looked at the pink music box tucked under Jonas' arm. "Sir?" he asked, pointing to the box.

"It has a special meaning for her. No value." He switched the box to the other hand. "I overheard a group say the vandals transported to the human world. Did you see anyone come up toward the transport station?" Jonas continued with the ruse.

"You know, sir, I didn't think of it at the time, but, yes, I was making my rounds and saw a band of three running. And they had a satchel with them. Looked like a yellow transport bag the Guardians use," answered Omar.

"Hmmm." Jonas looked at the ground, trying not to laugh. He was going to give Omar a piece of his mind, but later, and if they all survived the battle. Stupid to implicate a turned Guardian. *What the bloody hell was he thinking?*

AUDRAY MET RUPERT as he raced through the entryway. Catarina was shouting to him in Portuguese from their room. Rupert had one ear to her while he nodded to Audray.

"Can I talk to you?" Audray whispered.

"Dangerous. This whole thing is getting out of hand. She's got twenty-five new warriors arriving in the viewing room within the hour."

Audray wrinkled up her nose. "A mass suicide."

Rupert nodded. "Your Jonas has asked for me.

A loud scream punctuated the air as a fireball tumbled down the stairs. Audray realized it was the little Chinese girl, who had burst into flames. What was left of her head and feet lay in a puddle of black blood dripping off the bottom step.

"She's kind of getting postal now," Rupert said as he stared at the bloody scene with detached resignation. His body was quivering in fear, although Audray could see he was doing his best to compose himself.

"So, Rupert," Audray said, "You see what's in store for you? How long before you think this could be your body laying here?"

Rupert's shaky tone belied his words. "She won't harm me." Audray noticed he would not return her gaze. She stepped closer, which revealed the fear he could not hide in his eyes.

"Search your soul, Rupert. Look at her. She was a trusted servant of your wife's. A confidante as well. When will she find you expendable? Just ask yourself that question."

Rupert shuddered as Audray reached out to touch his arm. He was sweating, his left eye twitching and his face pale like he could vomit. At last he looked up the stairs to see if he was being watched, then looked down on Audray.

"What do you want? I am as trapped as you are."

"I can help you, but only if you help Jonas. Please, Rupert. The time is approaching where you'll not have the choice. You could be next. You know this. This is your chance to be free permanently from Catarina's grip."

He nodded, resigned.

"Now go. Go help him, please."

Rupert dashed out the front into the yard, leaving Audray leaning into the dark oak door embedded with etched glass. He grabbed two winged ones who were standing guard at the gate. All three disappeared down the cobblestone road and out of sight. Audray closed the door and leaned against it, with her eyes closed.

Love, he knows his time is short. He is bringing two of their minions, but he is not a warrior and I don't trust he'll do anything heroic."

She opened her eyes, and found Catarina staring back at her with dark eyes filled with hatred. "You flirt with my husband."

Audray tried to make light of it, but her nerves were frayed. She shook her head. "You honestly think Rupert is my type? I mean look at Jonas, and then look at Rupert. No comparison."

"Hmpf," Catarina returned.

"You forget. Before you came here I carried on an affair with his brother, Peter. Every time I look at Rupert's face, I think of all the disgusting things I had to do to that angel to have a chance at the Directorship."

"Yes, I've been told. Would have given anything to see it." She eyed Audray up and down. "You are nauseated still?"

"No. I'm fine. But tired."

"So why didn't you have Peter's child? You were....intimate...with him?"

"What a cruel twist of fate. You mean he never told you? Peter said he had been fixed as a human man. Those sorts of things transfer completely to the Underworld. Like plastic surgery, enhancements, that sort of thing. But regardless, I think what Jonas and I share is a one in a million. Fate, you might say."

"Makes no sense he would cut his manhood."

"There was no man there, Catarina. He was a boy inside a man's body. He didn't want to share the limelight with anyone, even his own kind."

"Then I suppose it's good he's dead." She studied Audray's face. "I would have had to hire someone else to eliminate him, of course."

Of course. Who could let a little rule about killing one's own family stand in one's way? Jonas was completely right. This woman could never be trusted, and anyone who got too close to her would burn in the Underworld.

AT THE BARRACKS, Rupert and the two winged angels appeared just outside the gate, not willing to ask permission and not willing to break in. Jonas came swiftly with Omar and four of his men.

Rupert glanced into all their faces. Jonas saw some intimidation resident there. "I have been sent by my wife." The statement caused a slight twitch in his left eye.

"Looks like there were three of them, and they went up to the human world. Rupert, I will need to go after them. But I cannot take these," Jonas pointed to the oversized dark angels who immediately shot a worried look to Rupert. Their wings flapped as if in irritation.

"Well, I don't believe they went up top," Rupert spat out. "Who saw them?"

Omar stepped forward. "Sir, I saw the three on their way to the transport station." He glanced at Jonas before adding, "They carried a yellow canvas satchel."

Jonas winced and swore under his breath.

"This is significant?" Rupert asked, looking back and forth between Jonas and Omar.

"Well, sir, they had a Guardian's bag, sir." Omar bowed his head and stepped back.

"So they were trying to definitely transport something to the human world. That what you're saying? Why the fuck would they want the seals?" Rupert shook his head. "I don't understand it."

"You underestimate their value, Rupert. An order affixed with these seals becomes instant law. Have you considered perhaps you and Catarina are not the only ones lusting after the Directorship?" Jonas said, hoping Rupert would take the bait.

"You've seen this with your own eyes, not been told of it?" Rupert directed his question to Omar.

Omar nodded confirmation, but Jonas could see he was having difficulty with the lie. "Well, there you have it. Looks like we are off on a fishing expedition," Jonas concluded.

"Not so fast. How the hell are *we* going to find them?"

"I have some friends who are friendly with Guardians. This sort of thing wouldn't happen with a Guardian transport bag unless they knew," Jonas offered. "Omar, you stay here and run things while I'm gone. I'll take you three and we'll leave now. Rupert, are you coming?"

"No. I've been asked to carry out a private mission, so I will be delayed. But then I'll join you in the search." Rupert leveled a gaze at Jonas.

Jonas could not risk further discussion of Rupert's plans, but was left with no option but to trust him. "I hope that you will return to protect what is in your best interest?"

The two men locked eyes again. Jonas hoped what he saw in Rupert's expression was resolve to do the right thing. But he knew it was a huge gamble.

"It is my vow," said Rupert.

Jonas and the three men ran for the corrugated iron shed of the transport station just at the end of the street. Before he slid back the steel door, Jonas stole a look at Rupert, who was talking on his cell phone to someone.

He hoped it was Audray, telling her Jonas was leaving the Underworld in one piece. Perhaps that would bring her one night of rest after all.

He got her message just as the transport limo door slammed shut. *Come back soon, Love. Go get Josh. He is the only one who can help.*

And that was what he had already decided to do.

Chapter 31

JOSH DIDN'T APPEAR surprised to see Jonas. He was playing chess with little Judy, who stiffened when she saw the dark angel.

"Didn't expect to see you playing chess, Miss."

Judy shot a guilty look at Josh, who stared into the empty tumbler by his seat at the table.

"I take it Melanie is not here?" Jonas asked him.

"Correct, my feathered friend," Josh said to the tumbler as he slurped the last of his drink. "I'm afraid I'm not a good bet, Jonas."

Jonas didn't want to acknowledge Josh and Judy had been getting it on, but he could smell the sexual tension. It wasn't his place to judge his former mentor. Josh's defect of character was deep in some regions of his soul, just as his sense of right and wrong was unshakable in others. Jonas was hoping the right combination would be with them today.

Josh walked over to Judy, pulled her up to standing and whispered something to the side of her face Jonas could not hear. She giggled and exited to the upper floor. Josh watched her ascend the metal stairway like it was his last taste of forbidden fruit.

Without looking at Jonas, he addressed him, "You've come here asking for my help. Can you see what a muck up I make of my own life? What the fuck do you want with the likes of me?"

"Josh, I don't judge this."

Josh held up a glass to Jonas, who nodded. "No doubt about it. I've missed those dark angels and what they can do." He shook his head as he poured their drinks. "I just can't leave them alone. I'm a deeply flawed individual, Jonas."

"Who seems to stumble upon doing the right thing more than one would guess. Josh you are *exactly* who we need. You are all I've got left. This fight will come to you eventually. If not today, next month, next year. There's a whole takeover being staged, the likes of which I've never heard about."

"Thought all that died with Peter."

"Peter was the test run. He was the pawn in this chess game."

"So who are the king and queen?" Josh asked as he handed Jonas his drink.

"Catarina, my twenty times great granddaughter, and her husband, Rupert Blade, Peter's brother. But I know Catarina is the one calling the shots, and Rupert is just her expendable pawn in this game. She has a desire for power the likes of which I've never seen before, Josh."

Josh took another sip and nodded. "Go on."

"Well, I think Rupert can be an ally. I think we can use him."

"What about all the stuff happening up top?

"It's like there are two factions, one below and one up top. They both want the same thing. I can't figure if they are working with each other or against each other. Catarina alluded to having help, but I don't really know."

"Let's hope they're not working together." Josh sat and motioned for Jonas to take the other red leather chair.

"I've made an appointment to meet that witch in an hour at Carl's pleading. Do you think I am in any danger?"

"Hardly, Jonas. But in her delicate condition, Audray is. And of course the other humans, me included, would be. So I'm grateful you didn't make this little rendezvous at my house."

"I wish I didn't need your help so much, sir. I'm meeting her to avoid all that, if possible.

"So what have we got?"

"They're holding Audray down in the Underworld. I escaped with a ruse they won't believe for long. I need you to assemble some people we can trust, like you did when we got rid of Peter. Since you've done Father a favor, can we count on him?"

"Only one who talks with him directly these days is Doris, the heavenly Guardians' taxi driver. I can call her. We can ask. Tell me what you want to have happen?"

"We just want to give up everything down there, live up here, if we can. At least until the baby is born. See if we can figure a way she can survive this pregnancy."

"Well, if the universe as we know it is screwed, that will be the least of her problems."

"You that pessimistic about the future? Honestly?" Jonas had never seen Josh so forlorn.

Josh's quick glance upstairs told Jonas he didn't have much time.

Jonas asked Josh the question that had been burning a hole in his stomach. "Just between the two of us. You ever know Claire and Audray were sisters?"

"Not. A. Clue. Still surprises me. Claire was so pure of heart. Still is. Audray, just was so—" Josh fretted, looking for the right word like he was sucking on a lemon. "So very preternaturally bad. She was made for the jobs I gave her."

Jonas gave him a fiery stare, fisting one of his hands on his knee.

"You know this to be true, man." Josh acted like he hadn't noticed, but Jonas was sure he did.

"Until now. She's changed, Josh. I like to think she's reverted back to her natural self that was altered, kicked around and damaged. The best part of her is coming out now. Maybe that's all Father needs to hear."

Josh stood up and stretched his back. "He doesn't work that way, Jonas. He's a bit asleep at the switch."

Jonas had heard the stories. He doubted Josh was correct. "I hear free will is a big thing to him."

"Yup. But I honestly don't understand how he decides to save this one, let this one fall."

"Maybe because he has all the time in the world."

"Could be. Maybe he believes time is his friend, not ours, but his." Josh stretched his arms out behind him like a cat.

"Make the call, Josh. I haven't got a lot of time. Neither does Audray." Jonas stood in front of the former dark angel, not wanting to intimidate him, but wanting him to know he was serious. "If you ever cared anything for Audray or me, you'll do this. I don't expect you want to save the world, but you'd be doing that too."

Josh laughed heartily. "Always up to me, isn't it? I'm so indispensible now as a human. Hated as a dark angel, I can't even be a normal fuckin' human. My appetites exceed my common sense. Like I said, I'd not bet on me."

"I have to. You're my last recourse. Otherwise we run, and how long do you think that would last, hmmm?" Jonas asked and stepped back. "Come on. Make the call to Doris right now. I'll go somewhere and give you guys some time while we wait. But hurry, man. You saw how sick she looks. And you know what they'll do if I don't get back down there soon."

"Very well."

Jonas watched as Josh pushed two numbers on his phone. It was a black sleek model he'd not seen before and suspected it might be some special hotline to Heaven. Josh cleared his throat, looked upstairs at little Judy, who appeared in one of his tee shirts that didn't cover the juncture of her legs. Josh gave her an appreciative glance and held up his forefinger.

"Love? This is your former dark angel boyfriend." He laughed as Doris squawked on the other end of the line. "No, I can picture it, but sorry darlin' we never had that chance." He cleared his throat again and rolled his shoulder. "I need you to get here as soon as you can. Your audience is requested." He listened again to something she was telling him.

Jonas couldn't tell what was being said, his heart was stuck in his throat.

"Jonas. Audray's Jonas. He's right here in my living room."

Josh listened.

"She's in the Underworld, babe. Held hostage."

Jonas could hear the squawking echoing throughout the living room. Judy disappeared with a sigh. Josh squinted and scratched his scalp.

"Babe. Look. Maybe this will change your mind. Audray is pregnant." Barely two seconds went by before Josh closed the phone and nodded. "Well, Jonas, you got your audience. She'll be here in an hour."

"Thanks. Look, I'll step outside and wait in the car."

"Not necessary," Josh said.

"But it's respectful. And that's what I want to be. Respectful. And thankful." Jonas shuffled through the living room, the kitchen and out the screened porch to the driveway. The wind blew, giving him the chills. He saw faces in the greenery that bordered Josh's rear yard, as if ghosts of dark angels and lost souls hung out around his house still, hoping for a second chance like Josh got. He figured it was his imagination.

True to Josh's word, Doris parked her cab right behind the Hummer. Her door squeaked as she extricated herself from behind the wheel. She stood before him after removing her cabbie cap to scrunch up her hair, which was flaming red, looking like Halloween straw in a candy corn basket of goodies. She replaced the cap. The deep brim cast shadows over her dark eyes. They were overly made up, her nail polish chipped but bright red, like the other times he'd seen her. He expected her to be angry with him, and he braced for some kind of blow. But her forehead was lined with folds that told him she was worried.

He started to say something, and she put her forefinger up to her mouth and summoned him inside.

They heard music echoing up the two-story living room, a light harp music with occasional accompaniment. The bedroom door upstairs was closed. Jonas saw Doris had made a note of it as well. She shrugged and gave him a smirk. "Everyone down here complains how fast things change. They don't really change at all down here. They never change in Heaven, either. I mean, day by day the same drama, the same bliss, the same orders and rescind of orders. Just like when I was in the military."

"I thought you had some training, with that flamethrower you carry in your transport."

"Oh that? I got an RPG now. Father doesn't know." She hit her forehead. "What the fuck am I talkin' about? He knows everything." She put her palms together and looked to the ceiling. "Sorry, old man, just couldn't help myself." She dropped her hands and chuckled. "I take certain liberties, as you've seen before. And here I am making fun of things, when the fate of the world hangs in the balance."

"Which is a change," Jonas whispered.

"NOT. HARDLY. It's always at stake. And somehow it always works out. So that's why I stay on the side with Father. Somehow it works out up there. Oh yeah, there are a lot of tears, hand wringing. You guys don't see the half of it!"

Jonas wished he had more time to spend with the little feisty cabbie Guardian angel.

"These girls are the most emotional beings in the universe. Falling in and out of love, trying to be perfect, gossiping, looking for eye candy in a world that restricts that. You'd think he'd learn. Only human nature, and these angels take with them some of their humanness, though The Wash strips it out. But it doesn't strip out everything."

"Okay, so did you know Audray and Claire were sisters?"

"Yes, I did."

"You never told Claire?"

"Wasn't allowed. Not that that is the big stopper for me. What good would it have done? Would have just messed up everything, or at least made things more complicated for her and Daniel."

Jonas must have looked puzzled.

"Figure it out, Jonas. Audray was Daniel's girlfriend before he met Claire. Claire is now his wife. Daniel got to sleep with both of them?"

"Oh."

"Look, I'm sorry if this is a needle in your gut."

"No. You're right."

"So can you imagine the family gatherings they'll have?" She tossed her head back and laughed so loud her cabbie hat fell off.

"You haven't seen mine." He was thinking of the Court and the women he had bedded there. "We both have a past."

"I'm thinkin' it was Father's plan all along. There really aren't any accidents, Jonas. Or are you just figuring that out?"

The upper bedroom door opened and Josh stood with his shirttails out barefoot, in jeans. "Hey there, sexy!" he called down to Doris.

Doris took a sniff of the air. "I smell forbidden love."

"Not!" Josh said as he danced down the stairway. "Wonderful to see you, dear."

They embraced, Josh kissing her on both cheeks, but Doris stepped back afterward, keeping her distance from the former dark angel "So, what's the plan?"

Jonas took his palms from his front pockets. "Audray wants to abandon the Directorship."

"The throne," Josh corrected.

Doris' face puckered and she spewed, "What the hell has gotten into all of you? You think Father is going to insert himself in this fray? Audray made her bed." She wiggled her eyebrows at Jonas. "Now she can lie in it."

"But the baby? The baby is innocent! You going to sacrifice the child?"

Doris sighed and sat down. With her elbows on her knees, slightly leaning forward, she angled her head and said, almost as if it caused her pain, "He hates that."

"Audray's body is changing. We've consulted some—" He wasn't sure he should tell her about the visit to the witch's cottage. "Some have told us she will die, and perhaps the baby too. We need information. We want to know so we can plan."

"We need a fuckin' miracle, is what we need," Josh muttered. "And I need another drink." He poured himself another tumbler and took a seat on the arm of the couch Doris sat on.

Jonas paced back and forth while scrubbing the back of his neck with his fingers.

"Doris, sweetheart, what do you think?" Josh asked in his most charming voice.

"Well, let me ask this. Jonas, what does Audray want?"

"To raise our child. To just live. To get to know her sister as her sister. We're done with things down there."

Doris was thoughtful.

"What aren't you telling us, Doris?"

She smiled. "I'm on your side, Jonas. I was always on Claire's side too, but then I had a better reason. I'd like her to get to know her sister as her sister. Yes, I would."

"What is it, then?" Josh knelt in front of the little cabbie.

"I can't, guys. But just know I'm on your side. I'd better get out of here and deliver the message." She bypassed Josh after gripping his shoulder, righted herself and walked toward the kitchen for the back porch door. "You lay low for awhile, if you can. Be safe. I'll see what I can do. In the end, it isn't up to me. But be smart. Make worthy decisions." She began to exit to the porch and then turned and addressed Josh, "And Josh, stay away from dark angels and their glamour for a few days. It's coloring your judgment and making you drink too much."

Chapter 32

JONAS FOUND THE coffee shop downtown and spotted Glenda immediately. His experience was nil when it came to witches, but he'd met his share of crafty, powerful women and she fit the bill right down to the deep burgundy low-cut dress worn to distract him. She might have been his type years ago. About two hundred years ago. He thought it odd that women underestimated a true man's self control. Not everything was animal instinct. Some women were just evil, and she was certainly one of those.

She rose, obviously pleased with herself for having snagged his attention. He focused on her eyes, remembering what Josh said, that he wasn't in danger. He could try to glamour her, but she probably had resources for that, so he played it straight.

"Let's get this over with and then you can stop preying on my friends."

"Ah, the professor and his woman. How nice. You are a true hero, just like your biography says."

"Fuck my biography. Can we just cut to the chase?"

"Please." She motioned to the highbacked chairs. They sat with a table between them. She had a mug with a teabag hanging down the side. "What would you like to drink?"

"I'd like a taste of my own freedom if you don't mind. Let's just get to the point. I am running out of time."

"Yes, I'm aware of that." She sipped her tea, not taking her eyes off him. "I'm sorry to say you have a paramour, but then, we wouldn't be talking today if you and Audray weren't a couple."

Jonas shrugged, getting impatient. He watched the street. He felt his control waning, and it wasn't coming from her powers. He was literally running out of time faster than he liked. He had not heard from Audray for several hours.

"Jonas, I might be in a position to help you."

That got his attention. He stared at the woman who seemed to enjoy his surprise.

"I've made an alliance with your great granddaughter. I'm sure by now you've figured that out."

"I suspected."

"I had to do certain things—things I wasn't happy doing. But I did them because I was directed to get you and Audray down to the Underworld so you could have a meeting with *her*."

"I'm listening."

"And it worked. But, I'm not stupid and I understand the woman is desperate to get her hands on the Directorship. However, I don't think it will stop there. She's asked for my support in taking control of the human world. I'm not sure this is a good plan. Or perhaps, there is still a little suspicion in my dark soul that this might cause some action on higher levels." She pointed to the ceiling.

"You mean the balance."

"Yes. She wants more than I think she'll get, ultimately."

"And if you fail to help her get that, she'll turn on you."

"Exactly. And she is more powerful than I."

Jonas nodded, examining his fingernails. Dare he begin to hope that perhaps one of his enemies could become an ally? He'd seen his share of double-crosses, so he held himself back from too much hope.

"As are you, Jonas," she continued.

"You know I do not have the vaporization skill she has."

"I have seen her winged creatures. Frightening. Hard to miss. Stirs up too much attention in the human world, and that is why I think she'll fail."

He didn't want to show his pleasure with this comment, but it was impossible to mask. "Really? You think she will fail?"

"Maybe not fail, perhaps bridled? Clipped? Let's just say I don't think she'll be able to deliver on her promises. I don't want the power. I want the protection."

"Then stop making alliances with the wrong people."

"I didn't even know about you until Catarina contacted me." She looked down at her burgundy fingernails. "I did a little research, and what I found was, well, interesting. So I dug deeper and that's when I found out who you really were."

"So why am I here?"

"I am in need of protection."

"I protect those worthy of protection."

"Is the safety of your lover and your baby enough for you? Or would you suggest something more worthy?"

That hit Jonas in the gut. "How can you guarantee she'll be protected?"

"I can't. You know that. But when the time comes, perhaps I can be another ally."

Chapter 33

CARL HAD TAKEN Jonas' warning to heart and wandered into a gun shop, hoping to purchase something for protection. He was informed of the waiting period.

We could all be dead by then.

Suddenly, he received an urgent message from Molly. *They've come for me. Stay away.*

There was no way Carl was going to do this.

When he arrived at the glass and metal structure built into the tall pine trees, he realized he'd been too late. Carl sprang from his car and dashed towards the doors to the library, which had been blown off. Crystals of shattered glass littered the lawn in front, as well as the cars and blacktop in the nearby parking lot. He could hear sirens wailing in the distance.

Carl's stomach contents almost erupted as he found blood spatter over the front desk, over the floor where people had run, slipped and fallen in pools of it. Several young bodies lay at unnatural angles on the cool granite tile. On his way to the reference desk he was already murmuring, "No! No!"

The place seemed vacant. Then Carl heard a message playing to his ears and his ears only. *Get Granny*, Molly's faint voice told him. *I'll be okay for now, but get Granny.*

Where are you, sweetheart?

Get out. Something's coming. Get out and get Granny.

Carl looked into the small wired window to the vacuum sealed and temperature controlled stacks room and saw a smudge of blood *on the inside.*

The door was shut, which meant it was locked. Several large gouges like those made with an axe were embedded in the wall and the door itself, but the lock had held. He could see they had gone for something stronger, and they'd be back to finish the job.

Through the wired window he saw her. She ran to him, tears streaming down her face. "Tell me how I can open this," he shouted.

"You can't. You must go get Granny."

He looked at her hand, which appeared to be bleeding. "Are you okay?"

"Yes. Yes. Go, Carl. I don't want you here when they come back."

"I don't want to leave you alone!"

Prefer you leave me alone. Safer. Go!!! Her telepathic message screamed in his ears.

Carl ran toward the stairwell to the staff exit. On the wall by the exit sign he saw a fire safety box with its glass shattered and contents splayed over the floor, including a fire extinguisher. He burst through the metal doors and flew downstairs, past the small coffee shop that was now abandoned, chairs overturned in what proved to be an obstacle course. Carl pushed on the metal bar to the door outside. The whoosh of warm fresh air filled the room as he tasted the possibility of freedom.

Making a long arc around a mound of grass and trees in a park-like sitting area, he doubled back to the parking lot and jumped into his car. Checking his rearview mirror, he didn't think he was followed, but couldn't say for sure.

Carl wondered if he should have checked the sky. Since this was a powerful black witch they were dealing with, did that mean she traveled by broom?

He knew exactly what direction he was headed, but wasn't completely sure how to get there.

Or if he'd be in time.

Chapter 34

AUDRAY WAS AWAKENED by sounds in the bedroom Catarina had banished her to. Fearing at first that someone had broken through the security to do her or the baby harm, she was surprised to see Rupert bent over and obviously trying to carefully tip toe toward her outstretched body on the bed.

"Shh. Audray. We don't have much time," he whispered.

"What's going on, Rupert?"

"I'm getting you out of here. We're going up top, where we think you'll be safer."

"What about Catarina?"

"She's newly created, Audray. Not sure if you remember your first days—"

"Who could forget them?" she whispered back. Her need for sexual conquest was off the charts and made it difficult to concentrate as a newly created dark angel in the Underworld. She rose and began to bunch pillows under the coverlets to make it look like she was still asleep. "So what's happened?"

"I plied her with some Sexual Apricot. A lot of it, by the way." He grimaced. "She's still learning about moderation. It got her so wound up, she passed out at Helena's. One of my men just brought me the news."

Audray wondered if it mattered to Rupert that his newly created dark angel wife probably had an appetite for anyone willing to have sex with her and wasn't going to be very discreet about it. "Are you okay with this?" She wanted to be reassured he was a true ally.

"Does it look like I have a choice?"

Rupert's breathing was labored. He was distracted and Audray could tell he was paralyzed with fear. This didn't make him an ally. She knew he'd run as soon as he had a ghost of a chance at survival. Audray knew they were running out of time, and knew he'd never stay for the fight. "How long will she be out?"

"Not long." With a moan, he added, "I imagine she'll wake and look for someone to burn over it." He pointed to his chest. "And I plan to be up top hoping to disappear or get a second chance."

"You get me out of here, and we'll do all we can. I can promise you that." She hoped the reassurance would ease his nerves enough to help him concentrate on the plan he'd devised.

He had brought a bright red cloak, which wasn't inconspicuous but was one of Catarina's, and if Audray was covered from head to toe the population would probably think it was the evil woman herself. Audray knew Catarina's cruelty had already begun to create rumors.

The stone streets were wet with the smell of Red-X and other exotic spices, as well as a healthy dose of human fluids of all kinds. Audray's nose began to twitch and she felt a sneeze come on, which wouldn't have been wise. She held her nose and huddled into the cloak as they scurried up the steps to the transport. Sounds of equipped men behind her at first worried her, but then she saw Rupert give them hand signals as they scattered out and created cover to the sides and behind them while a couple of Jonas' men scouted out front.

She could see the gray transport warehouse looming large from the top of the landing steps and for an instant felt relief, until she heard the screech of dark angels as they flapped their shredded black wings like bellows in an executioner's dungeon. One of them reared his head back as if he were going to shoot a fireball, treading air with the wings arched behind him. He was caught in the chest with a blast from one of Jonas' men and dropped in a heap, creating a huge ball of flames. The companion dark creature swung low and nearly clipped the cloak right off of Audray. She looked into his bloodied red eyes and saw recognition. Instead of charging at her further, he righted himself and began to take off toward Undertown. Fearful he'd report her escape, Audray pressed her right palm to the sky and a sputtering laser flash hit the bird in the eye, exploding his head as he too dropped to the ground.

The pain in her hand was nearly unbearable. She began to be sick to her stomach as she inhaled fumes of her scorched flesh.

"Does your other hand work?" Rupert asked in a near panic.

"I think so." Audray wouldn't look him in the eyes. She shared a glance with Jonas' man.

"Fuck, Audray, are you losing your powers? Rupert's voice broke like a teenage boy's.

"Forget about that now. We need to go," the soldier said. "It gets worse the longer we stay here. Come!" He ordered.

Rupert and the foot soldier helped her under the arm and together they rushed to the waiting transport. Audray was relieved to see several of the men went with them in the limo. As soon as the last door closed, the vehicle took off at what felt like the speed of light.

One of the men grabbed her wrist and wrapped it with a towel soaked in something that did take some of the pain away.

"Hold this tight around your palm and don't let any of the dirty air get to your wound. You will heal faster if you leave this on for at least an hour. But you will heal."

"Thank you," she said.

THE GUARD CINCHED it tighter, causing new pain. "It will work to accelerate the healing. Only painful for a few more minutes. You'll see."

"Where did you get this poultice?" she asked him as the transport purred through space.

"We carry them in our packs. An old remedy with herbs we grew and brought from the human world centuries ago. Fighting man's best friend."

A couple of the dark guards chuckled. She had expected something high tech and was relieved the old ways worked best, regardless of the realm.

The vehicle nearly reached the transport warehouse when they swerved abruptly to the right, nearly rolling over. Accompanying the deafening screeching of tires, shattering glass and metal crumpling was the frontal impact of the car as it slammed into a solid object. Two well strapped-in guards were holding onto Audray, so she didn't fly out one of the doors which had been ripped off its hinges in the crash. What was left of the vehicle finally came to a complete stop just outside the station. The driver had been pinned and her bloody body was smashed up against the metal grate protecting the passenger box. Rupert jumped out with the escorts, one of whom leaned in to grab her good hand. "Come on. We have to get out of here."

"I can trace."

"You can't take all of us, and I think you're going to need a small army," the guard announced. "Can you run?"

Before she could answer, another of Jonas' men whisked her off her feet and started running around the building into the warehouse village. Audray saw the pile of large boulders blocking the path the transport usually took. This had been an ambush. They headed to a cluster of abandoned structures for cover.

At the center of the arena-like courtyard lay the remains of the Director's home, reduced to charred rubble. It appeared to have been thoroughly picked over.

As they turned behind a large brick warehouse they saw the transport and the station explode into flames. Audray's heartbeat began to elevate. She saw spots in her eyes and leaned against the chest of the runner who held her. She was just about to pass out when they shifted her carefully to another runner, who picked up speed and nearly led the pack of men. She watched Rupert try to keep up, but realized how well trained and fit Jonas' guards were.

"Wait!" Rupert finally called out. "I need to get hold of Jonas." He was breathing heavily as he stopped. The rest of the men clustered around them, searching for enemies from all sides, including the air.

"We're here. Yes. She's safe for now. There are five of us, and Audray is nursing a wound from using her laser." Rupert listened and then handed the phone to Audray. She grabbed the lifeline to Jonas and everything right about her life.

"Are you okay?" she said to him just as he had said the same thing to her.

"My hand is healing. But I'm feeling faint, Jonas. Are you out of danger for now? She could hear the familiar sounds of Jonas' truck in the background.

"Coming to get you."

Within five minutes she saw the shiny black truck roar down the abandoned roadway leading back into town, Jonas and his long hair flying in the breeze. Though she tried to keep her eyes open, she collapsed into the arms of one of the guards. The man didn't flinch as she lost consciousness against his granite shoulder.

SHE AWOKE ON a large bed and instantly recognized Josh's room.

Jonas was speaking on the phone, trying to be soft about it. She uncovered herself from the comforter that had been placed over her and then remembered her burned hand. The bandage was still wrapped around it, but just as the guard had told her, the pain was greatly reduced and she could feel how quickly it had healed. She walked over to the door, which was slightly ajar.

Jonas' warm smile made her heart jump. Suddenly, all the uncertainty and pain of being separated from him, not knowing if he was safe, if there was anything that could be done to save the baby she was carrying, evaporated. As he took her in his arms, her world, the world she wanted to live in for the rest of her natural or unnatural life, was on its proper axis. She felt safe, even though there was still so much around them she did not understand.

After melting into his strong body until she stopped trembling, he whispered to the side of her face, "How are you holding up, baby?"

"I'm good now," she said as she squeezed him. "I don't want to ever be separated from you again." Staring into his eyes, she added, "Ever. No more separations, okay?"

"Not if I can help it," he said as he kissed her fully. When they lingered in tiny kisses, he pulled back. "Tell me the truth. Are you feeling better or worse than this morning?"

She thought about it before answering. She did feel more energy, less tired, more alive and her nerves were settled. The constant ache in her stomach from being nauseated was gone as well. Amazed, she answered him with a smile she hoped would reassure him, "I'm good. Really much better."

His shoulders rounded as he sighed, nodding his head. "That's good. That's good, baby. Maybe that's a sign this is where you belong."

"Was hoping for that."

"Me too."

"Rupert is the reason we escaped." She wanted to be sure Jonas knew how grateful she was.

"You feeling up to talking with us a bit?"

"Absolutely."

Clutching his hand, weaving her fingers between his, she was able to steadily descend the stairs to the little enclave of men. Josh was up in an instant to assist her to one of the red leather chairs by the fireplace, then took his place beside Judy on the loveseat. Jonas began.

"We've pieced together some facts that I hope bring us to a plan of some sorts. Josh and I believe Catarina will come here now, once she learns of Audray's escape, and," he cleared his throat, "Rupert's defection."

Audray saw Rupert flinch, close his eyes slowly and rub them.

The familiar chill of fear traveled up her back and made her shudder. "Go on."

"It seems my relatives have been scheming for centuries to gain power and control over many parts of the modern Western world. They stumbled upon information that led them to the conclusion I had survived and was alive in the Underworld. They sent spies and gathered information and one by one, converted themselves to dark angels, through invitation, through mass turnings."

"Call it for what it is, man. Mass suicides." Josh's voice was all business. "For the record, this was never the way."

"Their desire for domination over not only the Underworld, but the human world as well, has blinded them. It no longer is a family destiny. It is an addiction to power. The upper ranks of this family are in fact, warring against themselves, eliminating themselves, which is a good thing." Jonas glanced over at Rupert, who nodded his agreement. "Thus, no one is safe. Catarina wants dominion, obedience, and total submission by as many souls, dark or human, as she can possibly claim. She is fierce and doesn't think she can be stopped."

Audray looked around the room at the warriors sitting in front of her. The only person who would not return her gaze was redheaded Judy, who continued staring at her hands folded in her lap as she leaned into Josh.

Jonas continued, "She's made some allies here and she's counting on cooperation I'm not so sure she'll get. We may have a friend."

"Who, Jonas?" Audray asked.

"Glenda."

"The witch?"

"Yes, I spoke with her today."

Rupert spoke up. "When Catarina found out you were pregnant, her plans changed. She is totally focused on that baby, and you are that delivery vehicle until the child is far enough along. After that, she won't give a hoot what happens to you. She'll have the child." His eyes were sad. "It's her plan. I've heard it with my own ears."

Audray's veins felt cold, and she shivered again. Judy brought her a crocheted throw.

This last bit was difficult to swallow, knowing that the child she wanted so desperately to hold in her arms was going to be used as a pawn in an evil game of world domination. The dominions and needs of the greedy were not her concern. She would not allow her child to be used for anyone else's evil ends.

Even if she had to pay the ultimate sacrifice. She and Jonas shared a look she never wanted to have again. If they lost this battle, they would all go together.

Chapter 35

CARL RAPPED ON the heavy oak door of Drucilla's cottage. A tall, shirtless body builder-type man, answered the door. The man's hair was held back in a ponytail. He wore a red bandana around his neck.

"I need to talk to Drucilla."

He broke a wide smile, "Sorry pardner, she's gone. Visiting. Returns tonight. She didn't inform me there would be visitors. Who should I tell her called?"

He looked out into the clearing to see if anyone else had accompanied Carl.

"This isn't a social call," Carl began. "It's an emergency. Surely there's a way to reach her. It is a matter of life or death. Her granddaughter is in grave danger."

Carl was worried about Molly. He hadn't had any thoughts from her since he'd left the library. He told himself over and over again it didn't mean anything, that she was fine. Told himself perhaps the sealed room was the reason. Perhaps it worked like a media jamming frequency.

He flashed on a clear blue sky, the beach and the ocean – some of his favorite places, as if these images had been forced upon him. Just then, from the clearing of low shrubbery and forest, Drucilla emerged, carrying a red cape and basket, just like the Little Red Riding Hood story his mother used to read to him when he was young. Though she was clearly in her sixties or seventies, her angelic face belied an inner glow and cast a glamour, making him react to her as if she were a much younger woman. She had the same powers of mind over matter Molly did, but more intense.

"You look like an orphan at a witches' festival." She giggled like a little girl. "And for the record, I kept the calming thoughts clean. I can see Molly has intentions with you I'm not going to begin to delve into. *But I could!* So just be forewarned."

"I've only experienced this with Molly. I didn't know that—"

"Hogwash! Glenda used those powers too. It's just that with Molly you are in love with her, and Glenda scares the frogs out of you."

"That's an understatement."

"And most people don't know it, but they've come under the spells of witches during their lifetime. Ever bought too much at the store, especially when you had little or no money? Wanted something you'd given up for years and then suddenly craved? Here you thought it was your weak body doing this." She leaned in close enough Carl thought she might kiss him. "Witches. Having their way with you and laughing when you're gone."

Carl reflexively stepped back. "Molly needs you. We don't have much time, I fear."

"Yes, I got some confusing messages. I'm going inside to set this down, and then we'll leave. You know the way?"

"Just came from there," Carl said.

Drucilla walked through the door without opening it.

Carl was getting nervous, fisting and unfisting his hands, trying to catch his breath. He felt like he had to pee and vomit at the same time, and that wasn't a good thing.

She exited the door by opening it. Carl led her toward his vehicle, but Drucilla stopped him.

"I thought you said we didn't have much time."

"That's right."

She placed her arm around him and bowed her head. "Keep your eyes closed no matter what, until I say to open them. Pay no attention to the smells or sounds, just stay with me here, okay?"

Carl mumbled something. Before he could fully close his eyes he saw they had ascended to the sky several thousand feet. He immediately squeezed his eyes shut and thought he had passed out into a vivid dream. One of the many images he found was the seated form of Molly, waiting, in the corner of a room. As he saw her, she looked up and smiled.

Chapter 36

AUDRAY AND JONAS were sharing a few stolen moments, holding hands, and whispering alone. The guards had hidden themselves around the yard and down the street to form a perimeter of protection. Jonas explained their dark angel bodies would be able to detect any would-be intruder. He told her to expect minions, perhaps.

"Nothing subtle about Catarina. She has the fire and hatred her distant ancestor had. And now we have the fact that her husband, if he could be called that, has turned on her. She'll be blinded with rage."

Audray knew this to be true. "Except one thing isn't quite in her favor."

"What's that, my love," Jonas asked, kissing her softly on the lips, his dark eyes drinking in the sight of her. How she wanted to get lost in them forever.

"You've been a dark angel for three hundred years. Josh had been one. These guards, I'm guessing you don't have many that are recently turned."

"There's Rupert—"

"Who is not one of your trained guards. Even Peter had more training than he has. His proximity to Catarina only makes him a liability to her and a great asset to us. He doesn't have to fight. He has secrets."

Jonas leaned forward and kissed her ear. "And I have so much I want to say to you right now, it would distract us for a hundred years."

The familiar glamour of his breath was an elixir that made her feel strong and pure of spirit. Her love for this dark angel, who had been waiting his whole life to meet just her, was giving her courage. And for the first time, hope.

He read her mind and nodded. *Yes, love does that. Even with dark angels, love does that. Or so I've been told.*

She was sad for all the lonely years he had waited with no purpose in life except running away, staying to the shadows, and what a cost that had been to him and his soul.

All worth it, love. All worth the waiting. Time is irrelevant when you live forever.

"What happens, Jonas, if I'm turned human, and you remain immortal?"

He looked to the side of the house as a car drove up the driveway. "We'll wing it, love. I have no idea."

Rupert and Josh had been having a quiet conversation in the kitchen and beat them to the rear door at the porch.

Audray watched through the screen, her fingers on the metal netting, as she saw a young couple emerge. The girl was carrying an infant.

Claire!

Jonas was quick to grab Josh's arm. "What's this? Need you increase the stakes, bring someone else she cares about into this little circle of death?"

"Jonas. You don't know Claire very well. But if you did, you would understand I would spend the rest of my human life miserable if I didn't give her the opportunity to see Audray. As her sister, not her enemy."

Audray was out the rear door before any of them could grab her arm. She ran to Claire with arms outstretched, impacting the fresh-scented former Guardian angel and the pink bundle she was carrying with a bear hug. She heard Jonas swear behind her. "I couldn't believe it when I found this out, Claire." She withdrew to look down at the baby, and felt Claire's loving eyes on her. "I am so truly sorry I nearly ruined your life. I ruined your angel life." At last she examined Claire's face. "He told you?"

"Yes, that's why we're here." Claire's blue eyes radiated love. "It was welcome news."

Claire's hair was like golden straw, just as Audray had remembered it. The flood of memories doing things she was ashamed of came back, and she found it impossible not to cry.

"And as for ruining or almost ruining my life—on the contrary, Audray. You *gave* me my human life. You gave me this. Daniel. I would have never found him if it wasn't for your part in this. Don't you see? There are no accidents."

Claire's pure blue eyes watered, but Audray saw the strength of this former Guardian. Daniel stepped next to his wife and addressed Audray.

"Thank you. We thank you for this gift of today. We want to help all we can." He leaned forward and graced Audray's cheek with a tender kiss.

"And this is little Alondra. It means 'savior of mankind,'" Claire whispered.

The beautiful pink baby was rosy cheeked, but had her father's dark complexion and brown eyes. Her clear eyes studied Audray as if recognizing her.

"She's beautiful," was all Audray could say.

"Born on Christmas, can you believe it?" Claire smiled. "My little Christmas baby," she said as she kissed Alondra on the forehead.

"And now you will have one of your own." Claire reached out and touched her stomach. Blessings to you, Audray."

Jonas was at their backside and barking orders, breaking up the reunion. "I'm not happy about this. Now we have three more humans to defend and a whole lot more to lose. I'm not sure this was smart, but this is the hand we've been dealt."

"Yes, we must get inside," Daniel said. Wrapping an arm around Claire, they made their way up the steps to the kitchen. Audray walked behind them. She turned to Jonas.

"What's the plan?"

"Get ready for the onslaught. It could be a few, it could be thousands. I have no clue."

"She'll send the expendables first," Rupert blurted out. "Then she'll send her best. And when it's safe, or she thinks she's safe, she'll come."

"That's a strategy I'm familiar with. Old thinking."

"Usually effective," Josh said.

Claire turned around and drilled Josh a look no one would be able to misinterpret. "No more negative talk. We win this fight. And the next one and the next one if there is one. We fight until they are all destroyed."

Audray didn't want to mention that she doubted all the darklings of the Underworld could possibly be destroyed, especially by this little band of ill-equipped warriors.

No, they won't all be destroyed. Just until the balance between Heaven and the Underworld is restored. Jonas' thoughts soothed her.

"You're right," she whispered.

"The safest room in my house is the wine cellar," Josh said. "And there's a good several months' supply of food there, too." He leaned into an arched doorway that sucked open like the door on a large freezer. "I say Audray, Judy, Claire and the baby go down there and make themselves comfortable, while we save the world. All right with you, gents?"

Before he could be tagged, she watched Rupert slink off into the bushes. She doubted she'd see him again until after the dust settled, if then.

Jonas cursed again. Josh shook his head and shrugged.

Audray addressed the small gathering. "I should stay upstairs to help. My powers. You are going to need my powers."

"Not on your life. You go downstairs," Jonas was red-faced, the veins at the side of his neck extended, bulging. "You have what, one shot? At best? Is that worth the health of our child?"

She saw it was the truth. Audray gave Jonas a kiss she hoped wouldn't be her last, as Claire chastely kissed Daniel and he kissed the baby. Judy wrapped her legs around Josh's hips and placed a liplock on him that rivaled the suction sound of the cellar door. He spanked her behind as she slid down his front, waved with her fingers at the rest of the men standing awkwardly at attention. The women filed one by one into the cellar stairway as the large door was closed. Judy locked it from the inside.

The musky smell was ancient and familiar. Audray had been in many of them when she did Josh's bidding as a human assistant. Rows of dusty green and black bottles lined two walls, layered on rolling shelving that stacked four deep. The collection of wine was the largest Audray had ever seen.

"I had no idea he had all of this," she found herself saying.

"We actually spend quite a lot of time down here. He calls it his man cave." She giggled. "Not a tool or poster in sight!"

Claire nodded, gently swaying with the baby in her arms. "All he needs is some good wine and a large bed."

"And that we have!" Judy showed them an alcove with a stunning gold leaf fresco, sides adorned in tiny mosaics from some ancient temple or monastery. In the center of the space was a large master bed covered in satin pillows.

"You both should try to rest. No telling when we'll get another calm." The sisters agreed. Claire lay the baby between them as they placed their heads on the burgundy satin pillows and stared up at the painted copy of Botticelli's *Birth of Venus* on the ceiling.

Claire reached over and held Audray's hand. "Never thought this day would come, sister."

"Hope it's the first of many, sister."

"Me too," whispered Claire.

AUDRAY WAS AWAKENED by the sound of automatic gunfire and explosions that startled the baby. Claire was able to settle Alondra before she began to cry out. Audray went in search for a bathroom.

She found Judy sitting on the closed lid of the pot, on her cell phone. She abruptly closed the case when she saw Audray.

"Who are you talking to?" Audray asked, just as another blast shook the foundations of the house.

"A friend." She was evasive and Audray could see everyone had misjudged her. "You're talking to *her*, to them."

"Well, I would think you'd be more thankful, Audray. I wanted to make sure that with all the firepower going on upstairs, someone didn't accidentally decide to turn everything to glass. Her minions do disobey. Look at Rupert, that snake."

"The ones who disobey don't live very long, Judy."

"My point exactly. So I've just had to do a little insurance check-up."

"You honestly think you can negotiate with an evil witch like Catarina?"

"You think this little group could possibly defeat them?" She frowned, staring at her phone that gave off a ping. "That's the sound of freedom, Audray. I'm going to be given my true freedom, not the one Jonas tried to offer me. I'm hoping you'll be given the same, after…"

"What have you done?"

"I think I've saved your life, or at least the life of your unborn."

"What?"

"Don't you see? It's the only way you'll survive. She wants the baby you're carrying. She won't do anything to you for fear of hurting the child. That baby is very important."

Audray was sick to her stomach again and placed one palm on her belly. "She's never getting my baby."

"I don't think she can be denied."

"It won't happen, Judy. I'll die first."

"And then you'd be killing the child. Is it so bad to pay such a price for freedom, true freedom?"

"You understand you can't count on anything she promises. Freedom for now? Always looking over our shoulders? Even if she let Jonas live, you honestly think we'd be able to enjoy a life together somewhere else? I've thought about running away, but it would only be temporary."

"You fight, I think you will lose, Audray, and badly. Painful to think of it, really."

"Judy, surely you're not sporting a conscience. You care nothing for Josh? He has no worth to anyone and will be expendable."

"Josh is a wily devil and I think somehow he will survive. But I doubt he could protect anyone but himself. No, we're all on our own. Best thing is to cooperate, give her what she wants without a fight, and then live to war another day, if need be."

"It won't happen. You've misjudged all of us, Judy."

The young dark angel got up, stretched like the cat-like creature she was, tiring of her taunting of a favorite mouse. "Suit yourself. Don't say I didn't warn you." She left the bathroom.

The sounds of gunfire and explosions above them ceased and an eerie calm descended on them. Audray washed her face and hands and found Judy draped over a chair in the main room, reading a wine magazine. She casually looked up at her. "Everything better now?"

"Hardly," Audray said.

"Won't be long now," Judy quipped.

"Oh, we have just begun to fight, Judy."

"You have no faith. You'll see. You are the prize. You are in a good position to bargain for the life of those you love. Me, on the other hand, can only help deliver you to them. And that's what I've done."

"Done what?" Claire's raspy voice enveloped Audray from behind.

She turned and addressed her sister. "Judy's sold us out, Claire. She's made some sort of demonic deal with Catarina."

Holding the baby in her arms, the little former Guardian confronted their enemy. "You are more a fool than I thought before. You'll be the first she'll dispose of when she no longer needs you. You chose the wrong side."

The two sisters faced each other. "I'm not sure we can do anything but wait," Claire whispered. She leaned towards Audray and softly asked her, "Can you warn him?"

Audray nodded, turning away from Judy and closing her eyes. *Judy has betrayed us. Be safe, my love. She wants the baby.*

Jonas heartfelt answer came seconds later. *Save yourself and our child at all costs. We are restrained. Stay alive. I will figure a way somehow.*

The large oak door at the top of the stairwell was drawn open. Amidst smoke which quickly descended the metal stairway, sending an acrid scent of destruction, a lone figure appeared at the top, peering down on their little group.

Catarina.

"Your men are alive, for the moment. But they are in chains and shall remain that way until I have your full cooperation."

Claire stood close to Audray and they locked hands.

As Catarina began her first step down, Audray mustered what she could of her strength, raised her palm to the air and fired a laser at the dark angel, hitting her in the chest and knocking her back against the wall. Catarina screamed in pain, but did not fall. Although there was a scorched ring of fire on the ashen cloak she wore, the laser had not drilled through her body nor melted her flesh. The pain in Audray's palm was only half that compared to the sadness in her heart as she realized she'd lost the ability to vaporize.

Catarina's shrill voice boomed, sending bottles of wine bursting. "You fool! You wish to see what torture I can cause your Jonas? Your sister, you've even endangered your sister!"

She was breathing hard, gripping the metal railing as she righted herself. Audray deduced she was in some pain, although temporary.

Judy had scrambled to her feet, attempting to run to the stairwell to assist Catarina, who gave an evil grimace as she shot a red beam of fiery light at the young dark angel, leaving a gaping hole in her chest as she fell dead, charred black and bleeding on the stone floor of the wine cellar.

It wasn't much, but at least Audray could take comfort in the fact that she had judged Catarina correctly.

She heard Jonas whisper in her inner ear, *Good to know your enemies. Keep a level head, my love, and survive for Round Two.*

Chapter 37

THE CAMPUS APPEARED abandoned, which surprised Carl. As they descended rapidly to the grassy hill outside the library, they found the doors ajar.

"Molly is inside this building. I saw her as we flew," Carl said.

Drucilla sprang through the doors without touching the ground. Carl tried to keep up with her. As he ran through the lobby to the stacks, Drucilla was already at the stack doors, pulling them, her legs spread, one foot pressed against the side wall and the other against the other door. She yanked and yanked until she lost her grip and was thrown back, nearly toppling Carl in the fray. Her small bony body skidded on the smooth fabric of her skirt until she hit the back of the reception desk, stopping her travels.

Molly was at the window. "I have a pass key, but it will do me no good in here."

Drucilla said something under her breath. She righted herself, adjusted her skirt and top and walked through the wall of the vault. Carl remained outside, blinking. She exited the sealed room and produced the pass key, giving it to Carl.

"Sometimes it's so simple. I love it when that's the case."

Carl saw the damage to the doors and wondered if the key would work. They had not broken the seal, but someone had managed to make deep hatchet stabs into the metal-covered fiberglass doors, leaving gaping holes like slashes to a human body. He inserted the key, heard the reassuring sucking sound as the doors released.

Drucilla pushed him out of the way as if she were discarding a piece of dirty laundry. Molly was weaving as her grandmother grabbed her and started putting her hands on her neck, her belly, her back and then held her face to inspect her eyes. "You are all right, child? Did they drug or hurt you?"

"No. They never got to me."

Carl inserted himself, edging her grandmother away and nearly knocking her over. He held Molly against him, whispering in her ear, "Oh God, I am so glad you are unharmed."

Molly kissed him back, returned the squeeze he was giving her.

"So they're on their way, then? They'll be back?" Carl was searching the campus through the opened doorway. Only thing he saw moving was green shrubbery.

"I'm not picking up anything. They're off somewhere else. Some gathering…" Drucilla had placed her fingers at her temples.

"But I thought—" Carl started.

"Shhh!" Drucilla silenced him, holding her finger up in the air and bending her head. "Carl, your dark angels are attracting a lot of attention."

Carl's heart sank. He was too late to save Jonas and Audray. He had rescued Molly, but only because the attackers had been pulled off and sent another direction. The battle was raging elsewhere, and he had not done his job to warn Jonas. He righted an overturned chair and sat, placing his forehead to his palm. "I have no clue where they are. I feel like I have failed them. We said we'd help, and I failed them."

Drucilla hit him in the back of the head, practically sending him sprawling forward. "You big oaf. You think that kind of disturbance would escape me? Come." She stretched out her arms.

THEY WERE OFF, but this time he closed his eyes in time.

Just before they landed, Carl smelled smoke. Molly was tense and rigid, nearly jumping out of her skin as he touched her in the night air. A house was on fire in the foreground. It was a large home in a neighborhood with several other large mansions. Part of the oak tree in the front yard had ignited. They could hear sirens blaring.

Drucilla was bowed in concentration, her eyes closed, thumbs at her temples. "She's here. They're all here."

"What do we do?" he asked the older witch.

"Not sure she knows about our arrival. At least I'm hoping that's the case," she whispered back. "Get ready for something spectacular."

A loud clap of thunder and lightning sounded, illuminating the grounds around the house. They could see several large vehicles with heavily armed men standing nearby in a semicircle. Another group of men was handling several prisoners who were wrapped in black body bags of some sort and chained, inserting them into the vans.

The next flash of lightning gave Carl a glimpse of some dark winged creatures jockeying for position in the now-burning oak tree. As if on cue they squawked and screeched in unison as heavy hail came down upon the whole area. But as Carl looked closer, he could see it was raining snakes. The sheer number and weight of them pulled one of the winged creatures down from the tree as it tried to take flight. The animal hit the ground and screamed, fire and steam rising from the wave of dark snakes covering it. Occasionally a claw or wing would rise up, only to be taken down. The dying cries of anguish telegraphed a warning every creature on the ground would heed.

The other two creatures were circling overhead, stopping as if searching for a target. The armed men were trying to avoid the vicious serpents and ran to take cover in their vehicles. Some used automatic weapons, which appeared useless against the black horde as an even heavier rain of the creatures followed the first wave.

"We need to move back," Drucilla whispered. They were just outside of the rain of serpents, but retreated several steps further into the foliage of the house next door.

"Flesh-eating snakes. Yuck. Strictly thirteenth century witchcraft." Drucilla shuddered.

"Effective against humans, not much against the Underworld." Molly sniffed the air. "Grandmother, you smell her?"

"She's here, but she's not in this game for some reason. She's helping."

Molly snuggled close. It had been one more day of surprises. Allies from enemies. Enemies from allies. Snakes falling from the skies. If someone had told Carl a month ago he would fall in love with a witch, he'd not have believed them. And now this. What else was in store for them, he wondered. He felt totally inadequate for whatever was going to befall them.

Drucilla pulled Carl by his shirt lapel, her foul breath turning his stomach. "They've captured the dark prince, the one you seek. You will have to try to free him while I am busy."

"Where is he?"

"I feel his presence. There are several others as well who are alive. I'm guessing the packages they put into the vans. I cannot release those bonds. We are going to need his help."

"How?"

Molly spoke up. "We wait for the rain to stop, then I think I can get you to the vehicles."

Drucilla touched Molly's cheek. "Such a pretty thing. Shame we haven't had more time to spend together."

"We'll still have that time, Grandmother. You'll see. This isn't over yet."

Drucilla placed a palm on Molly's forehead, whispering an incantation, then did the same for Carl. "Now go, with my blessing."

Molly's arms were outstretched, fingers splayed as the snakes receded away from them, leaving behind dead and injured serpents. A commotion started near the house as a woman in black, not Glenda, was shouting orders. She was occupied with searing a path with a red laser light, scorching anything that moved.

The doors to one of the vans opened, and they were face to face with dark warriors who did not look of this world. Thinking quickly, Molly called out, "She's sent me to lead the way. I can protect you."

Just as she said this another of the dark winged creatures was brought down in a hail of screams, fraying Carl's nerves to the breaking point.

"Come quickly or they will overcome you," Molly told them.

Carl stood behind the side of the van until the three armed guards exited. She started toward the dark woman, spreading her arms out to disperse the serpents. When one of the men turned to close the doors, she shouted a command.

"Leave it. Their fate is not in our hands any longer." The man obeyed her and followed the others.

Carl jumped up into the back, finding Jonas bound and gagged. He quickly removed the rag from the dark angel's mouth.

"I cannot get these chains unlocked," he said to Jonas.

"You have a knife? You need to cut me out of this bag. My powers are diminished until I am free of it," Jonas barked.

Carl quickly produced his pocket knife and tried to slice open the bags, but the blade broke.

"Check their duty bag."

Carl found the nastiest serrated edged knife and allowed it to slice through the black fabric, which bled as if it were made of skin from an

Underworld creature itself, freeing the men inside. Jonas freed himself and his men from the chains.

"How many men have you brought?" Jonas asked.

Carl's heart sank. "There are two others. Molly, Drucilla…and…and me."

"Christ!" Jonas surveyed the ground outside the van and swore. "Couldn't you have found a soldier, someone who knows how to fight?"

Carl shrugged. "This is all we have. There wasn't—"

"Never mind," Jonas interrupted. "I've sent word to Audray that we're free. They're still in the cellar, but are being brought up top." He stepped on heads of snakes with his massive boots. "Careful not to let those nasties get you. They can't kill, but they have a swarm mentality, and together they can do you in. Carl, you'd best stay in the van."

"Not on your life," Carl shouted. "Molly's all alone."

"Not any longer. Everything is going to move very fast here. So stay close to me."

One of the men handed Carl a small laser weapon. "Careful not to get the heat on yourself. Only if one of them gets under your pants or on your body. I've set the focus to fine, but the thing will go fifty feet or more, so take care you don't shoot one of the good guys."

The weight of the weapon didn't seem to match the size of its firepower. He examined the trigger mechanism before Jonas reached over and flipped a red locking device. "You flick it with your thumb, like this," he demonstrated quickly. "Leave it on safety, just in case."

The other guard shrugged at the scowl Jonas gave him.

Entrusted now with something else he'd never encountered, a laser weapon from deep in the Underworld, Carl followed the three other warriors, his heart pounding in his ears.

Suddenly, a message from Molly exploded in his mind, turning him to stone. *Will love you forever. If not this lifetime, then the next.*

Chapter 38

THE MESSAGE JONAS received from Audray was bad news. *Jonas, my powers are nearly gone!* He froze, causing the soldier behind to collide with him.

He sent her back a warning, *Love, save your powers.*

His warrior training had him prepared for any eventuality, but this scenario, with so many variables had him reeling. He decided to just rely on his dark angel instincts, hoping that his years of experience would give advantage to his human training for battle. If it were just him, the actions he'd take without regard to his own soul would be automatic. But now he had something to live for. The dedication to a new love and the possibility he could care for and protect a family bouyed his bravado, but his common sense told him that with all he had to lose, he was perhaps more vulnerable than he ever had been.

And what would eternity be like if he failed to protect her? What if Catarina and her evil minions stole his birthright, his future, again? He'd made choices that had paid out consequences he'd had to live with for centuries. He would not allow this to happen again. He had to stay clear-headed, work with allies from different realms, trust people not yet vetted against not only one enemy, but opposing sides, crosses and possible double-crosses.

He was relieved to see armed guards holding Audray in the back porch of the house. She stood of her own will, firm and erect, queen of his heart. He knew the men were awaiting instructions to transport her away, probably to the Underworld. Claire stood beside her, calming the baby, also looking unharmed.

Dead or dying snakes littered the area between them as the fire in the house raged on. In a sonic boom that pierced the air, he heard his relative lay down the challenge.

"Bitch of the human world!" Catarina screamed to the heavens. Her bloodied face and shoulder giving off a ghastly cast. The healing process had begun, but her skin had bruised and puffed up, with one eye temporarily swollen shut. "Who choses snakes instead of warriors to guard her kingdom, who preys on humans like sexual toys—show yourself before I tire of this game and seek refuge from your stench of humanity."

Catarina was assaulted by a black-cloaked projectile, Glenda, who shrieked as she caused the dark angel to misfire, sending a huge burning branch of the oak tree in front of Josh's house to the ground. It was immediately covered with snakes as if the ravenous beasts were anticipating a juicy dark creature. The women tumbled, Glenda temporarily on top, raising them up into the air while she attempted to twist the head of Catarina, perhaps to decapitate her.

Jonas got out his weapon and shot at both of them. "Take the shot. Anyone take the shot," he barked. But the bodies went in and out of visibility, and when Glenda managed to throw Catarina off her, the angel passed through to the other side of the tree trunk unharmed. Their firepower veered off into trees of the neighboring houses. Catarina followed the trajectory of one shot from one of Jonas' men and fired a retaliatory laser which caught him squarely in the chest through his shield, and he was left a rubble of flesh. Next, Catarina turned her gaze on Glenda and gave her a sweet smile before Jonas saw the red in her eyes pool like molten lava.

Before she could get her shot off, a laser hit the side of her face, sending her hair in flames. The heat traveled to her shoulder and neck as she screamed and turned on the person who had launched against her. Jonas was coming to Audray's defense when he froze as he saw who Catarina was focused on.

Carl stood alone in the once-beautiful rose garden, his arm still outstretched, his weapon shaking. Catarina was forced down on one knee, but Jonas knew it wasn't a lethal blow and she would survive.

Without moving her eyes from Carl, Catarina, screamed her victory speech. "Ignorant, pathetic human. I cannot be killed, you fool. I am immortal."

Jonas inhaled, ready for his move. Her ghastly face was filled with hatred.

"Wait!" Molly ran from the bushes, standing in front of Carl. Desperately, Carl attempted to push her out of the way. Catarina might have been amused, but Jonas saw she was still in pain.

Ignorant humans indeed.

It was enough of a distraction that Jonas could fire his weapon at her. His two remaining guards did the same, but some sort of protection dome had been erected, effectively shielding her from their firepower.

"Fire and move," Jonas commanded. He didn't want any of them to be tracked. They all scattered and fired in quick succession, hoping their combined efforts would penetrate the shield, but to no avail.

From inside her protective dome, Catarina shouted, "Drop your weapon or I will fry the both of you together."

Carl hesitated. Molly pushed the gun down and helped him throw it on the ground.

"Clever girl."

For a few seconds everything stopped. Jonas saw Josh had been released from another of the vans by a couple of Jonas' men. Audray and Claire were being forced by Catarina's minions to leave the porch and march toward Catarina. Jonas was prepared to place his body between them.

But Catarina found him. "Why Grandfather, would you also kill your unborn? Is your pride and your love of your immortal life and your pathetic humans so great you would sacrifice the life of your family, again? Your ego is your downfall, Grandfather."

Audray and Claire were led to stand next to Catarina, just outside the protective dome. He hoped there would be no more firing of weapons, knowing some of his best sharpshooters were still in the shadows. The risk was not worth it. He knew what he had to do.

"I am yours. I am without a weapon," Jonas said as he dropped his weapon and walked forward, his arms in the air, his hands splayed.

Just as if he'd been stabbed in the chest, he felt Audray's tears as she realized he had offered himself up in a futile attempt to rescue her. But he was out of options. There wasn't any more time for anything else.

I am sorry, love.

Her response to him was swift. *No!*

The mess that was Catarina's face was made more horrific by the hatred she had towards him. He could see even the satisfaction of ending his life wouldn't be enough to satisfy her lust for blood. No doubt she had something very public and brutal in store for him, not quick. She would force Audray to watch. It gave him an idea.

He dropped to his knee and prayed for forgiveness, like he had done several centuries ago when he'd been knighted. "I am wrong to war against another member of my family, my many times great granddaughter," he began. "For this I should be punished. And it will be worth it if you will spare the life of my child, and the woman who is my only reason to live. You can take everything else of me you wish, but spare me the life of my woman and my child. Do that and I will be your slave for all eternity."

Catarina was annoyed as she brushed her face. A large piece of flesh still attached to long tendrils of hair fell onto her bodice. She flicked it to the ground. Jonas could see the healing process working, although he knew she was still in pain.

"You'd do that? Serve me like that idiot husband of mine, Rupert?"

"Yes."

"You would call *me* queen?"

"Of course, my queen."

"You would breed another heir?"

Jonas hadn't considered this. He hesitated too long.

"Ah! See? There are things you would not do."

"That I would not," Jonas looked up at her and then to Audray, hoping she'd see the truth in his eyes. "I have paid the price for that mistake before, I will not do it again."

Suddenly Drucilla appeared at the edge of the circle. "You evil bitch. Jonas holds more honor in his little finger than you would ever hold in a thousand lifetimes." Her little finger glowed for a second before a shimmer of crystals flew at Catarina, encapsulating her.

Catarina's countermeasures melted the golden veil, her eyes murderous and red. "Then die with honor, witch." The dark angel lowered the shield to send a pulsing beam at Drucilla, melting her quickly. Molly shrieked, but was held back by Carl. Catarina clasped her hands and chuckled. "You see? There is no hope. Time to die, all of you. I'm tired of this game of cat and mouse."

Jonas was nearly close enough to touch Audray, but the dark angel warned, "Stop now or it costs your bride a limb. Your choice, Grandfather." She backed up, reaching for Audray's bound hands, to pull her with her. Jonas saw the shield was still down. He mentally searched for a weapon, knowing she was fully exposed. Claire pushed Audray aside at the last minute, prepared to defend Audray's body with her own.

A large red liquid beam the diameter of an arm hit Catarina square in the chest, causing a gaping hole that surprised even her. Out of reflex, her eyes began the vaporization sequence but to no avail. Her face reddened as the red liquid found the heat within her own body and the dark angel exploded, leaving behind smoldering bloody rags.

"Couldn't stand that bitch," Doris said, lowering the flamethrower.

Audray collapsed into Jonas arms, safe at last.

Chapter 39

IN THE CHAOS afterwards, Jonas and two of his men carefully carried Drucilla's remains to the lawn of a nearby church yard. Audray watched as the fire at Joshua's house was put out. The former dark angel was shouting instructions to the fire crew as they tried to salvage as much as possible. She saw rescue workers take note of the scene, examining the large piles of dead and charred snakes, the bloody remains of the powerful dark angel as well as remains of two dark winged creatures and several other armed men. She knew the report to be filed would not make any sense, and no doubt Josh would have a hand in drafting something creative and nearly believable. Humans were his people now, after all.

Molly was beside herself with grief over the death of her grandmother, who had been the one to tip the scales in their favor, forcing the protective shield down. Carl went to the young witch, embracing her bended frame, but Molly was inconsolable.

"She wanted this for you, Molly. Believe me, she chose this," Carl whispered to her as he kissed her forehead and placed a blanket over her shoulders. "She'd want you to live your life and not to grieve."

"I can't help it."

Audray buried her face in Jonas' chest.

"Come, sister." Claire suddenly appeared from the darkness. Behind her, Daniel held Alondra tightly. "You need a place to rest. Daniel and I will bring you to our place, and then you can make your plans."

"I can't ask you to do that for me," Audray responded.

"But sister, you have no where else to go. Am I wrong?"

Jonas encouraged her to agree.

FRESHLY SHOWERED AND with some clothes Claire lent her, Audray felt like a new woman. Daniel had made strong coffee for him and Jonas. The two men were seated in front of the fireplace Audray knew only too well. A new painting adorned the wall above, replacing the one Audray had enjoyed when she was doing Josh's dark bidding. Daniel blushed and looked down at his coffee. The painting was just as bright as the jungle canvases he was known for, but these new ones looked like they'd been suffused with light from within.

"I like it, Daniel. These are lovely," she said as she examined the other canvases on an adjacent wall which led to the kitchen where Claire was working.

"You should see the ones he's been working on for the children's book series. I'll show you later. We've turned the attic into a studio. The light is perfect and he feels inspired to work there."

"As he should be, sister." Audray hugged Claire.

"You must rest, Audray. I can't imagine what this ordeal has done to you. How are you feeling?"

Audray was tired, but she didn't want to be without the company of her newfound sister. "I'm feeling well, thank you." She had so many questions she wanted to ask. "Do you remember our father at all, Claire?"

"Sadly, no."

"I'd give anything if I could have met him. I'm glad you didn't see what our mother had become."

"I hardly remember that time. The Wash is supposed to remove all our human memories. I thought perhaps when Father gave me back my human life some of those memories would remain. But I think now I'm glad for his gift of amnesia. My life really started when I became a Guardian."

"I can't see you living with or being any part of the mother I knew. How strange that two lives could be so different." She hesitated to explore more of what Claire knew of her past. "You know I found your grave. And the grave of our father. You are buried next to him. Perhaps I'll take you there to see it one day."

"Someday. I take things a day at a time now with Alondra. I'm not sure what we'll tell her of my past. But at some point she'll need to know."

They held hands in the kitchen, Audray rubbing the knuckles on the back of Claire's hand. "If I survive this—" Pain welled up inside her at the thought that perhaps she wouldn't be around to experience the life of her baby.

"You'll survive, Audray. You'll live to tell the tale to successive generations," Claire said lovingly and squeezed her hand. With her smooth still-angelic face and clear blue eyes, Audray found herself trusting and depending on Claire the more she was around her.

"But Josh said the mother doesn't usually—"

"Nonsense. Josh doesn't know everything. You know this for a fact, Audray, don't you?"

She nodded, placing her palms on her belly, rubbing the tiny bump she could feel. Or, maybe it was her imagination. Would she know this child? Would she be able to communicate with this child like she did with Jonas? Would this bundle of love cause her own death? She had more questions, but had no one to ask.

"You must have faith, Audray. Trust that there is a golden future for you out there. And for Jonas and your child. After all, we have no hard evidence to the contrary." Claire began preparing a plate of fruit. "Go and sit with Jonas and Daniel. And then I'm going to insist you take a nap."

Visitors were at the front door as Audray headed back to the living room. Jonas greeted several of his men, Omar among them, who reported the Underworld was in total chaos. They inquired whether Audray would be returning to restore order. Audray heard the angst in his thoughts as she told them that no, she would remain in the human world, for the time being. She saw Luke hanging in the background. "Luke? Should I appoint a successor?"

"As you wish, my queen."

"Luke would make an excellent Director," Jonas smiled in admiration at her choice.

"What about you, Jonas? The angels respect you," Luke asked.

Jonas placed his arm around Audray. "No. My place is here."

A battered yellow and black taxi cab pulled up into the driveway, and Audray recognized Doris behind the wheel. She was transporting Joshua and another man in the back seat. Audray couldn't help but run through the foyer to greet the Guardian and thank her properly. The hug she tried to bestow on the cabbie was shrugged off. Doris separated herself and stood stiffly, taking on a big gulp of air before she began.

"I'm not into the touchy-feely stuff, Audray, and I'm going to be real honest, I was ordered to watch over the little war we had this evening."

"By whom?" Josh and the other passenger had extricated themselves from the rear seat, but didn't come forward.

"I did," said the white haired gentleman standing next to Josh. *Father.*

Claire pushed by Audray and ran to the older gentleman. "You look well, my dear," he said before he enveloped her in his powerful arms.

Jonas came up behind Audray and embraced her. "All is as it should be, love. Have no fear. The battle is done, for now."

She melted into him, suddenly needing him more than she ever had. *We've survived, my love, but what of our future?*

We wait. We trust. We love each other. For now, that is all we can do.

With their arms about each other's waist, Father and Claire made their way over to Audray and Jonas.

"I usually keep my distance from dark angels, but I've made an exception here tonight," Father said. He dropped his arms from Claire's body.

"I provide the stage but I don't write the play, my new friends. It is your performance that makes it real. I give everyone a chance at redemption, just as the Underworld is a place to experience, um, the alternative."

"We've accepted our fate, sir. We have no regrets," Jonas spoke the words Audray was thinking.

"And then sometimes, a true miracle happens, surprises us all." Father's eyes lowered to Audray's belly. "May I?" he asked as he extended his palm toward Audray's stomach. She stepped to him and allowed him to place his hand on her there.

"Children are not my miracle, though I'd love to take credit for them. They are a true miracle, not one I created. Spontaneous. Perfect as life is perfect."

"What's to happen of us, Father?" Audray whispered. Jonas came up behind her, spooning his body against her backside, giving her the support her heart needed. He found her right hand and their fingers laced together. Whatever was going to be said, he was going to be there for her. Father removed his palm and crossed his arms, his face serious, with a small furrow to his brow.

"Is it your intention to raise this child in the human world?" he asked.

"In all honesty, I'd go wherever I must to raise this child. I want this child, Father," Audray answered him. "Perhaps that's not what you wanted to hear, but that is the truth, I think for both of us." She turned and Jonas gave back a nod of agreement. "Will I live to carry this baby to term, and will I live afterwards?"

"You would give up your dark angel lives for this child?"

"In a heartbeat," Audray answered him without hesitation, "As long as it won't damage the baby. If I need to die to bring this new life forth, I will willingly do that. But Father, is there a chance we can be a family?"

"The war goes on, Audray. It is far from over. In fact, it will never be over. How will you stay safe?"

"Is anyone ever guaranteed safety? Living, either as a human or a dark angel, is risky," Jonas inserted. "In the Underworld, there is no hope. Here, we have our love and with that comes a faith in a bright future. If you would allow such a thing," he continued.

"Allow it?" Father winked at Jonas. "As a matter of fact, I can't stop it!" He began to chuckle. "Give me your hands, children."

Audray was having difficulty holding back the tears. Her chest was heaving, her lower lip quivered. She thought holding her breath would stop her tears, but when Jonas squeezed her other hand, she lost it. Audray glanced up at Claire and found that Claire too was crying. In fact, everyone was crying, even Doris. The sounds of sniffling even came from Josh's direction. Father turned to him and smiled.

With Audray's small hand sandwiched between Jonas and Father's, she heard the words she would never forget.

"If it is human you desire, then it is human you both shall have. One special, limited lifetime to love, to raise your family, to pass on the faith you have in the human condition to others along your journey."

Golden threads encircled their hands as Father removed his, and Audray felt for the first time as a human woman, the skin of her beloved Jonas. Their fingers entwined and she looked to his tear-streaked face and felt the miracle of a bright loving future.

Chapter 40

THE CHATTER WAS light, but Jonas grew impatient as the hour grew long. His men picked up on his mood, and they each bade him farewell and good luck and promised to do what they could to protect him from the denizens of the Underworld, or to be his eyes and ears against any future war that might come to claim him. He thanked them for their loyalty and the hundreds of years of service they'd given him. It was harder to do than he'd expected.

He felt Audray's eyes on his back, and when he turned he saw her compassion for his plight. He jealously watched her private conversation with Josh, who had not stopped grinning since Father had said his farewell.

He regretted not having thanked Doris who he'd seen fawning over little Alondra along with the great man himself. The two of them left together. There was much more he wanted to learn about the feisty Guardian and suspected there was some interesting history there.

His muscles were sore and tight from the fight earlier. He felt the weight of his human body, something he'd forgotten those centuries ago, and knew he needed sleep. But his need to be at Audray's side was an even greater pull.

Claire led them to the master bedroom. Holding the baby, she opened the door to a soothing light green bedroom covered with Daniel's jungle canvases. He had the feeling they were walking into a

Brazilian rainforest, that some new adventure was at hand.

"We have a spare room, and have moved Alondra's things there. Please, sleep as long as you desire. You will need lots of rest to accept this new change in your bodies. No one here will disturb you."

"Thank you, sister."

"I am honored your first night and day as a new human will be spent in our house. Who could have predicted this?" Claire tilted her head and smiled at both of them. "Welcome home, for now. When you feel like it, we'll find you a more permanent home, but this will do for now, okay?"

"Thank you again," Jonas whispered, giving Claire a peck on the cheek.

With Claire gone and the door closed, Jonas looked at his human lover, not sure what she was feeling.

I am feeling the same, lover mine. I am needing you now more than ever. Nothing has changed.

Thrilled at this new revelation that they could still speak through telepathy, he cupped her face and whispered to her lips. "I haven't loved a human woman in over three hundred years." He nibbled on her lips. "I think I am the virgin here."

Audray's warm smile made his heart soar. "You are far from that, my love. But for this gift of being your first, I am honored."

Her lips tasted the same. Perhaps it was his imagination, but the salty tears that washed them he found intoxicating. He spread his thumbs over her cheeks one by one, and kissed her eyes. Her breathing was the same as he'd remembered. The perfume from her freshly washed body enveloped him as he slowly laced his fingers in her hair, pulling her to him, and then kissing the top of her head, the sides of her face, her ears, and then her neck as she rolled her head backward.

Her beautiful skin was smoother, more fragile. His fingers explored the top of her shoulder as he slipped the cotton sweatshirt off her head. He allowed his hands to feel the luxury of her long blonde curls. Her hands had dug under his shirt, pulling it apart, ruining the buttons, like the first time they'd made love. Except this time, it was Daniel's shirt, which barely fit him.

She was kissing his nipples, biting the little nubs, pushing her mound against his thigh. The pressure of her hardness against his weary muscles was delicious. He sunk his palms into the back of her pants and squeezed the flesh of her butt cheeks.

"How is this for you?" she whispered, her hot lips coating his, sucking at his lower lip, her steamy breath fueling his erection.

"So far, better," He whispered to her neck.

She moved her hands quickly to undo his pants and they fell to his ankles. She quickly took him in her palms and squeezed.

"Far better," he said with difficulty.

The thrill of the natural attraction they had for each other's bodies, the human chemistry, free of glamour and unenhanced by thoughts had him nearly dizzy with delight. He was going to pace himself, because he thought perhaps he should, in their present condition, but when she fell to her knees and took him in her lips he nearly came undone. He held her head to his groin and finally could hold back no longer.

I don't ever want you to stop.

He was sorry he'd said it. Of course they'd have to stop. Her sultry smile as she licked him from scrotum to his tip. "If you try to stop me, you'll fail." Then she took him completely, deeply into her mouth while telling him, *Up for the challenge, love?*

He was seeing stars and it was way too soon for this.

No worries, you'll have your way with me when I'm finished.

He thought of the battle scenes he'd been in over the centuries, the snakes he'd seen today, the decapitations and horrible things that had happened today...

It isn't going to work, lover. You'll explode in my mouth any minute now.

Reflex made him swear under his breath. He'd wanted to show his stamina as a human male, but instead everything he thought of sent him closer and closer to the edge. She brought him from her mouth and placed him in the center of her chest, between her breasts and squeezed them together.

Panic set in as he felt his balls constrict and begin to release. She allowed the head of his penis to lazily rub against her nipples, coating with his precum, letting him feel the hardness of her knotted nubs. Her look of need and longing pushed him through the gate as he arched back and began to spill, throwing his concerns to the side. Just as he began to spurt, she covered him once again with those luscious lips, sending him deep down her throat while she sucked and accepted all of him.

He'd barely finished when he abruptly changed positions, lifted her up and threw her on the bed. "My turn."

Audray gave out a little squeal of satisfaction as she found a pillow for her head and Jonas found another one for under her rear. He moved quickly to her mound, pulling back the lips of her hot sex, lapping the juices there, sucking on her nub and devouring her. His hot tongue found the juncture at the top of her leg where he sucked a bruise he hoped would hurt her slightly. His mental question was answered when she moaned, "Yes, my love."

Eager to stimulate her insides, he placed his forefinger at her opening. She rolled her pelvis to receive him and he held her back. She arched and pushed herself on him and he withdrew his hand so her frustration would build. Her need was growing wild and he loved seeing the fire burn inside her.

"Please, Jonas," she moaned as she touched herself and his cheeks, feeling the side of his tongue as he thrust inside her. "I need this, Jonas."

Just a little bit longer. I want to taste more of you, love. Just a little bit more, please. Her deep guttural plea nearly broke his heart, but he was on a mission now.

Patience... he said to her.

Is not a virtue. Fuck me, Jonas.

Only words would do as his response, "Ah, well when you put it that way, love, I shall indeed fuck you."

He climbed the bed raising her legs to rest on his shoulders, pushed the pillow underneath her plump little ass, spread her cheeks with his palms and inserted himself deep and to the hilt.

He felt her body turn to putty. He slowly arched and angled back and forth, changing positions, seating deep and holding, then changing his speed until he felt the delicious muscles inside her clamp down on him. Her body seized him, held him, but he wouldn't stop. His own groans filled the room as he felt himself slip again, sinking into her body deep and giving him more than he thought possible.

In the lazy hours that followed, Jonas earned his birthright several times, and was at last satisfied when he saw the new dawn coming through the sheer curtains. As he rose to close the darkening shades, his legs could barely carry his own weight.

He remembered what Claire had said, they'd need lots of rest to adjust to their new human form. He agreed with her completely. He wasn't going to let Audray out of his bed until he was good and ready to.

Perhaps he could stay here, with her, in this bed, for the rest of his human life, perfecting his human form. For as long as it was given him, he'd enjoy the woman he was created to love. It would be his new mission, full of hope and faith in that bright hereafter he now knew was possible.

The End

About the Author

NYT and USA Today best-selling author Sharon Hamilton's award-winning Navy SEAL Brotherhood series have been a fan favorite from the day the first one was released. They've earned her the coveted Amazon author ranking of #1 in Romantic Suspense, Military Romance and Contemporary Romance categories, as well as in Gothic Romance for her Vampires of Tuscany and Guardian Angels. Her characters follow a sometimes rocky road to redemption through passion and true love.

Now that he's out of the Navy, Sharon can share with her readers that her son spent a decade as a Navy SEAL, and he's the inspiration for her books.

Her Golden Vampires of Tuscany are not like any vamps you've read about before, since they don't go to ground and can walk around in the full light of the sun.

Her Guardian Angels struggle with the human charges they are sent to save, often escaping their vanilla world of Heaven for the brief human one. You won't find any of these beings in any Sunday school class.

She lives in Sonoma County, California with her husband and her Doberman, Tucker. A lifelong organic gardener, when she's not writing, she's getting *verra verra* dirty in the mud, or wandering Farmers Markets looking for new Heirloom varieties of vegetables and flowers. She and her husband plan to cure their wanderlust (or make it worse) by traveling in their Diesel Class A Pusher, Romance Rider. Starting with this book, all her writing will be done on the road.

She loves hearing from her fans:
Sharonhamilton2001@gmail.com

Her website is:
sharonhamiltonauthor.com

Find out more about Sharon, her upcoming releases, appearances and news from her newsletter, **AND receive a free book** when you sign up for Sharon's newsletter.

Facebook:
facebook.com/SharonHamiltonAuthor

Twitter:
twitter.com/sharonlhamilton

Pinterest:
pinterest.com/AuthorSharonH

Amazon:
amazon.com/Sharon-Hamilton/e/B004FQQMAC

BookBub:
bookbub.com/authors/sharon-hamilton

Youtube:
youtube.com/channel/UCDInkxXFpXp_4Vnq08ZxMBQ

Soundcloud:
soundcloud.com/sharon-hamilton-1

Sharon Hamilton's Rockin' Romance Readers:
facebook.com/groups/sealteamromance

Sharon Hamilton's Goodreads Group:

goodreads.com/group/show/199125-sharon-hamilton-readers-group

Visit Sharon's Online Store:

sharon-hamilton-author.myshopify.com

Join Sharon's Review Teams:

eBook Reviews:

sharonhamiltonassistant@gmail.com

Audio Reviews:

sharonhamiltonassistant@gmail.com

Life is one fool thing after another.

Love is two fool things after each other.

Reviews

PRAISE FOR THE
GOLDEN VAMPIRES OF TUSCANY SERIES

"Well to say the least I was thoroughly surprise. I have read many Vampire books, from Ann Rice to Kym Grosso and few other Authors, so yes I do like Vampires, not the super scary ones from the old days, but the new ones are far more interesting far more human then one can remember. I found Honeymoon Bite a totally engrossing book, I was not able to put it down, page after page I found delight, love, understanding, well that is until the bad bad Vamp started being really bad. But seeing someone love another person so much that they would do anything to protect them, well that had me going, then well there was more and for a while I thought it was the end of a beautiful love story that spanned not only time but, spanned Italy and California. Won't divulge how it ended, but I did shed a few tears after screaming but Sharon Hamilton did not let me down, she took me on amazing trip that I loved, look forward to reading another Vampire book of hers."

"An excellent paranormal romance that was exciting, romantic, entertaining and very satisfying to read. It had me anticipating what would happen next many times over, so much so I could not put it down and even finished it up in a day. The vampires in this book were different from your average vampire, but I enjoy different variations and changes to the same old stuff. It made for a more unpredictable read and more adventurous to explore! Vampire lovers, any paranormal readers and even those who love the romance genre will enjoy Honeymoon Bite."

"This is the first non-Seal book of this author's I have read and I loved it. There is a cast-like hierarchy in this vampire community with humans at the very bottom and Golden vampires at the top. Lionel is a dark vampire who are servants of the Goldens. Phoebe is a Golden who has not decided if she will remain human or accept the turning to become a vampire. Either way she and Lionel can never be together since it is forbidden.

I enjoyed this story and I am looking forward to the next installment."

"A hauntingly romantic read. Old love lost and new love found. Family, heart, intrigue and vampires. Grabbed my attention and couldn't put down. Would definitely recommend."

PRAISE FOR THE
SEAL BROTHERHOOD SERIES

"Fans of Navy SEAL romance, I found a new author to feed your addiction. Finely written and loaded delicious with moments, Sharon Hamilton's storytelling satisfies like a thick bar of chocolate." — Marliss Melton, bestselling author of the *Team Twelve* Navy SEALs series

"Sharon Hamilton does an EXCELLENT job of fitting all the characters into a brotherhood of SEALS that may not be real but sure makes you feel that you have entered the circle and security of their world. The stories intertwine with each book before...and each book after and THAT is what makes Sharon Hamilton's SEAL Brotherhood Series so very interesting. You won't want to put down ANY of her books and they will keep you reading into the night when you should be sleeping. Start with this book...and you will not want to stop until you've read the whole series and then...you will be waiting for Sharon to write the next one." (5 Star Review)

"Kyle and Christy explode all over the pages in this first book, [Accidental SEAL], in a whole new series of SEALs. If the twist and turns don't get your heart jumping, then maybe the suspense will. This is a must read for those that are looking for love and adventure with a little sloppy love thrown in for good measure." (5 Star Review)

PRAISE FOR THE
BAD BOYS OF SEAL TEAM 3 SERIES

"I love reading this series! Once you start these books, you can hardly put them down. The mix of romance and suspense keeps you turning the pages one right after another! Can't wait until the next book!" (5 Star Review)

"I love all of Sharon's Seal books, but [SEAL's Code] may just be her best to date. Danny and Luci's journey is filled with a wonderful insight into the Native American life. It is a love story that will fill you with warmth and contentment. You will enjoy Danny's journey to become a SEAL and his reasons for it. Good job Sharon!" (5 Star Review)

PRAISE FOR THE
BAND OF BACHELORS SERIES

"[Lucas] was the first book in the Band of Bachelors series and it was a phenomenal start. I loved how we got to see the other SEALs we all love and we got a look at Lucas and Marcy. They had an instant attraction, and their love was very intense. This book had it all, suspense, steamy romance, humor, everything you want in a riveting, outstanding read. I can't wait to read the next book in this series." (5 Star Review)

PRAISE FOR THE
TRUE BLUE SEALS SERIES

"Keep the tissues box nearby as you read *True Blue SEALs: Zak* by Sharon Hamilton. I imagine more than I wish to that the circumstances surrounding Zak and Amy are all too real for returning military personnel and their families. Ms. Hamilton has put us right in the middle of struggles and successes that these two high school sweethearts endure. I have read several of Sharon Hamilton's military romances but will say this is the most emotionally intense of the ones that I have read. This is a well-written, realistic story with authentic characters that will have you rooting for them and proud of those who serve to keep us safe. This is an author who writes amazing stories that you love and cry with the characters. Fans of Jessica Scott and Marliss Melton will want to add Sharon Hamilton to their list of realistic military romance writers." (5 Star Review)

www.ingramcontent.com/pod-product-compliance
Lightning Source LLC
Chambersburg PA
CBHW020406260626
47156CB00007B/2262